莎士比亚戏剧欣赏教程
A Course Book for Selected Readings of Shakespeare's Plays

主　　编：卢秋平
副主编：明　媚　廖　衡　乔　琼　沈国环
参　　编：范　丽　黄西林　李金云
　　　　　卢益霞　钱桂容　王　杨
　　　　　姚　刚　张　淳　周红霞

http://press.hust.edu.cn
中国·武汉

内 容 提 要

本教材分为两个部分。第一部分介绍莎士比亚的五大著名悲剧:《哈姆雷特》《罗密欧与朱丽叶》《李尔王》《麦克白》《奥赛罗》。第二部分介绍莎士比亚的五大著名喜剧:《威尼斯商人》《第十二夜》《仲夏夜之梦》《皆大欢喜》《无事生非》。每个单元的内容包括剧中人物介绍、背景知识介绍、剧情介绍、经典台词节选,以及关于所选戏剧的思考题,部分经典台词节选配有插图。本教程语言通俗易懂,旨在引导读者多角度分析莎士比亚的作品,了解其文学性和人文性,可作为专业课和通识课教材。

图书在版编目(CIP)数据

莎士比亚戏剧欣赏教程/卢秋平主编. —武汉:华中科技大学出版社,2024.3
ISBN 978-7-5772-0558-8

Ⅰ.①莎… Ⅱ.①卢… Ⅲ.①莎士比亚(Shakespeare,William 1564-1616)-戏剧文学-文学欣赏-高等学校-教材 Ⅳ.①I561.073

中国国家版本馆 CIP 数据核字(2024)第 046248 号

莎士比亚戏剧欣赏教程 卢秋平 主编
Shashibiya Xiju Xinshang Jiaocheng

策划编辑:刘 平
责任编辑:江旭玉
封面设计:原色设计
责任监印:周治超

出版发行:华中科技大学出版社(中国·武汉) 电话:(027)81321913
　　　　　武汉市东湖新技术开发区华工科技园　 邮编:430223
录　　排:华中科技大学出版社美编室
印　　刷:武汉开心印印刷有限公司
开　　本:787mm×1092mm　1/16
印　　张:13
字　　数:387 千字
版　　次:2024 年 3 月第 1 版第 1 次印刷
定　　价:48.00 元

本书若有印装质量问题,请向出版社营销中心调换
全国免费服务热线:400-6679-118　竭诚为您服务
版权所有　侵权必究

前　　言

　　本教材是为高等学校英语专业选修课编写的，也可以作为非英语专业的英语文学爱好者或者莎士比亚戏剧爱好者的阅读和欣赏材料。

　　本教材由两个部分组成，一共选取了莎士比亚的十部戏剧。第一部分选编了莎士比亚的五大著名悲剧：《哈姆雷特》(*Hamlet*)、《罗密欧与朱丽叶》(*Romeo and Juliet*)、《李尔王》(*King Lear*)、《麦克白》(*Macbeth*)、《奥赛罗》(*Othello*)。第二部分选编了莎士比亚的五大著名喜剧：《威尼斯商人》(*The Merchant of Venice*)、《第十二夜》(*Twelfth Night*)、《仲夏夜之梦》(*A Mid-Summer Night's Dream*)、《皆大欢喜》(*As You Like It*)、《无事生非》(*Much Ado about Nothing*)。每个单元都按照"剧中人物（中英文）—背景知识介绍—场景介绍—剧情介绍（中英文）—经典引文—引文的英文阐释及译文—思考题"这个顺序安排内容。部分经典引文配有插图，图文并茂，有助于读者更好地理解和记忆这些知识。

　　本教材的编写难免有欠缺之处，敬请读者海涵。欢迎大家提出宝贵意见，以供我们再版的时候改进。

Contents

Part One   Shakespeare's Great Tragedies

Unit 1   Hamlet /3

Unit 2   Romeo and Juliet /18

Unit 3   King Lear /34

Unit 4   Macbeth /50

Unit 5   Othello /71

Part Two   Shakespeare's Great Comedies

Unit 6   The Merchant of Venice /95

Unit 7   Twelfth Night /123

Unit 8   A Mid-Summer Night's Dream /143

Unit 9   As You Like It /161

Unit 10   Much Ado about Nothing /183

Part One
Shakespeare's Great Tragedies

Unit 1

Hamlet

1 Characters

Hamlet(哈姆雷特): Son of the late Danish king—old King Hamlet.

Claudius(克劳狄斯): The current king of Denmark, Hamlet's uncle and stepfather.

Gertrude(格特鲁德): Hamlet's mother.

Ghost of Hamlet's Father(哈姆雷特父亲的鬼魂)

Polonius(波洛涅斯): Lord Chamberlain[①] of King Claudius.

Ophelia(奥菲利娅): Daughter of Polonius.

Horatio(霍拉旭): Hamlet's best friend.

Laertes(雷欧提斯): Son of Polonius and brother of Ophelia.

Rosencrantz(罗森格兰兹), **Guildenstern**(吉尔登斯吞): Courtiers and schoolfriends of Hamlet. They become Hamlet's enemies by turning into Claudius' spies.

Marcellus(马西勒斯), **Bernardo**(勃那多): Guards for the royal castle of Elsinore.

Francisco(弗兰西斯科): Another guard.

Voltimand(沃尔蒂曼德), **Cornelius**(柯内留斯): Courtiers[②] who carry messages for the king.

Osric(奥斯里克): Another courtier, who tells Hamlet about the fencing match arranged for him and Laertes, and acts as the referee.

Reynaldo(雷奈尔多): Servant of Polonius.

Fortinbras(福丁布拉斯): Prince of Norway.

Players(戏剧演员): Actors who are arranged by Hamlet to perform a play about murder and usurpation.

Gravediggers(掘坟墓者): Two peasants who dig Ophelia's grave.

---

① A lord chamberlain is a person who manages a royal household. [(英国)王室的宫务大臣]

② A courtier is an attendant at the court of a monarch. [(尤指旧时的)侍臣,侍从,廷臣]

Yorick(约里克): Court jester① of old King Hamlet. His skull is dug out by one of the gravediggers in Act 5, Scene 1.

Claudio(克劳迪奥): Man who brings messages for the king and queen from Hamlet after Hamlet escapes back to Denmark from his trip to England.

2　Background

A major source for Shakespeare's *Hamlet* was Saxo Grammaticus (about 1150? -1220?)'s third and fourth books of *Gesta Danorum* (*The Deeds of the Danes*) in Latin Christiern Pedersen (1480-1554), a Danish humanist writer and printer who published the first edition of *Gesta Danorum* in Paris in 1514 with a different title: Historia Danica. Grammaticus wrote the book required by a priest named Absalon, archbishop of Lund from 1177 or 1178 to 1201. Lund (now part of Sweden) was then controlled by Denmark. *Gesta Danorum* narrates the stories of sixty Danish kings in Books 1 to 9 of the sixteen-volume work. Book 3 recounts the tale of Amleth (the model for Hamlet) who avenges Feng's murder of his father.

According to Grammaticus, Amleth lives on and becomes King of Jutland. The tale about Amleth was retold by François de Belleforest in 1572 in *Histoires Tragiques* (*Tragic Stories*).

Shakespeare's *Hamlet* is also likely based on a lost play referred to as *Ur-Hamlet* (the prefix ur- means original) by Thomas Kyd (1558-1594), and a surviving Kyd play, *The Spanish Tragedy* (also spelled *The Spanish Tragedie*). Kyd's presentation of the character Hieronimo could have inspired Shakespeare to portray Hamlet. Shakespeare critic and scholar Peter Alexander (editor of a popular edition of the complete works of Shakespeare, first published in 1951) insists that *Ur-Hamlet* was actually drafted by Shakespeare between 1587 and 1589 for the final version of the play. Another Shakespeare critic Harold Bloom agrees with Alexander in the book *Hamlet: Poem Unlimited* (published in 2003). Other possible sources for *Hamlet* are a Celtic tale of the tenth century about a warrior named Amhlaide and a Persian tale of the eleventh century from Abu Ol-Qasem Mansur's *The Book of Kings* (*Shah-nameh*).[1]

Hamlet is a product of the religious revolution Reformation in many aspects, and the skeptical humanism of the late Renaissance, maintaining that human knowledge had limits. For example, Hamlet had anxieties about discrepancy between appearance and reality, and his perplexity of religion (the sinfulness of suicide, the unfairness that killing a praying murderer would result in sending the murderer to heaven). These are under the direct influence of humanist thought. *Hamlet* has been staged and set in different periods of history since it was first written, from the late Middle Ages to modern-day.[2]

---

　　① A jester is a man employed in the past at the court of a king or queen to amuse people by telling jokes and funny stories. [(旧时宫廷中的)逗乐小丑,弄臣]

3 Settings

The main setting is Elsinore① Castle in eastern Denmark (Kronborg Castle in real life). Elsinore (Danish name Helsingør) is a real town located on the Øresund strait. In Shakespeare's time, Elsinore was a pivotal port which charged a toll for ship passage through the Øresund strait. [3]

4 Synopsis

The full title of the play is *The Tragedy of Hamlet, Prince of Denmark.*

Prince Hamlet has returned to Denmark from Germany where he is studying at the University of Wittenberg, to attend his father's funeral. It is alleged that his father was stung by a serpent one afternoon while sleeping in the garden as usual. Within a month, Hamlet's widowed mother, Gertrude, marries his uncle Claudius, the current king. Hamlet is perturbed by his father's abrupt death and his mother's hasty marriage to Claudius. He feels dejected and melancholy.

Horatio, Hamlet's bosom friend, comes to tell Hamlet that the guards Marcellus and Barnardo on watch at the top of the royal castle of Denmark, Elsinore, have seen the ghost of the deceased king twice, and that Horatio has seen the ghost on the third night. Hamlet is shocked. He follows Horatio to where the ghost has appeared, and sure enough, the ghost appears again at midnight, dressed in an armor. When the ghost beckons to Hamlet, Horatio and the guards try to stop Hamlet from following the ghost, fearing that the ghost might do harm to him. But Hamlet persists, resolute and hardy.

The ghost then reveals to Hamlet the truth of his death—Claudius poured poison into his ear while he was sleeping in the garden. He then makes Hamlet promise to revenge his death. But the ghost asks Hamlet not to hurt Gertrude although she proves false to their former affection.

Hamlet then pretends to be insane to avoid arousing suspicion of Claudius. Claudius doubts Hamlet's madness. He sends for Hamlet's schoolfriends Rosencrantz and Guildenstern to spy on Hamlet. Polonius, the king's counsellor, offers to find out Hamlet's insanity. After careful observation and according to Ophelia, Polonius' daughter's description, Polonius declares that the root of Hamlet's insanity is his love for Ophelia, who is warned by her brother Laertes against Hamlet's love. Laertes thinks that Hamlet's love for Ophelia is fickle because he cannot choose whom to marry but must yield to his duty as a prince.

Hamlet wants to prove the truth of what the ghost has told him for fear that the ghost might

---

① Elsinore is the royal castle of Denmark during the late Middle Ages (in European history, it refers to the period from about 1000 AD to 1450 AD).

be a devil in disguise to allure him to commit murder. At this time, some players are visiting the court and Hamlet asks them to stage a play named *The Mouse-trap* in which a duke of Vienna named Gonzago is murdered by Lucianus, a close relative of the duke, and Lucianus usurps the dukedom and marries Baptista, Gonzago's wife. Hamlet watches Claudius's reaction closely during the performance of the play. As expected, Claudius appears unrest when the play is on. He makes the players stop and leaves abruptly. This reaffirms Hamlet's suspicion. So he decides to kill Claudius at the ghost's behest.

Claudius makes Gertrude summon Hamlet and blame him for his recent words and behavior which displease and disturb the king and queen. Polonius is ordered to hide behind the tapestry to eavesdrop their conversation and then report it to the king. Hamlet is annoyed by Gertrude who refers to Claudius as his father. He accuses her of her betrayal of her late husband, his true father. Hamlet requires Gertrude to sit still and listen to him. Fearing that Hamlet might do harm to her in his "madness", Gertrude cries for help. Her cry creates a response from Polonius, who also cries "help". Mistaking him for Claudius, Hamlet stabs him through the tapestry with his sword.

By this time, Claudius has already sensed deeply the threat posed by Hamlet. He has sent for Rosencrantz and Guildenstern on a diplomatic mission to England and bring Hamlet with them. Claudius writes a secret letter to the king of England to have Hamlet murdered on his arrival. Polonius' death quickens the pace of this trip and they are sent to England immediately.

Ophelia becomes insane as a result of her father's death. Laertes has come back from France where he has been studying in the University of Paris. He is heartbroken to learn of his father's death and to see his sister in such a state. At first Laertes thinks that Claudius is responsible for his father's death and his sister's insanity, and he starts a rebellion. But Claudius tells him that Hamlet is the murderer. Laertes then vows to seek revenge against Hamlet. Claudius implies to Laertes that he has already revenged for Laertes, meaning that Hamlet will be killed on his arrival in England. But news about Hamlet's safe return to Denmark arrives. When they are on the ship, Hamlet steals the secret letter in the darkness and knows Claudius' scheme to ask the English king to cut off his head as soon as he arrives in England. Hamlet keeps the letter and writes a new one which instructs the English king to kill the messengers on their arrival. He signs and seals it and puts it back. Then they encounter some pirates and have a fight. During the fight, Hamlet boards the pirates' ship and their own ship sails on which carries Rosencrantz and Guildenstern to their deaths. When they know his identity as a Danish prince, they are merciful to him, hoping that he will do them a favor. So the pirates' ship brings Hamlet back.

Claudius then suggests that Laertes challenge Hamlet to a fencing match and Laertes will prepare a sword with a sharp point. Laertes says he will make the point dipped in poison so that when it brazes Hamlet, he will die. As a backup, Claudius will prepare a cup of poisonous wine for Hamlet in case he escapes the poisoned sword. While they are discussing this, news of

Ophelia's death has been heard. She was gathering flowers along a brook and had made a garland. When she was climbing onto a tree to hang her garland from a bending branch, the branch broke and she fell into the water and got drowned. Laertes is saddened more by this news. He comes upon Hamlet on the graveyard and they have a scuffle, although Hamlet says that he loves Ophelia too and is shocked by Ophelia's death. Claudius requires Laertes to keep calm and reminds him of the coming fencing match.

In the first two rounds of the fencing match, Laertes has got no chance to wound Hamlet, so he acts fiercely during the third one. He succeeds in hitting Hamlet this time. They scuffle and exchange their swords. Hamlet hits Laertes with the poisoned sword. Between the second and third round, Gertrude drinks the poisonous wine before Claudius is able to stop her from doing so. Now she is dying. Claudius says she swoons at the sight of blood, but she says faintly that it is because of the drink—she is poisoned, then she dies. Laertes reveals the chief villain of all this bloody scene. In a fury, Hamlet wounds Claudius with the poisoned sword and then forces him to drink the remainder of the poisonous wine. Claudius dies. Laertes forgives Hamlet for his father's death and then dies. As Hamlet is dying, Horatio picks up the poisonous cup and intends to commit suicide to follow Hamlet, but Hamlet stops him and bids him to live on to tell his story to the world. Before Hamlet dies, he says he will vote for Fortinbras, the Norwegian prince, for the Danish throne, and Fortinbras thinks he is rightful to claim the throne. At the beginning of the play, Horatio tells the guards that Fortinbras' father, the late Norwegian king, has challenged the old king Hamlet to a combat and slain by King Hamlet, and the Norwegian territory is seized by Denmark according to their agreement. Prince Fortinbras is now preparing for an invasion of Denmark to avenge his father's death and take back the lost territory. Claudius sends Fortinbras' uncle, the current king of Norway, a letter to make him stop his nephew's preparation for the invasion. Fortinbras' uncle agrees but asks for Claudius' permission to permit Fortinbras' army to march through Denmark on his way to invade Poland. Claudius agrees and Fortinbras is now on his march back from Poland triumphantly. The play ends with a military funeral for Hamlet to proclaim his greatness.

【剧情介绍】

在德国威登堡大学上学的哈姆雷特王子回到丹麦参加他父亲的葬礼,以及随后举行的母亲的婚礼。据说他的父亲是在花园里和平常一样午睡的时候被蛇咬了。不出一个月,他的母亲格特鲁德就嫁给了他的叔叔克劳狄斯,也就是现任国王。父亲的猝死和母亲的闪婚让哈姆雷特感到很困扰,并且沮丧、难受。

哈姆雷特的密友霍拉旭告诉他,哨兵马西勒斯和勃那多在皇城埃尔西诺守夜的时候,连着两晚看到了他父亲的鬼魂,第三个晚上,霍拉旭自己也看到了。哈姆雷特听闻后感到很惊讶,于是他就跟随霍拉旭来到他父亲鬼魂出现的地方,果然,午夜时分,那个鬼魂又出现了,穿着盔甲,朝着哈姆雷特招手。霍拉旭和哨兵们试图阻止哈姆雷特跟随鬼魂而去,因为他们担心鬼魂会伤害哈姆雷特,但是哈姆雷特很果敢,义无反顾地走到鬼魂跟前。

鬼魂告诉哈姆雷特他死亡的真相——克劳狄斯趁着他午睡的时候往他的耳朵里灌毒药,接着他让哈姆雷特为他报仇。他还提醒哈姆雷特不要伤害他的母亲,尽管她没有对自己的丈夫保持忠贞。

为了不引起克劳狄斯的怀疑,哈姆雷特只好装疯卖傻,但克劳狄斯还是怀疑他是否真的疯了,于是他吩咐哈姆雷特的两个同学——罗森格兰兹和吉尔登斯吞密切监视他。克劳狄斯的廷臣波洛涅斯主动提出试探哈姆雷特是真疯还是装疯。根据他的仔细观察,加上他的女儿奥菲利娅的描述,波洛涅斯认为,导致哈姆雷特发疯的根本原因是他对奥菲利娅的爱。奥菲利娅的哥哥雷欧提斯告诫她不要被哈姆雷特的爱情蒙蔽了双眼。他说哈姆雷特对她的爱只不过是逢场作戏罢了,身为王子的哈姆雷特是不能决定自己的结婚对象的。

考虑到那个鬼魂有可能是魔鬼的化身,是来引诱哈姆雷特犯罪的,哈姆雷特需要想办法证实鬼魂所说的是真实的。这时候,正好有一个剧团来到王宫。于是,他恳请演员们表演一部剧《捕鼠器》,这部剧讲的是维也纳的一个叫贡扎果的公爵被他的近亲卢西亚努斯杀害并且夺走了王位,贡扎果的妻子巴普蒂斯塔也改嫁给了卢西亚努斯。在他们表演这场戏的时候,哈姆雷特会密切注意克劳狄斯的反应。果然,在演出过程中,克劳狄斯显得局促不安,看到演出的后半部分,他命令演员们终止演出,然后就急匆匆地离开了。他的反应证实了哈姆雷特内心的怀疑,因此他决定照鬼魂的吩咐杀了克劳狄斯。

克劳狄斯让王后召见哈姆雷特并指责他最近的言行给国王和王后造成了不安和不悦。与此同时,波洛涅斯躲在挂毯后面偷听他们的谈话,以向国王报告。当格特鲁德称呼克劳狄斯为哈姆雷特的父亲时,哈姆雷特指责母亲不该背叛她已故的丈夫,也就是他真正的父亲。他让格特鲁德坐好并听他说话。格特鲁德害怕哈姆雷特因疯病发作而伤害她,于是大喊救命,这一来,躲在挂毯后面的波洛涅斯也大喊一声"救命",哈姆雷特以为是克劳狄斯躲在那里,于是一剑刺过去,刺死了波洛涅斯。

这时,克劳狄斯已经深深感觉到了哈姆雷特的威胁,于是他派遣罗森格兰兹和吉尔登斯吞带着他的密信去英国一趟。在信中,克劳狄斯叮嘱英国国王等哈姆雷特一到英国就把他杀掉。波洛涅斯的意外死亡使得克劳狄斯吩咐罗森格兰兹和吉尔登斯吞带着哈姆雷特立刻出发前往英国。

奥菲利娅无法接受父亲的死,她疯了。在法国巴黎大学读书的雷欧提斯回来了。父亲的死和妹妹的发疯让他心碎不已,起先,他以为造成这一切的罪魁祸首是克劳狄斯,于是他发动了叛乱,但克劳狄斯告诉他,杀死他父亲的凶手是哈姆雷特。雷欧提斯发誓要找哈姆雷特报仇,克劳狄斯暗示雷欧提斯,他正在帮他除掉哈姆雷特——他的英国之行就是他的死亡之旅。出人意料的是,哈姆雷特竟然活着回到了丹麦。原来,哈姆雷特在船上趁着黑夜偷看了克劳狄斯写给英国国王的密信,得知了他的计谋,于是他重新写了一封信,签名后封好放回去,换掉了之前的那封,他在信中请求英国国王把送信人杀掉。接着,他们的船在航行中遇到了海盗,在打斗中,哈姆雷特上了海盗的船,他们的船则载着克劳狄斯的两个亲信继续驶向英国去迎接他们的死亡。海盗得知了哈姆雷特的王子身份,知道他不会亏待他们,于是他们把哈姆雷特送回了丹麦。

克劳狄斯建议雷欧提斯和哈姆雷特来一场击剑比赛,雷欧提斯可以准备一把尖锐锋利的剑,并且在剑上涂抹毒药,克劳狄斯则准备一杯毒酒给哈姆雷特,确保哈姆雷特必死无疑。他们正在商量计策的时候，奥菲利娅的死讯传来。她在河边采花，编了一个花环，当她爬到树上，打算把花环挂在一根弯曲的树枝上时，树枝断了，她不幸掉到河里淹死了。妹妹的死让雷欧提斯的伤痛雪上加霜。在妹妹的墓地，雷欧提斯遇到了哈姆雷特，尽管哈姆雷特声称他非常爱奥菲利娅，雷欧提斯还是愤怒地和哈姆雷特扭打在一起。克劳狄斯提醒雷欧提斯保持冷静，准备接下来的击剑比赛。

在击剑比赛的前两场，雷欧提斯无法伤到哈姆雷特，第三场一开始，他就咄咄逼人地挥舞着他的剑，所以这次他成功地用剑刺伤了哈姆雷特，在打斗过程中，他们交换了剑，那把毒剑同样刺伤了雷欧提斯。在第二场的休息时间，格特鲁德无意中喝了那杯毒酒，克劳狄斯没来得及阻止她，所以第三场比赛过程中，格特鲁德就倒在了地上，克劳狄斯还撒谎说她晕血，但格特鲁德指着毒酒，说酒有问题，然后就停止了呼吸。在雷欧提斯死之前，他向哈姆雷特坦白了他和克劳狄斯的计谋，并且原谅了哈姆雷特。霍拉旭端起剩下的毒酒准备一饮而尽，他想跟随哈姆雷特一起奔赴死亡，但被哈姆雷特制止了。哈姆雷特让霍拉旭活下来，把他的故事讲给世人听。哈姆雷特还说，他要为挪威王子福丁布拉斯继承丹麦王位投上一票。在戏剧开头的时候，霍拉旭给守夜的哨兵讲到，福丁布拉斯的父亲，也就是已故的挪威国王，曾经挑战过老国王哈姆雷特，他们之间立下盟约，如果挪威国王被击败的话，挪威就臣服于丹麦，结果挪威国王被老哈姆雷特王杀死了，挪威国土就被他占领了。福丁布拉斯决定夺回被丹麦占领的国土。克劳狄斯给现任挪威国王，也就是福丁布拉斯的叔叔写信，请他阻止福丁布拉斯进攻丹麦，作为交换，克劳狄斯同意了攻打波兰的福丁布拉斯的军队从丹麦经过，如今，福丁布拉斯的军队已从波兰凯旋。在本剧的末尾，丹麦为纪念哈姆雷特的壮举而为其举行了军人式的葬礼。

5　Famous quotes

【Quote 1】

Polonius
Yet here, Laertes? Aboard, aboard, for shame!
The wind sits in the shoulder of your sail and you are stayed for.
There, my blessing with thee.
And these few precepts in thy memory look thou character.
Give thy thoughts no tongue,
nor any unproportioned thought his act.
Be thou familiar but by no means vulgar.
Those friends thou hast, and their adoption tried,
grapple them unto thy soul with hoops of steel,
but do not dull thy palm with entertainment
of each new-hatched, unfledged comrade.

Beware of entrance to a quarrel, but being in,
bear't that th' opposèd may beware of thee.
Give every man thine ear, but few thy voice.
Take each man's censure but reserve thy judgment.
Costly thy habit as thy purse can buy,
but not expressed in fancy—rich, not gaudy,
for the apparel oft proclaims the man,
and they in France of the best rank and station
are of a most select and generous chief in that.
Neither a borrower nor a lender be,
for loan oft loses both itself and friend,
and borrowing dulls the edge of husbandry.
This above all: to thine own self be true,
and it must follow, as the night the day,
thou canst not then be false to any man.
Farewell. My blessing season this in thee. [4]
(Act 1, Scene 3)

[**Polonius** (played by Felix Aylmer) speaking to Laertes (played by Terence Morgan) in a 1948 film directed by Laurence Olivier.]

⬥ Paraphrase

Polonius

Still here, Laertes? Get going, get going—shame on you!
The wind gusts in the sails of your ship,

and yet it is forced to wait for you.
Here, I give you my blessing.
And I'll give you a few rules to live by
in order to maintain your good character.
Keep quiet about your own thoughts,
and don't act on any idea you haven't fully thought through.
Be friendly but not too friendly.
Hold onto those friends you have that you know are trustworthy,
with all your heart.
But don't go shaking hands with every new,
unknown person you meet.
Try not to get caught up in any fights or arguments.
But, if you do become involved,
act to make sure that those you're facing respect you.
Listen to everyone, but give advice to few.
Hear every man's opinions,
but keep your own judgments to yourself.
Buy the most expensive clothes you can afford
—but buy clothes that are high-end, not gaudy,
because clothes make the man.
And that is especially true in France.
Neither borrow money nor lend it
—because lending money to a friend
usually results in the loss of the money and the friend,
while borrowing makes people reckless with money.
Above all: be true to yourself,
which carries with it the natural result that
you won't be false to anybody else.
Goodbye. May my blessing help you remember my advice. [5]

◇ 原文译文

波洛涅斯

还在这儿，雷欧提斯！上船去，上船去，真好意思！风息在帆顶上，人家都在等着你哩。好，我为你祝福！还有几句教训，希望你铭刻在记忆之中。不要想到什么就说什么，凡事必须三思而行。对人要和气，可是不要过分狎昵。相知有素的朋友，应该用钢圈箍在你的灵魂上，可是不要对每一个泛泛的新知滥施你的交情。留心避免和人家争吵；可是万一争端已起，就应该让对方知道你不是可以轻侮的。倾听每一个人的意见，可是只对极少数人发表你的意见;接受每一个人的批评,可是保留你自己的判断。尽你的财力购置贵重的衣服,可是不要标新立异,必须富丽而不浮艳,因为服装往往可以表现人格;法国的名流要人,就是在这点上显得最高尚,与众不同。不要向人告贷,也不要借钱给别人;因为债款放了出去,往往不但丢了本钱,而且失去了朋友;向人告贷的结果,是容易养成因循懒惰的习惯。尤其要紧的,你必须对你自己忠实;正像有了白昼才有黑夜一样,对自己忠实,才不会对别人欺诈。再会!愿我的祝福使这一番话在你的行事中奏效。[6]

【Quote 2】

Hamlet

I will tell you why. So shall my anticipation prevent your discovery,

and your secrecy to the king and queen moult no feather.

I have of late—but wherefore I know not

—lost all my mirth, forgone all custom of exercises,

and indeed it goes so heavily with my disposition that this goodly frame,

the earth, seems to me a sterile promontory;

this most excellent canopy, the air

—look you, this brave o'erhanging firmament,

this majestical roof fretted with golden fire

—why, it appears no other thing to me than

a foul and pestilent congregation of vapors.

What a piece of work is a man!

How noble in reason, how infinite in faculty!

In form and moving how express and admirable!

In action how like an angel,

in apprehension how like a god!

The beauty of the world.

The paragon of animals. And yet, to me,

what is this quintessence of dust?

Man delights not me.

No, nor woman neither,

though by your smiling you seem to say so.[7]

(Act 2, Scene 2)

◆ Paraphrase

Hamlet

I'll tell you why.

That way you won't have to reveal anything,

and you can preserve the secrecy

you promised to the king and queen.

Lately, for reasons I don't now,

I've lost all my joy, stopped exercising,

and feel so depressed that the entire world seems to be empty to me.

This beautiful canopy, the sky—look at it,

this splendid overarching sky,

a majestic roof adorned with golden sunlight

—why, to me it seems like nothing more than

a foul collection of diseased air.

What a masterpiece each human is!

How noble in his ability to think, how unlimited in abilities,

how attractive in his body and movement,

how angelic in action, how godlike in understanding!

The most beautiful thing in the world.

The perfect ideal, standing above all other animals.

And yet, for me, what are humans like, except dust?

Men don't delight me.

No, women neither

—though your smiles seem to suggest that's what you were thinking.[8]

◆ 原文译文

哈姆雷特

让我代你们说明来意,免得你们泄露了自己的秘密,有负国王、王后的委托。我近来不知为了什么缘故,一点兴致都提不起来,什么游乐的事都懒得过问;在这一种抑郁的心境之下,仿佛负载万物的大地,这一座美好的框架只是一个不毛的荒岬;这个覆盖众生的苍穹,这一顶壮丽的帐幕,这个金黄色的火球点缀着的庄严的屋宇,只是一大堆污浊的瘴气的集合。人类是一件多么了不得的杰作!多么高贵的理性!多么伟大的力量!多么优美的仪表!多么文雅的举动!在行为上多么像一个天使!在智慧上多么像一个天神!宇宙的精华!万物的灵长!可是在我看来,这一个泥土塑成的生命算得了什么?人类不能使我发生兴趣;不,女人也不能使我发生兴趣,虽然从你们现在的微笑之中,我可以看到你们在这样想。[9]

【Quote 3】

Hamlet

[soliloquy①] To be, or not to be? That is the question
—Whether 'tis nobler in the mind to suffer
the slings and arrows of outrageous fortune,
or to take arms against a sea of troubles,
and, by opposing, end them?
To die, to sleep—no more
—and by a sleep to say we end the heartache
and the thousand natural shocks that flesh is heir to
—'tis a consummation devoutly to be wished!
To die, to sleep. To sleep, perchance to dream
—ay, there's the rub,
for in that sleep of death what dreams may come
when we have shuffled off this mortal coil, must give us pause.
There's the respect that makes calamity of so long life.
For who would bear the whips and scorns of time,
th' oppressor's wrong, the proud man's contumely,
the pangs of despised love, the law's delay,
the insolence of office, and the spurns
that patient merit of th' unworthy takes,
when he himself might his quietus make with a bare bodkin?
Who would fardels bear,
to grunt and sweat under a weary life,
but that the dread of something after death,
the undiscovered country from whose bourn no traveler returns,
puzzles the will and makes us rather bear those ills we have
than fly to others that we know not of?
Thus conscience doth make cowards of us all,
and thus the native hue of resolution
is sicklied o'er with the pale cast of thought,
and enterprises of great pitch and moment
with this regard their currents turn awry,

---

① A soliloquy is a speech in a play in which a character, who is alone on the stage, speaks his or her thoughts. (戏剧独白)

and lose the name of action. [10]

(Act 3, Scene 1)

[Hamlet (played by Laurence Olivier) making his famous soliloquy in a 1948 film directed by Laurence Olivier.]

◆ Paraphrase

Hamlet

To live, or to die? That is the question.
Is it nobler to suffer through all the terrible things fate throws at you,
or to fight off your troubles, and,
in doing so, end them completely?
To die, to sleep—because that's all dying is
—and by a sleep I mean an end to all the heartache
and the thousand injuries that we are vulnerable to
—that's an end to be wished for!
To die, to sleep. To sleep, perhaps to dream
—yes, but there's the catch.
Because the kinds of dreams that might come in that sleep of death
—after you have left behind your mortal body
—are something to make you anxious.
That's the consideration that makes us suffer
the calamities of life for so long.
Because who would bear all the trials and tribulations of time
—the oppression of the powerful, the insults from arrogant men,
the pangs of unrequited love, the slowness of justice,

the disrespect of people in office,
and the general abuse of good people by bad
——when you could just settle all your debts using
nothing more than an unsheathed dagger?
Who would bear his burdens,
and grunt and sweat through a tiring life,
if they weren't frightened of what might happen after death
——that undiscovered country from which no visitor returns,
which we wonder about and which makes us prefer
the troubles we know rather than fly off to face the ones we don't?
Thus, the fear of death makes us all cowards,
and our natural willingness to act is made weak by too much thinking.
Actions of great urgency and importance get thrown off course
because of this sort of thinking,
and they cease to be actions at all. [11]

◇ 原文译文

哈姆雷特

生存还是毁灭，这是一个值得考虑的问题；默默忍受命运的暴虐的毒箭，还是挺身反抗人世的无涯的苦难，通过斗争把他们扫清，这两种行为哪一种更高贵？死了，睡着了，什么都完了，要是在这一种睡眠之中，我们心头的创痛，以及其他无数血肉之躯所不能避免的打击，都可以从此消失，那正是我们求之不得的结局。死了，睡着了，睡着了也许还会做梦；嗯，阻碍就在这儿：因为当我们摆脱了这一具腐朽的皮囊以后，在那死的睡眠里，究竟将要做些什么梦，那不能不使我们踌躇顾虑。人们甘心久困于患难之中，也就是因为这个缘故；谁愿意忍受人世的鞭挞和讥嘲、压迫者的凌辱、傲慢者的冷眼、遭轻蔑的爱情的惨痛、法律的迁延、官吏的横暴和费尽辛勤换来的小人的鄙视，要是他只需用一柄小小的刀子就可以清算他自己的一生？谁愿意负着这样的重担，在烦劳的生命的压迫下呻吟流汗，倘不是因为惧怕不可知的死后，惧怕那从来不曾有一个旅人回来过的神秘之国，是它迷惑了我们的意志，使我们宁愿忍受目前的折磨，不敢向我们所不知道的痛苦飞去？这样，重重的顾虑使我们全变成了懦夫，决心的炽热的光彩，被审慎的思维盖上了一层灰色，伟大的事业在这一种顾虑之下，也会逆流而退，失去了行动的意义。[12]

6　Questions for discussion

(1) What is Hamlet's view of death?
(2) What is the significance of Hamlet's soliloquy?
(3) What causes Hamlet's tragedy?

(4) What do you know about Shakespeare's humanistic ideas revealed in this play?

(5) What do you think of the female characters in this play?

(6) What are the major themes of this play?

(7) Do you think Polonius' advice practical?

7　References

[1][2][3]　Hamlet Study Guide[EB/OL]. https://www.litcharts.com/lit/hamlet.

[4][7][10]　Shakespeare W. Hamlet[M]. New York: Simon & Schuster, 1992.

[5][8][11]　Hamlet: Shakespeare Translation[EB/OL]. https://www.litcharts.com/shakescleare/shakespeare-translations/hamlet.

[6][9][12]　威廉·莎士比亚. 莎士比亚悲剧五种[M]. 朱生豪,译. 北京:人民文学出版社,2020.

Unit 2

Romeo and Juliet

1　Characters

Romeo（罗密欧）：Son of the Montagues, one of the protagonists of the play.

Juliet（朱丽叶）：Daughter of the Capulets, another protagonist of the play.

Montague and Lady Montague（蒙塔古老爷和太太）：Male and female heads of the household of Montague.

Capulet and Lady Capulet（凯普莱特老爷和太太）：Male and female heads of the household of Capulet.

Escalus（埃斯喀勒斯王子）：Prince of Verona.

Paris（帕里斯）：Young nobleman, kinsman of Escalus.

Nurse of Juliet（朱丽叶的保姆）：Juliet's wet nurse when she was an infant. She acts as Juliet's attendant, confidante, and messenger in the play.

Mercutio（默古修）：Kinsman of the prince and friend of Romeo.

Benvolio（班伏里奥）：Nephew of Montague, cousin and friend to Romeo.

Tybalt（提伯尔特）：Nephew of Lady Capulet.

Friar Laurence（劳伦斯神父）：Franciscan priest[①] who marries Romeo and Juliet.

Friar John（约翰神父）：Another Franciscan priest, a minor character whose mission is to carry a letter to Romeo.

Balthasar（巴尔萨泽）：Servant of Romeo.

Sampson（桑普森），**Gregory**（格雷戈里）：Servants of Capulet.

Peter（彼得）：Assistant of Juliet's nurse.

Abraham（亚伯拉罕）：Servant of Montague.

Apothecary（药剂师）：Man who sells Romeo a deadly poison.

Rosaline（罗萨琳）：Niece of Lord Capulet and the girl with whom Romeo is smitten before he meets Juliet. She doesn't show up in the play, but is mentioned by Romeo, Benvolio, Mercutio, and Friar Laurence.

[①]　Franciscan priest is a robed Catholic monk who follows a regimen established by St. Francis of Assisi.

Page of Paris（帕里斯的侍从）: Young man who serves Paris and waits for him while he is visiting Juliet's grave.

2　Background

Shakespeare's *Romeo and Juliet* is mainly based on *The Tragicall Historye of Romeus and Juliet*, Arthur Brooke's long narrative poem written in 1562, which in turn had been based on a French translation of Matteo Bandello, an Italian writer's tale. [1]

In the early Renaissance period, Italy was split into several smaller city-states warring with one another frequently. Most of Italy belonged to the peasant class and social inequality was profound. Wealthy families such as the Montagues and Capulets were also politically powerful in the cities. They were preoccupied by parochialism and arrogance, and their children were not allowed to choose their marriage partners. [2]

3　Settings

The plot takes place mainly in Verona and partly in Mantua, Italy, in the Renaissance Period.

The play takes place first in Verona, Italy, on a Sunday morning in July and ends four days later in the same city. Verona is in northern Italy. The ruler of Verona at the time of the story was Bartolomeo della Scalla, who died in 1304. Part of the play takes place in Mantua where Romeo is banished. Mantua is in the Lombardy region of Italy, south of the Swiss border. [3]

4　Synopsis

In Verona, there are two noble families, the house of Capulet and the house of Montague. The two households have maintained a feud to such an extent that even their servants cannot bear to meet each other in the streets without a quarrel or a fight.

The play opens with Sampson and Gregory from the house of Capulet walking in the streets when they meet Abraham and another servant from the house of Montague. Sampson bites his thumb, an obscene gesture in Shakespeare's time, at them, which provokes Abraham. They start to quarrel and swing their swords at one another. Benvolio, another member of the house of Montague, shows up. He draws his own sword to stop them from fighting. Tybalt, Lady Capulet's nephew, enters onto the scene and blames Benvolio for the situation, then Tybalt attacks Benvolio and a fierce fight ensues. Soon Capulet and Montague arrive and get ready to fight each other. Prince Escalus enters and is furious to see them disrupt the peace of the city for a third time. He rules that if they start another fight, they will pay for the strife with their lives.

Next enters Romeo, a gentle and handsome young man who is lovelorn. He is sad because his love for Rosaline, Lord Capulet's niece, is unrequited. Rosaline has sworn to be a virgin. Benvolio finds Romeo and promises to help Romeo out of his lovesickness.

Now it is in Capulet's house. Capulet rejects Count Paris' request for Juliet's hand, saying that she is not yet full fourteen. But if Juliet consents to marry him, Capulet will give him permission. Capulet then gives his servant Peter a list of guests to be invited to a feast held in Capulet's house. Capulet invites Paris to the party because there will be many beautiful young women present. If Paris still wants to marry Juliet after having met those beautiful young women, Capulet will consider consenting to their marriage.

Benvolio manages to persuade Romeo to attend the party, hoping that he might fall in love with another beautiful girl so that he will not be obsessed with Rosaline. Romeo tells Benvolio that no other girl can outshine Rosaline. But Benvolio insists that Romeo will find another girl there.

Finally, Romeo, Benvolio, Mercutio and several other men of their house come to the party under facemasks, though Romeo and Mercutio had ominous dreams last night and Romeo has a premonition that his participation of the feast will cause his untimely death. Soon Romeo notices Juliet and exclaims how beautiful she is. He is eager to know who she is and asks a servant who doesn't know her either. When Romeo is talking, Tybalt hears his voice and recognizes he is a Montague. He declares that he will kill the intruder, but he is stopped by Capulet who warns him not to break the peace agreement that Capulet and Montague have made in the presence of Prince Escalus.

Romeo approaches Juliet. He takes Juliet's hand and expresses his fondness for her. Juliet is also smitten with Romeo. When Juliet's nurse finds Juliet and tells her that her mother wants to talk with her, Juliet leaves reluctantly. Romeo then asks the nurse who Juliet's mother is and the nurse tells him that she is Lady Capulet. Romeo is astonished to have fallen in love with a daughter of his family's enemy. Despite this, when the party draws to a close, Romeo lingers on. He sneaks into Capulet's orchard and spots Juliet confessing her love for Romeo to herself on the balcony. Overhearing her confession of love and expression of her dilemma, Romeo cannot help but blurting out his wish to be baptized again if his family name prevents her from loving him. Juliet is shocked to hear another voice all of a sudden in the darkness. When she knows it is Romeo, she urges him to leave, for fear that he will be discovered by her kinsmen and killed by them. But Romeo is fearless. He tells Juliet that nothing will prevent him from loving her. He is even willing to give up his family name for their love. Then they exchange vows of love for each other. Juliet says if Romeo really loves her and intends to marry her, they should arrange the time and place for this. She will wait for his message tomorrow. When the nurse calls for Juliet again and again, she bids Romeo good night and Romeo parts with Juliet begrudgingly.

Early the next morning, when Friar Laurence is searching for herbs, weeds and flowers to make tinctures and potion, Romeo comes to seek his help. Friar Laurence has heard of Romeo's love for Rosaline and thinks he needs help to win Rosaline. Unexpectedly, Romeo tells Friar Laurence that he has forgotten Rosaline's name completely and it is Juliet that he truly loves now. He wants Friar Laurence to marry them secretly as soon as possible. Friar Laurence warns Romeo, "Wisely and slow. They stumble that run fast." But Romeo consents to do so in the hope that their marriage will resolve their family feud.

Romeo meets Juliet's nurse and tells her to bring Juliet a message that requests her to come to the church to be married by Friar Laurence in the afternoon. While the nurse is away running errands, Juliet has been waiting for her return anxiously. She immediately demands the news from Romeo on seeing her back. The nurse tells her to go to Friar Laurence's chambers in the afternoon where a husband is waiting to make her a wife. Meanwhile, the nurse will go back to meet Romeo's servant who will give her a rope ladder for Romeo's use at night.

When the two lovers meet in Friar Laurence's chambers, they are excited and embrace each other. Friar Laurence admires their love but wonders how long their passion will last. Then he marries them.

It is a hot day. Benvolio, Mercutio, and Mercutio's page are walking in the street when they happen upon Tybalt with a few other Capulets. Tybalt provokes Mercutio by asking him if he has consorted with Romeo. At this time, Romeo comes up and Tybalt tells Mercutio that "his man" is approaching. Mercutio is offended. Tybalt then calls Romeo a villain when Romeo comes near. Romeo is not angry. Instead, he tries to make Tybalt calm down. He says he loves Tybalt's family name as he loves his own. He says this because he has been married to Juliet secretly. Mercutio cannot bear to see Romeo's submission and draws his sword. Tybalt corresponds and they begin to fight. Romeo tries to stop them in vain. Tybalt stabs Mercutio mortally. Mercutio curses the two families before his death. Romeo feels very sorry for his friend's death. When Tybalt enters the square again later on, Romeo approaches him and says that one of them must die to join Mercutio in heaven. The two draw their swords and fight. Tybalt is killed.

The two families' heads and the prince arrive and Lady Capulet demands severe punishment for the murder of Tybalt. As Tybalt has killed Mercutio first, the prince rules that Romeo be banished to Mantua and he must leave immediately. If he is found, he will be sentenced to death.

Romeo feels regretful for what he has done, and to be exiled is worse than death because he has to separate from his newly wedded wife. Friar Laurence comforts him that he will announce his marriage publicly and speak for him to the prince and try to win his forgiveness. He will also help make the two families come to terms with peace, so that he will be allowed to come back to be reunited with Juliet. Before all this is done, Romeo must stay in Mantua patiently. Romeo complies with Friar Laurence's advice and will go to Juliet's bedroom for the night with the rope ladder he has prepared for the night. Then he will leave early tomorrow morning for Mantua so that he will not be discovered.

After Romeo leaves for Mantua the next day as planned, Lady Capulet comes to Juliet and tells her to get ready for her marriage to Paris on Thursday. It is Monday. Paris and Lord Capulet have just reached an agreement on the date of the marriage. They all think the marriage will help soothe Juliet's grief over the loss of her cousin Tybalt. But Juliet tells her mother that she would rather marry Romeo, her enemy, than Paris. When she sees there is no hope for her to defy her father's decision, she goes to seek Friar Laurence's help. Friar Laurence gives Juliet a vial of potion for Juliet to drink on Wednesday night. After she drinks it, her breath will stop. Her face will turn pale and her body will become stiff like a corpse. She will be carried on an uncovered funeral bier to the family catacombs, dressed in her best clothes. The simulate death will last as long as forty-two hours. Friar Laurence will send Romeo a letter to inform him of this plan, so that he will wait in the vault for Juliet to wake up. Then Romeo will take Juliet back to Mantua to live.

Everything goes on as they have expected. But the letter for Romeo goes awry. Friar John, who is supposed to have brought the letter to Romeo, comes back and gives the letter back to Friar Laurence—he went to find another friar to accompany him to Mantua, but this friar had visited the sick people infected by the plague. Consequently, both of them were isolated and not allowed to go to Mantua. Meanwhile, Balthasar, Romeo's servant, has witnessed Juliet's funeral. He hurries to Mantua and tells Romeo about Juliet's "death". Romeo goes to an apothecary and buys some strong poison before he comes back to Verona with Balthasar.

When Romeo starts to open the door of the tomb, he is discovered by Paris, who is visiting Juliet's grave to mourn for her untimely "death". Paris prevents Romeo from prying open the door. Romeo requests Paris to let him proceed and says that he doesn't want to hurt Paris, but Paris won't listen. His persistent intervention and his intention to arrest Romeo as a criminal provokes Romeo and they begin to fight. Paris is killed and Romeo pries open the grave door and enters. He kisses his beautiful Juliet and drinks the poison.

Friar Laurence enters the crypt and is shocked to find that both Paris and Romeo are dead. Juliet wakes up and asks the friar about her husband. Friar Laurence tells her that Romeo is dead. He asks her to go out with him and he will send her to a nunnery. Juliet refuses to leave and Friar Laurence hurries away when he hears the watch coming. Juliet kisses Romeo's lips to see if there is any remainder of the poison that can kill her too. As the noise comes nearer, Juliet decides to act fast. She notices Romeo's dagger and takes it and stabs herself without hesitation.

The watchmen, Paris' page, Balthasar, the prince, Capulet and Lady Capulet, and Montague come, and Friar Laurence is caught by the watch on his way to leave the graveyard, because he looks suspicious—he is trembling and weeping with tools in his hands, tools for entering the crypt. The friar tells them all that has happened, and Balthasar confirms what he has said with Romeo's letter for his father. The prince blames Capulet and Montague, whose enmity has led to so many deaths. Then Capulet offers Montague his hand and the two families are reconciled. Montague declares that he will erect a gold statue of the true and faithful Juliet. Capulet responds that he will make a statue of Romeo as well.

【剧情介绍】

在维罗纳，有两大贵族世家：凯普莱特家族和蒙塔古家族。这两大家族世世代代都处于一种敌对状态，他们之间的仇恨非常深，就连两大家族的仆人们在街上偶遇时都会发生争吵或者打斗。

本剧开始的时候，凯普莱特家族的两个仆人——桑普森和格雷戈里在街上行走的时候遇到了蒙塔古家族的两个仆人，其中一个叫亚伯拉罕。桑普森对着蒙塔古家族的两个仆人咬大拇指，激怒了亚伯拉罕，于是他们就吵了起来，并且拔出剑来对着对方挥舞。这时，蒙塔古家族的班伏里奥也来了，他拔出自己的剑，试图阻止双方打斗。凯普莱特太太的侄子提伯尔特也出现了，他指责班伏里奥应该对眼下的情形负责，接着他就攻击班伏里奥，于是一场恶斗开始了。不久，凯普莱特老爷和太太，以及蒙塔古老爷和太太都赶来了，两位老爷也准备参与这场恶斗。此时，埃斯喀勒斯王子赶来了。他怒斥这两个家族破坏了维罗纳的和平。他宣布，只要他们之间再次发生斗殴，他们将会付出生命的代价。

接着出现了本剧的焦点人物之一，温和俊美的罗密欧。他正在害相思病，他爱上了凯普莱特老爷的侄女罗萨琳，可是罗萨琳不爱他，并且她还发誓不嫁人。班伏里奥找到了罗密欧，他答应凯普莱特老爷和太太要治好罗密欧的相思病。

在凯普莱特老爷家里，帕里斯伯爵请求凯普莱特老爷把女儿朱丽叶嫁给他，被老爷拒绝了。他的女儿还没满十四岁呢。不过，他说假如朱丽叶本人同意嫁给他的话，他没意见。接下来，凯普莱特老爷递给仆人彼得一份名单，让他去邀请名单上面的人参加他们家的舞会。他也邀请了帕里斯，因为宾客里面有很多年轻漂亮的女子，假如帕里斯见到她们之后还是只想娶朱丽叶的话，那么凯普莱特老爷就考虑答应他的请求。

班伏里奥努力劝说罗密欧去参加凯普莱特老爷家的舞会，这样的话，兴许他会看上某一个漂亮的女子，从而不必钟情于罗萨琳。罗密欧说任何女子都掩盖不了罗萨琳的光芒。不过，班伏里奥还是认为罗密欧会碰到让他心动的女子。

罗密欧、班伏里奥、默古修以及他们家族的好几个人一起戴着面具来参加凯普莱特家族的舞会。尽管罗密欧和默古修头天晚上都做了不吉利的梦，罗密欧还有一种不祥的预感：这场舞会会让自己断送性命。舞会开始了，罗密欧很快就注意到了朱丽叶并赞叹她的美。他很急切地向一个仆人打听她是谁，不过这个仆人也不认识她。这时，提伯尔特正好听到罗密欧说话，立刻辨认出他是蒙塔古家族的人。他扬言要杀了这个擅自闯进舞会的人，但是凯普莱特老爷拦住了他，并提醒他不要破坏了这两大家族当着埃斯喀勒斯王子的面立下的和平约定。

罗密欧慢慢靠近朱丽叶。他握住她的手，向她表达自己对她的喜爱。朱丽叶也被罗密欧迷住了。这时，朱丽叶的保姆找到她，告诉她赶紧去她妈妈身边，凯普莱特太太有话对她说，朱丽叶不情愿地离开了罗密欧。罗密欧就问保姆谁是这个女孩的妈妈，当他得知这个女孩的妈妈就是凯普莱特太太的时候，他怔住了，他没想到自己爱上了仇家的女儿。尽管如此，舞会接近尾声，罗密欧还是不愿离去。他溜进了凯普莱特家族的果园，正巧看到了朱丽叶在房间的阳台上喃喃自语，述说着自己对罗密欧的爱慕，当罗密欧听到朱丽叶说到她进退两难的时候，他忍不住脱口而出，说自己宁愿重新接受洗礼，改掉他的姓氏，因为就是他的姓氏使得他们不能相爱。猛然从黑暗中传来的声音把朱丽叶吓了一跳,当她看清是罗密欧的时候,立即提醒他赶快离开,如果她的家人发现了罗密欧,事情会更糟糕。可是罗密欧毫不畏惧,他说没有什么可以阻挡他对朱丽叶的爱,他甚至可以放弃他的姓氏。于是,两个年轻人互相倾诉着对对方的爱恋。朱丽叶说,如果罗密欧真的爱她并想娶她,他们可以商定时间和地点结婚,她会在第二天等罗密欧的消息。当保姆再三催促朱丽叶进房间的时候,朱丽叶只好告别罗密欧,罗密欧也只好依依不舍地离去。

　　第二天一大早,劳伦斯神父正在采集鲜花和草药,这些能用来制作药酒和酊剂,罗密欧找上门,请劳伦斯神父帮忙。神父听说了罗密欧喜欢罗萨琳的事情,还以为他是来请神父帮忙让他追到罗萨琳的,没想到,他对神父说他已经把罗萨琳这个名字彻底忘了,他现在爱的女孩是朱丽叶,所以想请神父为他们秘密主婚,越快越好。神父告诫他要聪明些,慢慢来,跑快了容易摔跤。不过,考虑到这两个年轻人的联姻也许可以化解两大家族的积怨,神父就同意帮这个忙。

　　朱丽叶的保姆找到罗密欧,带走了他留给朱丽叶的口信,让朱丽叶下午到教堂来,劳伦斯神父会为他们主持结婚仪式。当保姆外出跑腿时,朱丽叶在焦急地等着保姆回来。一看到保姆,朱丽叶就迫不及待地打听消息。保姆告诉她,下午罗密欧会在教堂里等着朱丽叶参加婚礼。与此同时,保姆会折回去找罗密欧的仆人拿绳梯,供他们晚上幽会的时候用。

　　当两个热恋中的年轻人在教堂里再次见面的时候,他们激动得紧紧抱在一起。劳伦斯神父赞叹他们的爱,但他担心他们的激情持续不了多久。很快,他就为两个年轻人主持了结婚仪式。

　　有一天,天气很热,班伏里奥、默古修及其侍童走在街上的时候,遇到了提伯尔特以及凯普莱特家族的几个人。提伯尔特问默古修是否还和罗密欧做朋友,这惹怒了默古修。这时罗密欧走了过来,于是提伯尔特对默古修说"他的男人"来了。默古修被提伯尔特恶心到了。接着,提伯尔特又称呼走过来的罗密欧为恶棍。罗密欧不但没有生气,反而劝说提伯尔特要冷静,他还说他爱提伯尔特的家人就如同他爱自己的家人一样。他这样说是因为他和朱丽叶已经秘密结婚了。默古修看到罗密欧一副奴颜婢膝的样子,感到难以接受,于是他拔出了剑,提伯尔特也拔出了剑,一场恶斗开始了,罗密欧试图阻止他们,但没能成功。提伯尔特给了默古修致命一击。临死之前,默古修诅咒了两大家族。罗密欧为他好朋友的死难过,当提伯尔特再次出现在广场的时候,罗密欧走到他跟前说,今天他们两个必须有一个去天堂陪伴默古修,接着,他们俩都拔出了剑搏杀起来,提伯尔特被罗密欧刺死。

　　两大家族的家长和王子都赶来了。凯普莱特太太要求严惩杀死提伯尔特的凶手。由于提伯尔特杀人在先,王子判定将罗密欧流放到曼图亚,并且他必须立刻离开维罗纳。如果罗密欧还在这个城市逗留,他就难逃死罪。

　　罗密欧很后悔自己太冲动。对他来说,流放比死更让他难受,因为他不得不和他的新婚妻子分开。劳伦斯神父安慰罗密欧说,他将会公开他们已婚的事实,然后去找王子求情以获得他的原谅,他还会争取两大家族的和解,这样一来,罗密欧就可以回到维罗纳和他的妻子团聚了。在这之前,罗密欧必须老老实实待在曼图亚。罗密欧接受了神父的劝告，他准备晚上先爬绳梯到朱丽叶那里过夜，第二天凌晨便动身去曼图亚，这样就没人会发现他。

第二天，罗密欧按照计划启程，前往曼图亚，凯普莱特太太来到朱丽叶跟前，让她准备好周四嫁给帕里斯。现在是周一。帕里斯和凯普莱特老爷刚刚就结婚的安排达成一致。他们认为，朱丽叶和帕里斯结婚，就可以冲淡表兄提伯尔特之死带给她的悲伤情绪。朱丽叶对妈妈说，她宁愿嫁给她的仇人罗密欧，也不愿意嫁给帕里斯。当她发现抗婚无效的时候，她去找劳伦斯神父寻求帮助。神父给了她一瓶药，告诉她周三晚上喝下药，她的呼吸就会停止，脸色会变得苍白，身体也会变得僵硬，如同死去一般。她的家人就会为她穿上最华丽的衣服，把她放在没有盖的棺木里，安置在他们家的墓穴里，这种假死状态会持续42小时。神父会派人送信给罗密欧，告诉他这个计划，以便他在朱丽叶苏醒过来之前赶回维罗纳，并且在墓地等待她醒过来，然后他们再双双返回曼图亚。

一切都按照计划进行。然而，不幸的是，给罗密欧的信出了岔子。去送信的约翰神父把劳伦斯神父写给罗密欧的信原封不动地带回来了。约翰神父和另一位神父一起去送信时，中途去看望过感染了瘟疫的病人，结果他们俩都被隔离起来，不允许进入曼图亚。与此同时，罗密欧的仆人巴尔萨泽目睹了朱丽叶的葬礼。他快马加鞭赶到曼图亚，告诉罗密欧这个噩耗。罗密欧找到药剂师买了剧毒药，然后和巴尔萨泽一同赶回维罗纳。

罗密欧砸开朱丽叶家的墓穴门的时候，被赶来"吊唁"的帕里斯发现了。帕里斯不让罗密欧砸门，罗密欧好言相劝，让帕里斯不要管他，并对帕里斯说他不想伤及无辜，但是帕里斯就是不听，继续阻止罗密欧进入墓穴，并且扬言要将罗密欧这个罪犯抓起来。这激怒了罗密欧，两个人动起手来，罗密欧杀死了帕里斯。接着，他打开墓穴来到朱丽叶的棺木旁边，他亲了一下美丽的朱丽叶，便喝下毒药离开了人世。

劳伦斯神父也来到了墓穴，他发现帕里斯和罗密欧两个的尸体时大吃一惊。这时，朱丽叶已经醒过来了，她问神父她的丈夫怎么样了。神父告诉她，罗密欧已经不在人世了。神父劝说朱丽叶赶紧和他一同离开墓穴，他会送她去修道院。朱丽叶不愿跟他走。此时，外面传来守夜人的说话声，劳伦斯神父只得赶紧先行离去。朱丽叶吻了吻罗密欧的嘴唇，试图舔到一些残余的毒药，让毒药毒死自己。随着外面传来的声音越来越近，她加快了动作。这时，她正好看到罗密欧身上有一把匕首，于是她毫不犹豫地抽出匕首，刺进了自己的身体。

所有人都赶过来了：守夜人、帕里斯的侍童、王子、凯普莱特老爷和太太、蒙塔古老爷，以及从墓地逃出去的劳伦斯神父（他的神情非常可疑，哭哭啼啼的，身体颤抖着，手里拿着掘墓的工具）。神父被迫讲出了事情的前因后果，巴尔萨泽证实了神父所言，并以罗密欧写给蒙塔古老爷的信佐证。王子谴责凯普莱特和蒙塔古两位老爷，就是他们彼此之间的仇恨导致了这么多人的死亡。于是，凯普莱特老爷向蒙塔古老爷伸出手来，两人握手言和，两个家族的仇恨终于得以化解。蒙塔古老爷宣布，他将为忠贞的朱丽叶建造一座黄金雕像，而凯普莱特老爷也宣布，他也将为罗密欧建造一座雕像。

5　Famous quotes

【Quote 1】

The Chorus
Two households, both alike in dignity,
in fair Verona, where we lay our scene,
from ancient grudge break to new mutiny,
where civil blood makes civil hands unclean.
From forth the fatal loins of these two foes,
a pair of star-cross'd lovers take their life;
whose misadventured piteous overthrows,
doth with their death bury their parents' strife.
The fearful passage of their death-mark'd love,
and the continuance of their parents' rage,
which, but their children's end, nought could remove,
is now the two hours' traffic of our stage;
the which if you with patient ears attend,
what here shall miss, our toil shall strive to mend. [4]
(Prologue)

◆ Paraphrase

In beautiful Verona, where our play takes place,
there are two families, both equally noble.
From their old grudge there is an outbreak of new fighting,
in which they stain their refined hands with fellow citizens' blood.
A pair of ill-fated lovers from the deadly bloodlines of
these two feuding households commit suicide.
Their sad and tragic deaths put an end to their parents' fighting.
Now, for the two hours in which we are onstage,
we will present the story of their love and death,
which was the only thing that could stop their families' rage.
If we've left anything out of this prologue,
just listen with patient ears
—we will work to make everything understood. [5]

Unit 2　Romeo and Juliet

◇ 原文译文

　　故事发生在维罗纳名城,有两家门第相当的巨族,累世的宿怨激起了新争,鲜血把市民的白手污渎。是命运注定这两家仇敌,生下了一对不幸的恋人,他们悲惨凄凉的陨灭,和解了他们交恶的尊亲。这一段生生死死的恋爱,还有那两家父母的嫌隙,把一对多情的儿女杀害,演成了今天这一本戏剧。交代过这几句挈领提纲,请诸位耐着心细听端详。[6]

【Quote 2】

Mercutio

True, I talk of dreams,
which are the children of an idle brain,
begot of nothing but vain fantasy,
which is as thin of substance as the air
and more inconstant than the wind,
who woos even now the frozen bosom of the north,
and, being angered, puffs away from thence,
turning his face to the dew-dropping south. [7]
(Act 1, Scene 4)

[Mercutio (on the left, played by John McEnery) talking about dreams to Romeo (on the right, played by Leonard Whiting) in a 1968 film directed by Franco Zeffirelli.]

◇ Paraphrase

Mercutio

True. I'm talking about dreams,
which are produced by a brain that's doing nothing.
Dreams are born of no more than empty fantasy,

which lack substance like air,
and are more unpredictable than the wind,
which can blow on the frozen north and
then suddenly get angry and blow south.[8]

◇ 原文译文

对了,梦本来是痴人脑中的胡思乱想;它的本质像空气一样稀薄;它变化莫测,就像一阵风,刚才还在向着冰雪的北方求爱,忽然发起恼来,一转身又到雨露的南方来了。[9]

【Quote 3】

Romeo
I fear too early,
for my mind misgives some consequence yet hanging in the stars
shall bitterly begin his fearful date with this night's revels,
and expire the term of a despisèd life closed in my breast
by some vile forfeit of untimely death.
But he that hath the steerage of my course,
direct my sail. On, lusty gentlemen.[10]
(Act 1, Scene 4)

(Romeo talking about his premonition in a 1968 film directed by Franco Zeffirelli.)

◇ Paraphrase

Romeo
I fear we're going to arrive too early.

I have a feeling this party tonight is fated to set in motion
some awful destiny that will result in my own untimely death.
But whoever's in charge of my fate can steer me where they want.
Let's go, my lusty friends![11]
(Act 1, Scene 4)

◇ 原文译文

我怕也许是太早了；我仿佛觉得有一种不可知的命运，将要从我们今天晚上的狂欢开始它恐怖的统治，我这可憎恨的生命，将要遭遇残酷的夭折而告一结束。可是让支配我的前途的上帝指导我的行动吧！前进，勇敢的朋友们！[12]

【Quote 4】

Romeo

He jests at scars that never felt a wound.
But soft! What light through yonder window breaks?
It is the east, and Juliet is the sun.
Arise, fair sun, and kill the envious moon,
who is already sick and pale with grief,
that thou, her maid, art far more fair than she.
Be not her maid since she is envious.
Her vestal livery is but sick and green,
and none but fools do wear it. Cast it off!
It is my lady. Oh, it is my love.
Oh, that she knew she were!
She speaks, yet she says nothing. What of that?
Her eye discourses. I will answer it.
—I am too bold. 'Tis not to me she speaks.
Two of the fairest stars in all the heaven,
having some business,
do entreat her eyes to twinkle in their spheres till they return.
What if her eyes were there, they in her head?
The brightness of her cheek would
shame those stars as daylight doth a lamp.
Her eye in heaven would through the airy region stream so bright
that birds would sing and think it were not night.
See how she leans her cheek upon her hand.

Oh, that I were a glove upon that hand
that I might touch that cheek! [13]
(Act 2, Scene 2)

(Romeo viewing Juliet in the orchard in a 1968 film directed by Franco Zeffirelli.)

◇ Paraphrase

Romeo
He jokes about scars from wounds he's never felt.
But wait! What light is that in the window over there?
It is the east, and Juliet is the sun.
Rise, beautiful sun, and kill the jealous moon,
which is already sick and pale with grief because
Juliet, her maid, is more beautiful than she is.
Don't be her maid, since she's jealous.
The moon's virginity makes her look sick and green,
and only fools hold on to their virginity.
Throw it off. It is my lady. Oh, it is my love.
Oh, I wish she knew I loved her. She's talking,
but isn't saying anything.
Why is that? Her eyes are speaking.
I'll respond—no, I am too bold. It's not to me she speaks.
Two of the most beautiful stars in the sky had to go off on some business,
and begged her eyes to twinkle in their place until they return.
If her eyes were in the sky and the stars were in her head,
the brightness of her cheeks would overwhelm the stars,
just as daylight outshines a lamp.
And her eyes in the night sky would shine so brightly that
birds would start singing, thinking it was day.

Look how she leans her cheek against her hand.
I wish I were a glove on that hand,
so I could touch her cheek.[14]

◇ 原文译文

没有受过伤的人才会讥笑别人身上的创痕。轻声！那边窗子里亮起来的是什么光？那就是东方，朱丽叶就是太阳！起来吧，美丽的太阳！赶走那妒忌的月亮，她因为她的女弟子比她美得多，已经气得面色惨白了。既然她这样妒忌着你，你不要忠于她吧，脱下她给你的这一身惨绿色的贞女的道服，它是只配给愚人穿的。那是我的意中人。啊！那是我的爱。唉，但愿她知道我在爱着她！她欲言又止，可是她的眼睛已经道出了她的心事。待我去回答她吧；不，我不要太鲁莽，她不是对我说话。天上两颗最灿烂的星，因为有事他去，请求她的眼睛替代它们在空中闪耀。要是她的眼睛变成了天上的星，天上的星变成了她的眼睛，那便怎样呢？她脸上的光辉会掩盖了星星的明亮，正像灯光在朝阳下黯然失色一样；在天上的她的眼睛，会在太空中大放光明，使鸟儿误认为黑夜已经过去而展开它们的歌喉。瞧！她用纤手托住了脸，那姿态是多么美妙！啊，但愿我是那一只手上的手套，好让我亲一亲她脸上的香泽！[15]

【Quote 5】

Juliet

O Romeo, Romeo! Wherefore art thou Romeo?
Deny thy father, and refuse thy name.
Or, if thou wilt not, be but sworn my love,
and I'll no longer be a Capulet.[16]
(Act 2, Scene 2)

[Juliet (played by Olivia Hussey) expressing her dilemma in a 1968 film directed by Franco Zeffirelli.]

◇ Paraphrase

Juliet

Oh, Romeo, Romeo, why must you be Romeo?
Deny your father and give up your name.
Or, if you won't change your name,
just swear your love to me and I'll give up being a Capulet. [17]

◇ 原文译文

罗密欧啊,罗密欧!为什么你偏偏是罗密欧呢?否认你的父亲,抛弃你的姓名吧;也许你不愿意这样做,那么只要你宣誓做我的爱人,我也不愿再姓凯普莱特了。[18]

【Quote 6】

Juliet

'Tis but thy name that is my enemy.
Thou art thyself, though not a Montague.
What's Montague? It is nor hand, nor foot,
nor arm, nor face, nor any other part belonging to a man.
O, be some other name!
What's in a name?
That which we call a rose by any other word would smell as sweet.
So Romeo would, were he not Romeo called,
retain that dear perfection which he owes without that title.
Romeo, doff thy name, and for that name,
which is no part of thee. Take all myself. [19]

(Act 2, Scene 2)

◇ Paraphrase

Juliet

Only your name is my enemy.
You'd be yourself even if you ceased to be a Montague.
What's a Montague, after all?
It's not a hand, foot, arm, face, or any other body part.
Oh, change your name!
What's the significance of a name?
The thing we call a rose would smell as sweet
even if we called it by some other name.

So even if Romeo had some other name,

he would still be perfect.

Romeo, take off your Name

—which really has no connection to who you are

—and take all of me instead.[20]

◇ 原文译文

只有你的名字才是我的仇敌,你即使不姓蒙塔古,仍然是这样的一个你。姓不姓蒙塔古又有什么关系呢? 它又不是手,又不是脚,又不是手臂,又不是脸,又不是身体上任何其他的部分。啊! 换一换姓名吧! 姓名本来是没有意义的;我们叫作玫瑰的这一种花,要是换了个名字,它的香味还是同样的芬芳;罗密欧要是换了别的名字,他可爱的完美也绝不会有丝毫改变。罗密欧,抛弃了你的名字吧;我愿意把我整个的心灵,赔偿你这一个身外的空名。[21]

6 Questions for discussion

(1) What causes the tragedy of Romeo and Juliet?

(2) If you were Romeo or Juliet, what would you do in their situations?

(3) What do you think of Friar Laurence's plans to bring Romeo and Juliet together?

(4) What's Mercutio's interpretation of dreams and what is yours?

(5) What are the major themes of this story?

(6) What other famous love stories with tragical endings do you know, in Chinese or English culture?

7 References

[1] Romeo and Juliet:Work by Shakespeare[EB/OL]. [2023-12-07]. https://www.britannica.com/topic/Romeo-and-Juliet.

[2][3] Romeo and Juliet Study Guide[EB/OL]. https://www.litcharts.com/lit/romeo-and-juliet.

[4][7][10][13][16][19] Shakespeare W. Romeo and Juliet[M]. New York: Simon & Schuster, 2004.

[5][8][11][14][17][20] Romeo and Juliet:Shakespeare Translation[EB/OL]. https://www.litcharts.com/shakescleare/shakespeare-translations/romeo-and-juliet.

[6][9][12][15][18][21] 威廉·莎士比亚. 莎士比亚悲剧五种[M]. 朱生豪,译. 北京:人民文学出版社,2020.

Unit 3

King Lear

1 Characters

Lear(李尔王): King of England.
Goneril(贡纳尔): Eldest daughter of Lear.
Regan(里根): Second daughter of Lear.
Cordelia(科迪莉亚): Youngest daughter of Lear.
Duke of Burgundy(勃艮第公爵): Suitor of Cordelia.
King of France(法兰西国王): Suitor of Cordelia, who marries her although she is disowned by Lear.
Duke of Cornwall(康沃尔公爵): Regan's husband.
Duke of Albany(奥尔巴尼公爵): Goneril's husband.
Earl of Kent(肯特伯爵): Faithful friend of Lear, who is disguised as Caius after he is banished by Lear and continues to serve him.
Earl of Gloucester(格洛斯特伯爵): Old man whose eyes are gouged out by Cornwall.
Edgar(埃德加): Gloucester's elder son.
Edmund(埃德蒙): Gloucester's younger bastard son.
Fool(弄臣): Jester loyal to Lear.
Doctor(医生): Physician who treats Lear at Dover.
Oswald(奥斯瓦德): Steward of Goneril.
Captain(队长): Employee of Edmund.

2 Background

When *King Lear* was written (1604-1607), King James VI ruled Scotland and England. He tried to make the parliament approve the union of Scotland and England into one nation. It was James who first used the term "Great Britain" to describe the unity of England, Scotland, and Wales. Speaking to the parliament, he kept mentioning the misfortunes caused by the disunion of England under King Leir. The historical context of this play reminds us of the history of King Leir and the question of union/disunion of Great Britain in the playwright's own time.[1]

The most likely sources of Shakespeare's *King Lear* were the anonymous *The True Chronicle History of King Leir and His Daughters* (1594), Raphael Holinshed's *Chronicles of England, Scotland and Ireland* (1587), Sir Philip Sidney's *Arcadia* (1590, Chapter 10, Book 2), and a Dutch pamphlet entitled "Strange, Fearful and True News Which Happened at Carlstadt in the Kingdom of Croatia" (a source for the information on eclipses in Act 1, Scene, 2.)[2]

3 Settings

The action takes place in ancient Britain. The places include the castles of King Lear and the Earl of Gloucester, the palace of the Duke of Albany, a forest, a heath, a farmhouse near Gloucester's castle, a French camp near Dover, a British camp near Dover, and fields near Dover.[3]

4 Synopsis

The English King Lear is now eighty years old. He wants to retire, so he decides to divide his kingdom and hand it over to his three daughters. How much each of them inherits will depend on how much she pleases him. Whoever flatters him most will get the biggest part. The eldest daughter, Goneril, declares that she loves Lear more than she does wealth, liberty and any valuable things and that she loves him as much as she loves life itself. She loves her father so much that words fail to express it. Lear is pleased to hear this and Goneril inherits one third of his kingdom. The second daughter, Regan, says that her elder sister has expressed her love for her father. She adds that she loves her father to such an extent that she disregards joy in her life. Her sole happiness that she values is his father's love. Lear feels flattered and imparts another third to Regan. The youngest daughter of Lear, Cordelia, feels nervous and worried because she lacks a glib tongue that her sisters have. Her love is more sincere and weightier than words. When Cordelia's turn comes, Lear asks her what she can tell him to get a larger part of his kingdom than her sisters have, because she is his favourite daughter. To his displeasure and disappointment, Cordelia replies "nothing"—she will say nothing to win his kingdom. Lear gives Cordelia another chance, saying that "nothing" will bring her nothing. Cordelia explains that she does love him, honour him and obey him. She loves him according to her duty as a daughter, but how can it be possible that he is her only love as her sisters have claimed that they only love him? She points out a fact that after she is married, her husband will take part of her love. Lear is so furious at her blunt words that he disinherits and disowns her, saying that her honesty will be her only dowry. He then divides the part that he has kept for Cordelia between his two sons-in-law, the Duke of Albany and the Duke of Cornwall. When the earl of Kent intercedes on Cordelia's behalf and insists that Lear redress his unwise decision, Lear banishes him.

The Duke of Burgundy, one of Cordelia's suitors, pleads with Lear to materialize his offer of dowry as he has promised so that he will marry her, but Lear is adamant. Burgundy withdraws his courtship and leaves. The other suitor, King of France, willingly accepts Cordelia as his wife and queen. He says to Burgundy that love is not love when it mingles with irrelevant matters, and that Cordelia's virtues are the most valuable dowry. Lear bids France to take Cordelia away because he doesn't want to see her anymore. Cordelia bids farewell to her sisters, reminding them to live up with their claimed love for their father, and leaves with the French king for France.

Lear tells Goneril and Regan that he will alternate months living with them, together with his 100 knights as his followers. When he comes to live with Goneril first, however, he and his men are not welcome. Goneril tells her steward Oswald to neglect Lear. She complains that Lear and his followers are so rowdy and cause chaos in her house and demands that Lear cut down the number of knights to half. Lear is shocked by Goneril's coldness and ingratitude. He feels insulted and infuriated too. Then he storms out of Goneril's palace, cursing her. By this time, Kent has disguised as a commoner named Caius and come into Lear's service. Lear bids Kent to send his letter to Regan that he has been illtreated by Goneril and will go to live with her. Meanwhile, Goneril dispatches Oswald to deliver her letter to Regan in which she tells Regan about their father's foolish behaviour, rude words and violent temper.

Receiving the letters from the king and Goneril and hearing that Lear is on his way to her place, Regan thinks it would be best for her to be away from home. She and Cornwall, her husband, go to the Earl of Gloucester's castle. Gloucester has two sons. One is the younger one, Edmund, who is a bastard, and the other is Edgar, the elder. Gloucester loves both, but Edmund cannot inherit his property as an unlawful son. Edmund then tricks Gloucester into believing that Edgar wants to murder Gloucester, and when he stops him from doing so, Edgar wounds him and escapes (In fact Edmund gets Edgar in a mock fight during which he tells Edgar to flee because their father is somehow offended by him. After Edgar leaves, he wounds himself). Gloucester is angered. He sentences Edgar to death and declares Edmund his only legitimate heir. Regan and Cornwall welcome Edmund into their service. By this time, Kent/Caius and Oswald as messengers have also arrived at Gloucester's castle from different directions. Oswald supposes Kent a servant of Gloucester's house and asks him where to stable their horses. Kent speaks rudely to Oswald, calling him names like "rogue", "rascal", "villain", "bastard", and so on. Oswald is surprised. He asks Kent why he slanders him. He doesn't think that Kent knows him. Of course, Kent knows him. He abuses Oswald because he serves Goneril who maltreats the king. Kent challenges Oswald to a fight. He draws his sword and strikes Oswald, who cries for help. Edmund, Cornwall, Gloucester and some servants enter. After hearing Oswald's narration of how Kent has wronged him, Cornwall orders the servants to bring the stocks and lock Kent in. Gloucester suggests him against doing so, otherwise, the king will be insulted if his royal servant is treated like that. But Cornwall and Regan insist.

Lear arrives and feels humiliated to learn that Regan shuns meeting him on the pretext of being sick and weary, and to see his messenger's legs are put in the stocks. He insists on summoning Cornwall and Regan who turn up reluctantly. Lear complains about the ill-treatment in Goneril's house, but Regan suggests that he go back to ask for Goneril's forgiveness, dismiss half of his knights and stay with her for the rest of the month. Goneril also comes here, and Lear blames her for breaking his heart. He refuses to go back to Goneril's place, calling her a disease in his flesh and "a pimple", "a sore" and "a raised tumor" in his blood. He expresses his intention to live with Regan. Regan says that it's expensive and dangerous to maintain fifty knights, and she would only accept twenty-five. He says in this case, he will go back to live with Goneril because she can let him maintain fifty, so her love seems to be double that of Regan's. Then both daughters agree that he doesn't need even one single knight as they have plenty of servants to tend to him. They can put up with living him, but none of his knights. Lear cannot bear anymore. He exits in the imminent storm, weeping and cursing his two daughters, and calling them "unnatural hags". Regan orders the door to be shut against Lear. Lear's Fool follows him, though Lear has started to lose his sense. Kent pays a gentleman to go to Dover to deliver his message to Cordelia what sufferings her father has experienced.

Gloucester expresses to Cornwall and Regan that he wants to help the king and provide him shelter. This irritates those who takes his ownership of his own house. Gloucester then tells Edmund to stand on the king's side and that he will find the king and help him secretly. But after Gloucester exits, Edmund says he will inform against his father so that he will get what his father will lose. When Cornwall learns of Gloucester's stand on the king's side, he charges him with treason and declares that he will pay for his betrayal. Regan demands that he be hanged and Goneril demands that his eyes be plucked out. Cornwall bids the servants to find Gloucester, who is now with the king, the Fool, Kent and Edgar. They are sheltering from the storm in a hovel where Edgar has been staying. He disguises as the poor Tom, a beggar and madman, to stay safe from being captured and killed. Gloucester doesn't recognize him. Cornwall sends Edmund away to inform Albany of the landing of the French army and preparing for the war so that he will not witness his father's punishment. When Gloucester is brought in, Cornwall asks him what he has done to help the king. Gloucester replies that he has the king brought to Dover. Cornwall is enraged and gouges Gloucester's eyes, but he receives a fatal strike by one of his own servants who cannot bear to see Cornwall's cruelty. The servant is then killed by Regan. Gloucester calls Edmund for help, only to be told by Regan that it's useless to call Edmund because he hates Gloucester, and it is right Edmund who reveals Gloucester's treason to them. It's not until then does Gloucester realize that he has wronged Edgar who has been slandered by Edmund.

Edgar is grieved over his father's suffering. He continues his disguise as the beggar to help Gloucester who wants him to lead the way to Dover where there is a cliff, and the old man wants to commit suicide there. But the place that Edgar leads him to is in fact flat ground. When Gloucester jumps, he only falls. Edgar pretends to be a stranger who has witness his "jumping off the cliff" and speaks to him in another voice that it is a miracle that he has survived. It must be the gods who have saved his life. He should from now on have a carefree and peaceful mind. They come upon Lear and feels sorry for the king's loneliness and insanity. Cordelia has learnt of his sufferings and sends some gentlemen to look for him while the French army is entering England to avenge Lear's maltreatment. The gentlemen find Lear and brings him to the French camp. Cordelia requires a French doctor to cure Lear of his insanity.

After Lear is taken away, Oswald come upon Gloucester. Regan has given an order that whoever kills Gloucester will gain her favour because wherever he goes, people pity him and turn against them. But instead of killing Gloucester, Oswald is killed by Edgar. Before he dies, Oswald asks Edgar to help him to deliver a letter to Edmund. Edgar opens the letter and finds it was written by Goneril who wants Edmund to kill Albany so that they can marry. Goneril doesn't love Albany. He has blamed Goneril for her cruelty to her father. He has learnt of Gloucester's blindness and declares that he will avenge his lost eyes. He refuses to partake in their evil deeds. Later Edgar hands the letter over to Albany.

Albany has also heard of Edmund's betrayal of his father. He despises Edmund but has to fight with him against their common enemies—the French army. They win the battle. Lear and Cordelia are taken prisoner. Albany wants to be merciful to Lear and Cordelia, but Edmund has given his captain a secret order to have Lear and Cordelia hanged to make it appear that they hang themselves. Albany has read Goneril's letter to Edmund and now he charges him with treason and summons someone to challenge Edmund and prove that he is a traitor. Edgar responds to the summon and wounds Edmund mortally, then he reveals his true identity. He tells them that before he comes, he has told their father who he is. The old man has mixed feelings of grief (over Edmund's betrayal) and joy (to see Edgar alive) so intensely that he dies. The dying Edmund admits to all the evil things he has done, including his promise to both Goneril and Regan to marry them. Regan is a widow and seems to be justified to marry Edmund. Out of jealousy, Goneril has poisoned Regan. Now that her conspiracy is revealed, she has committed suicide. Edmund says that now the three of them will be united in death. But before he dies, Edmund wants to do something good. He tells them to go to the prison to save Lear and Cordelia's life. But it is too late. Lear is holding Cordelia's body in great grief. The captain has already hanged Cordelia and Lear has killed the captain. He is so grieved over Cordelia's death that he dies. Albany asks Edgar and Kent who has also revealed his true identity to help him rebuild the country, but Kent says he will follow the king, his master.

【剧情介绍】

李尔王是英国的国王,已经 80 岁了。他想退位,并把领土分割,交给他的三个女儿和女婿们掌管。至于每人可以得到多少,将取决于她们取悦父王的程度,最大的一份会给让他最开心的女儿。大女儿贡纳尔说她对父王的爱胜过她对财富、自由以及一切珍贵物品的喜爱,她热爱父王如同她热爱生命本身一样。她的这种爱是任何语言都无法表达出来的。

李尔王对贡纳尔的表白很满意,就分给了她三分之一的国土。二女儿里根说她姐姐的话表达的也正是她想要对父王说的,她补充说,她生活中的所有快乐都比不上她对父王的爱更让她快乐。她人生最大的幸福便是父王对她的爱。李尔王听闻此言,也高兴地分给里根三分之一的国土。轮到小女儿科迪莉亚的时候,她十分紧张,因为她说不出两个姐姐那样的甜言蜜语,她的爱是真诚的,分量之重是语言表达不出来的。所以,当李尔王问她会说些什么话来取悦他以得到比她两个姐姐更多的时候,这个最让他疼爱的女儿居然只说了一句"没什么"——她说不出什么来取悦父王而得到他的国土,李尔王非常不快,也很失望。他决定再给她一个机会,提醒她如果她说不出什么她就什么也得不到。科迪莉亚解释说,她爱父王,尊敬父王,听父王的话。她会对父王尽孝道,可是她怎么可能做到姐姐们所说的那样父王是她们唯一的爱呢?她指出一个事实:一旦她结婚,她的丈夫就会得到她一部分的爱。科迪莉亚耿直的言语激怒了李尔王,他宣布和她断绝父女关系,对她说就让她的诚实为她做嫁妆,并且把原本留给她的那份也分给了另外两个女婿——奥尔巴尼公爵和康沃尔公爵。肯特伯爵为科迪莉亚求情,恳请李尔王重新考虑他的决定,李尔王不但不接受肯特伯爵的建议,反而将他流放了。

　　科迪莉亚有两个追求者,一个是勃艮第公爵,另一个是法国国王。勃艮第公爵恳请李尔王按照之前的约定为科迪莉亚准备嫁妆,这样他就娶科迪莉亚为妻,可是李尔王坚决不改变他的心意,勃艮第公爵只好放弃求婚,然后离开了。法国国王非常愿意娶科迪莉亚,让她做自己的王后,并说如果爱情夹杂其他不相关的东西,就不是真正的爱情了。他还说,科迪莉亚的美德就是她最珍贵的嫁妆。李尔王让法国国王赶快把科迪莉亚带走,因为他永远也不想再看到她了。科迪莉亚和姐姐们说再见,叮嘱她们一定要遵守她们的承诺好好爱她们的父王,然后跟随她的丈夫去了法国。

　　李尔王告诉贡纳尔和里根,他会带上随从——100个骑士——轮流在她们家住一个月。头一个月,李尔王在贡纳尔家住,然而贡纳尔并不待见他们。贡纳尔甚至吩咐她的管家奥斯瓦德不要搭理她的父王。她还抱怨李尔王和他的随从太吵了,把她家搞得一片混乱。她还让李尔王把他的随从数量减少一半。李尔王被贡纳尔的冷酷无情和忘恩负义震撼到了,同时也感到很受伤和愤怒。于是他一边诅咒着贡纳尔,一边气冲冲地离开了她的家,准备去投奔他的二女儿里根。他派遣装扮成平民留在他身边为他效劳的肯特伯爵去送信给里根,告知她他们受到贡纳尔的虐待,打算去她家住。与此同时,贡纳尔也给妹妹写了一封信,让奥斯瓦德送过去,贡纳尔在信中向妹妹描述了父王愚蠢的行为、粗鲁的语言和暴躁的脾气。

　　里根收到父王和姐姐的信,得知父王要来她家,她想自己还是不在家最好。于是里根和她的丈夫康沃尔一起来到格洛斯特伯爵家。格洛斯特有两个儿子。小儿子埃德蒙是他的私生子,大儿子叫埃德加。格洛斯特对两个儿子一样疼爱,但埃德蒙是私生子,不能继承父亲的财产,于是埃德蒙设计让父亲相信埃德加要杀他,埃德蒙在试图阻止埃德加伤害父亲的时候受伤了,埃德加也逃走了(事实上,埃德蒙让埃德加和他假装打斗,他告诉埃德加,他们的父亲不知何故在生埃德加的气,他让埃德加离开家,不要继续惹父亲生气。等到埃德加走了之后,埃德蒙就使用了苦肉计)。听完埃德蒙的诉说,格洛斯特气坏了。于是,他宣布判处埃德加死罪，埃德蒙将成为他唯一的继承人。里根和康沃尔欢迎埃德蒙为他们效劳。这时，肯特伯爵（化妆成凯厄斯）和奥斯瓦德作为李尔王和贡纳尔的信使，也从不同方向来到了格洛斯特家。奥斯瓦德以为肯特伯爵是格洛斯特家的仆人，就问他拴马的地方在哪里。肯特伯爵骂他是无赖、流氓、恶棍、杂种。奥斯瓦德很诧异地问肯特伯爵为什么要诋毁他，他应该不认识自己才对。肯特伯爵当然认识奥斯瓦德。他大骂奥斯瓦德，是因为他觉得奥斯瓦德是贡纳尔的走狗，他伺候的主人虐待自己的亲生父亲李尔王。肯特伯爵还挑战奥斯瓦德，要和他决斗，他拔出剑袭击奥斯瓦德，后者大喊救命。埃德蒙、康沃尔、格洛斯特带着几个仆人过来了，听完奥斯瓦德诉说在肯特伯爵那里遭受的冤屈，康沃尔就命令仆人拿来枷锁把肯特伯爵锁上。格洛斯特劝说康沃尔不要这样做，毕竟肯特伯爵是国王的人，他这样做等于侮辱国王，但是康沃尔和里根不理会他的劝告。

李尔王也来了。当他听说里根自称又病又累不肯接见他，还看到他的信使被套上枷锁，李尔王感到受了侮辱。他坚持让康沃尔和里根出来见他，这两个人才不情愿地出来了。李尔王告诉他们贡纳尔如何虐待他，可是里根建议他还是回到姐姐家，向她道歉以得到她的原谅，并且把他的骑士数量减掉一半，然后把这个月住满。这时，贡纳尔也来了。李尔王谴责她伤透了他的心，骂她是自己肉体上生出来的病痛，是疱，是疮，是他血液里的一个肿瘤。他说他将和里根一起生活。可是里根说养活50个骑士费用太高，并且存在安全隐患，如果将骑士数量减少到25个，她才勉强可以接受。听罢，李尔王说他还不如去和贡纳尔生活，好歹贡纳尔还会养他的50个骑士，李尔王表示贡纳尔对他的爱是里根的两倍。可是接下来，两个女儿一致认为她们的父王一个骑士也不需要，毕竟她们的家里都有足够数量的仆人来伺候他。她们只同意养父王一个人。李尔王再也无法忍受了，他迎着即将到来的暴风雨夺门而去，诅咒着他的两个女儿，骂她们是忘恩负义的老妖婆。里根命人关上大门。李尔王的弄臣跟在他身边。李尔王渐渐疯了。肯特伯爵花钱请人带信给科迪莉亚，告知她李尔王的不幸遭遇。

格洛斯特对康沃尔和里根说他想去找国王，让他有个遮风挡雨的地方，这些话惹怒了康沃尔和里根，他们把格洛斯特赶出了他自己的家。格洛斯特让埃德蒙也站在国王这边，他告诉儿子，他会找到国王并且偷偷帮助他。等他走了之后，埃德蒙说他要告发自己的父亲，这样他会得到父亲失去的一切。得知格洛斯特的背叛，康沃尔判定他犯了叛国罪，并说他将为自己的背叛付出代价。里根要求将格洛斯特绞死，贡纳尔则要求把他的眼珠挖出来。康沃尔派他的仆人找到了格洛斯特，这时他正和国王、国王的弄臣、肯特伯爵以及埃德加一起。他们找到了一个避雨的棚屋，这里正是埃德加藏身的地方。为了不被逮捕和杀害，埃德加把自己打扮成了乞丐和疯子，改名为汤姆。格洛斯特没有认出他。康沃尔派埃德蒙给奥尔巴尼送信，告知他法国军队已经登陆了，让他准备战斗。康沃尔把埃德蒙支开，是避免他目睹父亲受刑。格洛斯特被带进来后，康沃尔问他是如何帮助国王的，格洛斯特说他已经把国王送到了多佛。康沃尔一怒之下挖出了格洛斯特的眼珠，不过他在作恶的时候，遭到他自己的仆人给他的致命一击，这个仆人实在看不下去他的残忍行为，这个仆人也因此被里根杀了。格洛斯特呼喊埃德蒙救他，可是里根告诉他不要做无用的叫唤，告发他叛变的人正是埃德蒙,因为埃德蒙恨他。直到这时,格洛斯特才幡然醒悟,埃德加是无辜的,他冤枉了这个儿子。

埃德加看到父亲遭受的痛苦,心里非常悲痛。他继续扮成乞丐,陪在他的身边。格洛斯特请埃德加把他带到多佛的悬崖那里,准备跳下悬崖自尽。可是埃德加把他带到的地方却是平地。当他纵身一跳的时候,只摔了一跤。埃德加假装成一个刚刚目睹了他"跳崖"过程的路人。他换个声音和格洛斯特说话,告诉他居然跳崖还没死,简直是一个奇迹,一定是神在帮助他。如此看来,他内心应该得到宁静,能无忧无虑地活下去。他们见到了李尔王,对孤身一人、已经发疯的李尔王非常同情。科迪莉亚已经得知了父王的不幸遭遇,派人找到了他。法国军队已经踏上了英国的国土,准备为李尔王遭受的不幸报仇。科迪莉亚的人找到李尔王后把他带到法国的军营。科迪莉亚吩咐法国的医生治好她的父王。

李尔王被带走医治,奥斯瓦德遇到了格洛斯特。里根早已下令,杀了格洛斯特的人将会得到她的恩宠,因为只要格洛斯特活着,不管他到哪里,他都会获得人们的同情,反过来人们就会反抗造成他不幸的人。本来想杀害格洛斯特的奥斯瓦德反而被埃德加杀了。临死之前,奥斯瓦德拜托埃德加将一封信送到埃德蒙手上。埃德加打开信,发现是贡纳尔写给埃德蒙的,她吩咐埃德蒙把奥尔巴尼杀了,然后他们两个就可以结婚了。贡纳尔不爱奥尔巴尼。奥尔巴尼指责她不该如此对待自己的亲生父亲。奥尔巴尼听说格洛斯特眼睛被挖的消息,他决定替他报仇。奥尔巴尼不肯和他们一起作恶。后来,埃德加把这封信交到了奥尔巴尼的手上。

奥尔巴尼还得知了埃德蒙对他父亲的背叛。尽管他鄙视这个人,但为了对付共同的敌人,也就是法国军队,奥尔巴尼不得不和埃德蒙并肩作战。结果,英国军队赢了,李尔王和科迪莉亚都成了俘虏。奥尔巴尼想宽恕李尔王和科迪莉亚,可是埃德蒙早就给他的队长下了密令,让其将这两个人绞死,还要伪装成他们是自缢身亡的。奥尔巴尼看了贡纳尔写给埃德蒙的信后,宣布埃德蒙犯了叛国罪。他问有没有人愿意讨伐这个叛徒,来证实他就是叛徒,埃德加响应了奥尔巴尼的讨伐命令,对埃德蒙拔出了剑并给了他致命一击。接着,他就说出了自己的真实身份。他还说,在他来这里讨伐埃德蒙之前,他也告诉了他父亲格洛斯特他是埃德加,老伯爵悲喜交加,悲的是他有一个埃德蒙这样背叛他的儿子,喜的是被他冤枉的大儿子埃德加还活着,由于悲喜过度,老伯爵不幸离开了人世。埃德蒙承认了他所犯的一切过错,包括他向贡纳尔和里根两个女人承诺过要娶她们。里根现在是寡妇,可以名正言顺地嫁给埃德蒙。出于嫉妒,贡纳尔毒死了里根,如今她和埃德蒙的奸计败露,她也只好了结自己的性命。现在,他们三个终于可以去天堂团聚了。不过,埃德蒙在死之前想弥补他的罪过,他让他们赶紧去监狱挽救李尔王和科迪莉亚。然而,已经来不及了,李尔王抱着科迪莉亚的尸体进来了,科迪莉亚被队长杀害,李尔王把那个队长杀了,可是他无法挽回科迪莉亚的生命。李尔王悲伤过度而死。奥尔巴尼希望埃德加和已经亮明真实身份的肯特伯爵帮他重整他们的国家,可是肯特伯爵说他将随他的主人也就是李尔王而去。

5 Famous quotes

【Quote 1】

Gloucester

These late eclipses in the sun and moon portend no good to us.
Though the wisdom of nature can reason it thus and thus,
yet nature finds itself scourged by the sequent effects.
Love cools, friendship falls off,
brothers divide, in cities mutinies, in countries discord,
in palaces treason, and the bond cracked 'twixt son and father.
This villain of mine comes under the prediction
—there's son against father.
The king falls from bias of nature
—there's father against child.
We have seen the best of our time.
Machinations, hollowness, treachery, and all ruinous disorders
follow us disquietly to our graves.
Find out this villain, Edmund.
It shall lose thee nothing. Do it carefully.
And the noble and true-hearted Kent banished,
his offense honesty! 'Tis strange, strange. [4]
(Act 1, Scene 2)

◆ Paraphrase

Gloucester

These recent eclipses of the sun and moon are evil omens for us.
Though science can explain how they happen,
They are still omens, and bad things always follow eclipses.
Love loses its passion, friendships fall apart,
brothers become enemies, riots break out in cities,
civil wars begin, treason infiltrates palaces,
and the bond between fathers and sons is broken.
This villainous son of mine fits the prediction of the bad omens
—that's son against father.
The king goes against his former nature

—that's father against child.
The best part of our age has passed.
Schemes, emptiness, treachery, and chaos will follow us loudly to our graves.
Find out the truth about this villain, Edmund.
It won't damage your reputation. Just do it carefully.
And the noble and true-hearted Kent has been banished,
for the crime of being honest! It's strange, strange. [5]

[Gloucester (played by Norman Rodway) speaking to Edmund (played by Michael Kitchen) in a 1982 film directed by Jonathan Miller.]

◇ 原文译文

最近这一些日食、月食果然不是好兆头;虽然人们凭着天赋的智慧,可以对它们做种种合理的解释,可是接踵而来的天灾人祸,却不能否认是上天对人们所施的惩罚。亲爱的人互相疏远,朋友变为陌路,兄弟化成仇敌;城市里有暴动,国家发生内乱,宫廷之内潜藏着逆谋;父不父,子不子,纲常伦纪完全破灭。我这畜生也是上应天数;有他这样逆亲犯上的儿子,也就像我们王上一样不慈不爱的父亲。我们最好的日子已经过去;现在只有一些阴谋、欺诈、叛逆、纷乱,追随在我们的背后,把我们赶下坟墓里去。爱德蒙,去把这畜生侦查个明白;那对你不会有什么妨碍的;你只要自己留心一点就是了。——忠心的肯特又被放逐了!他的罪名是正直!怪事,怪事![6]

【Quote 2】

Edgar
I heard myself proclaimed,
and by the happy hollow of a tree escaped the hunt.
No port is free,
no place that guard and most unusual vigilance
does not attend my taking.

Whiles I may 'scape,
I will preserve myself,
and am bethought to take the basest and most poorest shape
that ever penury in contempt of man brought near to beast.
My face I'll grime with filth,
blanket my loins, elf all my hair in knots,
and with presented nakedness outface the winds and persecutions of the sky.
The country gives me proof and precedent of Bedlam beggars,
who with roaring voices strike in their numbed and mortified bare arms
pins, wooden pricks, nails, sprigs of rosemary,
and with this horrible object from low farms,
poor pelting villages, sheepcotes, and mills,
sometime with lunatic bans, sometime with prayers,
enforce their charity.
"Poor Turlygod!" "Poor Tom!"
—That's something yet. Edgar I nothing am.[7]
(Act 2, Scene 3)

[Edgar (played by Anton Lesser) making his soliloquy in a 1982 film directed by Jonathan Miller.]

◇ Paraphrase

Edgar
I heard myself declared an outlaw,

and I was lucky to escape those hunting me by hiding in the trunk of a tree.
No port or road is safe for me,
and everywhere people are watching and waiting to arrest me.
But I'll survive as long as I can avoid being captured.
I've decided to disguise myself as the filthiest,
lowliest beggar that was ever hated by man.
I'll smear my face with dirt, wear a loincloth,
make my hair tangled and knotted,
and face the wind and bad weather almost naked.
I've seen in this country beggars who come from insane asylums,
who shriek and stab pins, skewers, nails,
and sprigs of rosemary into their numb and deadened arms.
With this horrible spectacle,
along with their insane curses and occasional prayers,
they force lowly farmers and poor villagers to give them alms.
"Poor Turlygood!" "Poor Tom!"
They call themselves.
That's at least something to be.
I'm nothing when I'm known as Edgar. [8]
(Act 2, Scene 3)

◇ 原文译文

　　听说他们已经发出告示捉我；幸亏我躲在一株空心的树干里，没有被他们找到。没有一处城门可以出入无阻；没有一个地方不是警卫森严，准备把我捉住！我总得设法逃过人家的耳目，保全自己的生命；我想还不如改扮为一个最卑贱穷苦，最为世人所轻视，和禽兽相去无几的家伙；我要用污泥涂在脸上，一块毡布裹住我的腰，把满头的头发打了许多乱结，赤身裸体，抵抗着风雨的侵凌。这地方本来有许多疯乞丐，他们高声叫喊，用针、木锥、钉子、迷迭香的树枝，刺在他们麻木而僵硬的手臂上；用这种可怕的状态，到那些穷苦的农场、乡村、羊棚和磨坊里去，有时候发出一些疯狂的诅咒，有时候向人哀求祈祷，乞讨一些布施。我现在学着他们的样子，一定不会引起人家的疑心。可怜的疯叫花子！可怜的汤姆！虽然有几分像，但我现在不再是埃德加了。[9]

【Quote 3】

King Lear
O, reason not the need!
Our basest beggars are in the poorest thing superfluous.
Allow not nature more than nature needs,

— 045 —

man's life's as cheap as beast's.
Thou art a lady.
If only to go warm were gorgeous,
why, nature needs not what thou gorgeous wear'st,
which scarcely keeps thee warm.
But, for true need
—you heavens, give me that patience, patience I need.
You see me here, you gods, a poor old man,
as full of grief as age, wretched in both.
If it be you that stir these daughters' hearts against their father,
fool me not so much to bear it tamely.
Touch me with noble anger.
And let not women's weapons, water drops,
stain my man's cheeks!
No, you unnatural hags,
I will have such revenges on you both that all the world shall
—I will do such things
—what they are yet I know not,
but they shall be the terrors of the earth.
You think I'll weep?
No, I'll not weep. [10]
(Act 2, Scene 4)

[Lear (on the right, played by Michael Hordern) speaking to Goneril (the taller one on the left, played by Gillian Barge) and Regan (the shorter one on the left, played by Penelope Wilton) in a 1982 film directed by Jonathan Miller.]

◆ Paraphrase

Lear

Oh, don't be so logical about needs!
Even the poorest beggars have at least something they don't need.
If you only allow people to have what they need to survive,
then a man's life becomes as cheap as an animal's.
You are a fashionable lady.
If you dressed only to stay warm,
then you wouldn't need the gorgeous clothes you're wearing,
as they hardly keep you warm at all.
But as for my true needs
—may the heavens give me endurance, the endurance that I need.
You see me here, you gods, a poor old man,
as wretched in his grief as he is in his frailty.
If it's you who inspire these daughters to turn against their father,
then at least don't make me such a fool
as to take their insolence without protesting.
Give me noble anger,
and don't let any womanly① tears stain my man's cheeks!
No, you unnatural hags,
I'll have such a revenge on you both that the whole world will...
I'll do such things...
I don't know what things I'll do yet,
but they will be terrible.
You think I'll weep?
No, I won't weep. [11]

◆ 原文译文

啊！不要跟我说什么需要不需要；最卑贱的乞丐，也有他的不值钱的身外之物；人生除了天然的需要以外，要是没有其他的享受，那和畜类的生活有什么分别。你是一位夫人；你穿着这样华丽的衣服，如果你的目的只是为了保持温暖，那就根本不合你的需要，因为这种盛装艳饰并不能使你温暖。可是，讲到真的需要，那么天啊，给我忍耐吧，我需要忍耐！神啊，你们看见我在这儿，一个可怜的老头子，被忧伤和老迈折磨得好苦！假如是你们鼓动这两个女儿的心，使她们忤逆她们的父亲，那么请你们不要尽是愚弄我，叫我

---

① In Shakespeare's time, a man who betrayed emotions was looked down upon as highly effeminate.

默默忍受吧;让我的心里激起了刚强的怒火,别让妇人所恃为武器的泪点玷污我的男子汉的面颊!不,你们这两个不孝的妖妇,我要向你们复仇,我要做出一些使全世界惊讶的事情来,虽然我现在还不知道我要怎么做。你们以为我将要哭泣;不,我不愿哭泣,我虽然有充分的哭泣的理由,可是我宁愿让这颗心碎成万片,也不愿流下一滴泪来。[12]

【Quote 4】

King Lear

Poor naked wretches, whereso'er you are,
that bide the pelting of this pitiless storm,
how shall your houseless heads and unfed sides,
your looped and windowed raggedness,
defend you from seasons such as these?
Oh, I have ta'en too little care of this!
Take physic, pomp.
Expose thyself to feel what wretches feel,
that thou mayst shake the superflux to them
and show the heavens more just. [13]

(Act 3, Scene 4)

(**Lear in the storm in a 1982 film directed by Jonathan Miller.**)

◆ Paraphrase

Poor homeless wretches, wherever you are,
Suffering through this pitiless storm
—with no roof over your heads,
no fat on your ribs, and only rags for clothing:
how will you defend yourselves against such weather?
Oh, when I was king I should have done more for you!

Cure yourself, men who live in luxury.

Expose yourself to feel what the poor and homeless feel,

so you can give them the surplus wealth you don't need,

and make the world a more just place. [14]

◆ 原文译文

衣不蔽体的不幸的人们,无论你们在什么地方,都得忍受着这样无情的暴风雨的袭击,你们的头上没有片瓦遮身,你们的腹中饥肠雷动,你们的衣服千疮百孔,怎么抵挡得了这样的气候呢?啊!我一向都没有想到这种事情。安享荣华的人们啊,睁开你们的眼睛,到外面来体味一下穷人所忍受的苦,分一些你们享用不了的福泽给他们,让上天知道你们不是全无心肝的人吧![15]

6　Questions for discussion

(1) What is the main plot and what subplots can you find?

(2) What is your attitude towards Edmund? Do you think he is an utter villain?

(3) How do you feel for King Lear? Do you think he deserves his treatment by Goneril and Regan?

(4) Make a comparison between King Lear and the Earl of Gloucester.

(5) What is the use of disguise in the play?

(6) How does filial piety differ in Western and Chinese cultures?

7　References

[1][2][3]　King Lear Study Guide[EB/OL]. https://www.litcharts.com/lit/king-lear.

[4][7][10][13]　Shakespeare W. King Lear[M]. New York: Simon & Schuster, 2015.

[5][8][11][14]　King Lear: Shakespeare Translation[EB/OL]. https://www.litcharts.com/shakescleare/shakespeare-translations/king-lear.

[6][9][12][15]　威廉·莎士比亚. 莎士比亚悲剧五种[M]. 朱生豪,译. 北京:人民文学出版社,2020.

Unit 4

Macbeth

1　Characters

Macbeth(麦克白): Nobleman of Scotland, the Thane of Glamis and later thane of Cawdor, and ambitious army general in Scotland. The historical Macbeth was an eleventh-century Scot who took the throne in 1040 after killing King Duncan Ⅰ, his cousin, in a battle near Elgin in the Moray district of Scotland. In 1057, Duncan's oldest son, Malcolm, killed him in battle and ended his reign. Malcolm assumed the throne as Malcolm Ⅲ.[1]

Lady Macbeth(麦克白夫人): Wife of Macbeth, who eggs Macbeth on to kill Duncan.

Duncan(邓肯): King of Scotland.

Malcolm(马尔科姆): Elder son of Duncan, the Prince of Cumberland, and Duncan's designated heir to the throne.

Donalbain(道纳班): Younger son of Duncan.

Banquo(班柯): Army general of Scotland. The historical Banquo is recounted as an accomplice to murder King Duncan with Macbeth. Shakespeare portrayed Banquo as Macbeth's innocent victim possibly because James Ⅰ, the King of England, was Banquo's descendant.[2]

Three Witches(三个巫婆): Or weird① sisters as they are called in the play, who predict Macbeth will become the king.

Macduff(麦克达夫): Scottish nobleman and the Lord of Fife.

Lady Macduff(麦克达夫夫人): Wife of Macduff.

Son of Macduff: One of the Macduff children.

Lennox(雷诺克斯): Nobleman of Scotland.

---

① Weird is derived from the Anglo-Saxon word wyrd, meaning fate. Thus, the witches appear to represent fate, a force predetermining destiny. The first writer to represent fate as three old women is the Greek poet Hesiod (8th century, B. C.). Hesiod refers to them as goddesses: Clotho, Lachesis, and Atropos. Clotho was in charge of weaving the fabric of a person's life. Lachesis determined a person's life span and destiny. Atropos cut the threads of the fabric of life when a person's life came to an end. No one—not even the mightiest god—could change the decisions of the Fates. Collectively, the Greeks called them Moirae (referred to as Parcae in Latin). The given name Moira means fate.

Angus(安格斯): Scottish nobleman.
Ross(罗斯): Scottish nobleman, thane.
Fleance(弗里恩斯): Son of Banquo.
Siward (希沃德): Earl of Northumberland, general of the English forces.
Young Siward(小希沃德): Son of Siward.
Gentle-woman(侍女): Lady Macbeth's attendant.
Seyton(塞顿): Servant of Macbeth.

2 Background

When Queen Elizabeth died in 1603, King James of Scotland came to the English throne. James patronized Shakespeare's theatre troupe which became the King's Men. *Macbeth* can be considered as an expression of Shakespeare's gratitude to the king. For example, Banquo was a historical figure, King James' ancestor. In Shakespeare's play, Banquo is innocent, who doesn't participate in Macbeth's murder of the king and his other evil deeds, which can be interpreted as a kind of compliment given to King James' ancestor. [3]

Shakespeare's *Macbeth* is mainly based on Raphael Holinshed's (? -1580?) *The Chronicles of England, Scotland and Ireland* (popularly known as *Holinshed's Chronicles*), the first edition of which was published in 1577 in two volumes and the second in 1587. Shakespeare referred to the second edition. He may also have referred to Samuel Harsnett's *A Declaration of Egregious Popish Impostures* (1603), George Buchanan's *Rerum Scoticarum Historia* (1582) and published reports of witch trials in Scotland. The Gunpowder Plot of 1605 may also have been considered by Shakespeare. [4]

3 Settings

The plot takes place in Scotland and England during the eleventh century.

Macbeth takes place mainly in northern Scotland, namely, at or near King Duncan's castle at Forres, at Macbeth's castle on Dunsinane Hill in the county of Inverness, at Macduff's castle in the county of Fife, and in countryside where three witches meet. It also takes place briefly in England where Malcolm stays and gathers an English army to fight Macbeth. [5]

4 Synopsis

Macbeth, the Thane of Glamis, and Banquo, another general of the Scottish army, have defeated the Norwegian invaders helped by the Scottish rebels, Macdonald and the Thane of Cawdor. Macbeth has defeated Sweno, the Norwegian King and killed Macdonald. On their way back to the camp, Macbeth and Banquo encounter three witches who hail Macbeth the Thane of Cawdor and prophecy that he will be king hereafter. Regarding Banquo, though he will not be king, his descendants will. Macbeth is full of fear and wonder. He is astonished how the witches have the information, but they vanish. Then Ross and Angus, two noblemen come and bring the news that the old Thane of Cawdor is sentenced to death and Macbeth is made the new Thane of Cawdor. Duncan, the Scottish King, Malcolm and Donalbain, his two sons, and other noblemen are at a camp near the battlefield. Duncan tells Macbeth that he deserves more than he has awarded for his exploits, and that they will spend the night at Inverness, Macbeth's castle.

Macbeth sends his wife Lady Macbeth a letter about the prophecy and the King's coming. Having read the letter, Lady Macbeth is afraid that Macbeth is too kind to take the action of murdering the King to become King himself. When they are all at Inverness, Macbeth does hesitate to kill the King because he is a good king who is well-liked by the people and who has honoured him. Lady Macbeth mocks Macbeth for his cowardice and questions his manhood. She says she has breastfed a baby and it is sweet to love a baby. But if she decides to end its life, she would dash out its brain even if it was smiling at her. Macbeth asks her what if they fail. She assures him that they won't. She will get the guardsmen of the King's room drunk to make it easy for Macbeth to kill the King.

Late that night in Macbeth's castle, Banquo has trouble to get to sleep, disturbed by what the witches have said. He doesn't want to be a slave to ambitions. Macbeth hopes that Banquo will help him in time due and he will reward him for his help. Banquo agrees, but not at the sacrifice of his honour. Macbeth sees a bloody dagger floating in the air before he commits the murder. He is disturbed. Lady Macbeth says she would have killed the King herself hadn't the sleeping Duncan looked like her father. Nevertheless, Macbeth has done the deed. When Lady Macbeth notices that the daggers are still in Macbeth's bloody hands, she asks him to put them back, but he dare not go back to the bloody scene. Lady Macbeth offers to go herself and plants them on Duncan's attendants to frame them. After Macbeth killed the King, he cannot pray and is unable to sleep.

When Macduff, the Thane of Fife, and Lennox, another nobleman, come to see the King early in the morning, they are talking about strange signs on the previous night. Lennox says he heard wind blowing wildly and owls hooting—omens of destruction and chaos. Then Macduff finds the King has been murdered and he wakes up the others in horror. He asks Lennox and Macbeth to go to have a look themselves. They exit and soon come back. Lennox says the King's guardsmen are the murderers because their faces and hands are bloody, and the bloody daggers are on their pillows. Macbeth kills the confused guardsmen who are not fully awake from their drunkenness, explaining that he was outrageous at that moment. They wake up the others and summon a meeting to discuss what has happened. Malcolm and Donalbain are terrified. They fear that they will be the next victims, so they decide to flee, Malcolm to England and Donalbain to Ireland, thinking that it will be safe for them to escape separately. Their escape makes others suspicious of their culpability for the murder of their father. Macbeth is made King. Banquo suspects that Macbeth fulfils the witches' prophecy by foul plays.

Now Macbeth feels unrest when he thinks of the prophecy regarding Banquo. If his descendants become kings, what's the point of what he has done for the throne? He decides to have him and his sons murdered. He summons two assassins and tells them that Banquo is to blame for their miserable lives and eggs them on to avenge their poverty and misery, otherwise, their manhood is questionable. The men reply that they will follow Macbeth's command. Macbeth tells them that he has invited Banquo and some other noblemen for a feast that night. They can waylay him and his son Fleance on the way and kill them. When the two killers are carrying out the murder, they are joined by a third sent by Macbeth to consolidate the action. However, they just fulfil part of the conspiracy—Banquo is killed, but Fleance has fled, making him suspicious of his role in the murder of his father.

When they are at the feast, one of the killers comes back to report to Macbeth what has happened. Macbeth then comes back to the table, but his seat is taken by Banquo's ghost. Macbeth speaks to the ghost that he didn't kill him and asks the ghost not to shake his bloody head at him but to vanish. While he is talking to the ghost, the other noblemen feel weird because they cannot see the ghost. Lady Macbeth explicates for Macbeth that he has had such fits since his childhood, then she tells Macbeth to stop his behaviour like this and show his manhood. After the feast is over, Macduff leaves for England to join Malcolm who at first doubts that Macduff is Macbeth's henchman, but when he is assured of Macduff's loyalty to him, he welcomes him. Macbeth dispatches a messenger to get Macduff back, but he rebuffs the messenger, who leaves with a gesture of a threat for Macduff. Macduff asks the King of England, Edward, to gather an army to fight against Macbeth.

Macbeth goes to the witches for information about his fate. They display three apparitions in front of him: a floating head, a bloody baby out of the womb of a woman, and a child wearing a crown and holding a tree in his hand. Meanwhile, they warn Macbeth to beware Macduff. But they make Macbeth believe that he is invincible by telling him that no man born of a woman will do him harm and that he will not be defeated until Birnam Wood moves to Dunsinane. Since every man was born by a woman and a forest cannot move, he should be safe. At last, Macbeth asks the witches if Banquo's heirs will become kings. The witches conjure up eight kings walking in a line, followed by Banquo's ghost, then the witches disappear.

Macbeth sends killers to Fife, Macduff's castle to kill his wife, children and servants. Ross brings the tragic news to Macduff, who determines to avenge the slaughter. In Macbeth's own castle at Dunsinane, a gentlewoman and a doctor are attending to Lady Macbeth, who has sleepwalked for several nights. In her sleep walking, she keeps washing her hands, saying that who would have expected that the old man has so much blood. The doctor says that Lady Macbeth's disease is beyond his ability to cure and that he will not tell others what he has heard.

Malcolm raises an army of ten thousand men commanded by the English general Siward.

They invade Scotland and arrive at Birnam Wood. Malcolm commands the soldiers to cut off a branch as a screen to hide their numbers, and they move on. The Scottish noblemen leave Macbeth and join Malcolm's army. They say that those who stay are not out of love for Macbeth but out of fear. As Macbeth is waiting for the impending English army, he hears a woman's cry. His servant Seyton goes to find out what has happened. He returns to tell Macbeth that Lady Macbeth has died, and it seems that she has committed suicide. Macbeth gives a soliloquy of the emptiness and meaninglessness of life. At this time, a servant rushes in and tells Macbeth that he sees Birnam Wood moving. Macbeth begins to fear. When the army has arrived at Dunsinane, they throw away the branches. The first to fight with Macbeth is Siward's son. Young Siward offers to go first to fight with Macbeth who is arrogant to say that no man of woman born can harm him. Though Siward fights bravely, Macbeth kills him easily. But it is easy for the English army to seize Macbeth's castle because it is almost defenseless. Macduff is searching for Macbeth to avenge his family. When they meet, Macbeth still claims that he is unvanquishable because Macduff was born by a woman. Unexpectedly, Macduff tells him that he was taken out of his mother's womb untimely by Caesarian section. Hearing this, Macbeth is fearful and doesn't want to fight anymore. But Macduff says if he surrenders, he will be mocked by all the Scottish people. Macbeth has to resume fighting. Macduff kills him and chops off his head. Malcolm is hailed as King of Scotland. He promotes the thanes to earls and pledges to bring back peace and order to the country.

【剧情介绍】

麦克白是格莱米斯的领主，他和班柯都是苏格兰将军。他们刚刚战胜了苏格兰叛乱者——考德领主麦克当纳带领的挪威侵略军。麦克白打败了挪威国王斯威诺并杀死了麦克当纳。在回营的路上，麦克白和班柯遇到了三个巫婆，她们称呼麦克白为考德领主，还预言他将成为苏格兰王。至于班柯，尽管他自己当不了国王，但他的后代会。麦克白听闻这些预言感到很纳闷，并且心生恐惧，不知道她们何出此言，正要进一步询问，她们已经消失得无影无踪。这时，苏格兰贵族罗斯和安格斯赶过来，告诉他们上任考德领主被判死刑，麦克白成为新的考德领主。苏格兰王邓肯、他的两个儿子马尔科姆和道纳班，还有其他一些贵族都在战场附近的一个军营里。苏格兰王对麦克白说，他取得的功绩配得上更多的荣誉，他还告诉麦克白，他们一行人将在因弗尼斯麦克白的城堡过夜。

麦克白派人给他的夫人送信，告知她巫婆的预言以及国王一行人将在他们家过夜的消息。麦克白夫人读了他的来信，唯恐麦克白心太善，下不了手杀死苏格兰王，他就当不了国王。当那些人都来到因弗尼斯之后，麦克白确实下不了决心手刃苏格兰王，因为他是一个宅心仁厚、受人爱戴的好国王，并且对麦克白也很尊重。麦克白夫人取笑他是一个懦夫，缺乏男子气概。她说她曾经为一个婴儿哺乳过，怜爱婴儿的感觉很美好，可是如果她想了结这个婴儿的性命的话，即便婴儿冲着自己微笑，她也可以让他肝脑涂地。麦克白问她万一谋杀失败怎么办，她向麦克白保证，她会把国王的侍卫们灌醉，然后麦克白再动手，这样就万无一失了。

当晚，深夜时分，班柯总感觉睡不着，因为他心里一直在想白天那些巫婆说过的话。他不想受野心摆布。麦克白希望班柯在适当的时候能够搭把手，当然他会厚待班柯。班柯答应了，但他说这种帮忙不能以牺牲自己的名誉为代价。麦克白在行凶之前，他看到空中悬着一把血淋淋的利剑，他内心慌乱了。麦克白夫人说，假如不是国王熟睡的样子让她想起了自己的父亲，她都可以亲手杀了他。不过，麦克白还是按照计划杀了苏格兰王，来到夫人跟前时，他手里还拿着带血的匕首。夫人让他赶快把匕首放回去，可是他说他不敢回看那个血腥的场面。于是，麦克白夫人就把那些匕首拿回去，放在邓肯的侍卫身旁，以嫁祸给他们。杀了国王之后，麦克白无法祷告，也睡不着觉了。

第二天一早，法夫领主麦克达夫和另一个名叫雷诺克斯的贵族来参见国王，他们边走边说着头一天晚上发生的一些奇异的景象。雷诺克斯说，他听到狂风乱吼和猫头鹰的啼叫声，这些都是象征毁灭和混沌的不祥之兆。接着，麦克达夫发现国王被杀害了，他惊恐不已，赶忙叫醒其他人，还让雷诺克斯和麦克白去看已经死去的国王。雷诺克斯说谋杀者是国王的侍卫，因为他们的脸上和手上都沾满了鲜血，那把血淋淋的匕首就在他们睡觉的枕头上。麦克白趁机把这些一身酒气，仍然稀里糊涂的侍卫杀了，解释道他一时气愤不已，就了结了他们的性命。马尔科姆和道纳班感到毛骨悚然，他们担心下一个受害者就是他们，所以准备赶紧逃跑，马尔科姆逃往英国，道纳班逃往爱尔兰，他们觉得分开逃亡的话风险小一些。他们的逃跑不由得使人怀疑他们和他们父王的死脱不了干系。于是，麦克白就当上了国王。班柯怀疑麦克白为了让巫婆们的预言成为现实而不择手段。

接下来，麦克白只要一想到那些关于班柯的后代将成为国王的预言就心生不安。如果班柯的后代为国王的话，那现在麦克白自己为了当上国王而做的这些有什么意义呢？于是，他决定把班柯和他的儿子都杀了。他命令两个杀手去完成这个任务。他挑唆这两个人找班柯报仇，因为导致他们俩贫困和不幸的人正是班柯，如果他们不去的话，就算不上男人了。于是，这两个人说他们听从麦克白的安排。麦克白告诉他们，当天晚上他会邀请包括班柯在内的一些贵族到他的城堡赴宴，杀手们可以在半路伏击班柯和他的儿子弗里恩斯并将他们杀掉。在他们执行命令的时候，麦克白又给他们增添了一个人手，以确保他们圆满完成任务。然而，他们的任务只完成了一半，因为他们只杀了班柯，弗里恩斯逃走了。但他的出逃却使他成为杀死父亲的嫌疑人。其中一个杀手向正在参加晚宴的麦克白汇报情况，等麦克白重新回到餐桌的时候，他发现他的座位上坐着班柯的鬼魂。他对鬼魂说不是他杀的班柯，并恳请鬼魂不要对着他摇晃那血淋淋的头，请求鬼魂快点消失。当他说这些话的时候，贵族们都感到怪异，因为他们都看不到鬼魂，只有麦克白可以。麦克白夫人赶紧替他解围，说麦克白小时候就有这种间歇性发作的胡言乱语的疯病。接着，她提醒麦克白注意自己的行为，要表现出自己的男子气概。宴会散场后，麦克达夫离开苏格兰去了英格兰，与马尔科姆碰面。起先，马尔科姆还怀疑麦克达夫是麦克白派来的奸细，但在证实了麦克达夫对自己的忠心之后，马尔科姆接纳了他。麦克白派人去命令麦克达夫回来，遭到他的拒绝。信使示意他将为此付出代价。麦克达夫请求英格兰国王爱德华集合一支军队去攻打麦克白。

麦克白再次找到三个巫婆去询问他的命数。巫婆为他展示了三个鬼魂。第一个是一个漂浮的脑袋，第二个是从一个女人肚子里拿出来的带血的婴儿头，第三个是手握树枝、头戴王冠的男孩。然后，巫婆提醒麦克白要提防麦克达夫。但她们又为麦克白营造了一种假象，他似乎天下无敌，因为巫婆对他说，只要是女人所生的人就伤不到他，没人能够打败他，除非伯南森林向邓西纳恩移动。由于每个人都是女人所生，并且森林不可能会移动，所以麦克白应该是平安无事的。最后，麦克白问巫婆班柯的后代是否真的会成为王。她们立刻用咒语唤起八个国王组成的队伍出现在麦克白面前，班柯的鬼魂在后。接着，巫婆们消失了。

麦克白派杀手去麦克达夫位于法夫的城堡，将他的妻儿和仆人都杀害了。罗斯领主把这个噩耗带给麦克达夫，麦克达夫发誓要报仇雪恨。在邓西纳恩麦克白自己的城堡里，麦克白夫人的女佣还有一名医生在照顾她，她已经连续梦游好几个晚上了，并且她总是重复洗手的动作，还喃喃自语说没想到那个老头居然会流这么多血。医生说，他对麦克白夫人的病情无能为力，不过他不会把她说过的那些话传出去。

马尔科姆集合了一支大约一万人的军队攻打苏格兰的麦克白，主帅是英国的希沃德将军。经过伯南森林的时候，马尔科姆指挥士兵们砍下树枝作为掩护，以免向敌军暴露他们的人数，苏格兰的贵族们都离开麦克白而加入马尔科姆的队伍。他们说，留在麦克白身边的人并非出于爱戴，而是出于惧怕。当麦克白等待着英军到来时，他突然听到女人的哭声。他的仆人塞顿去打探消息，回来禀告麦克白说，是他的夫人去世了，看上去好像是自杀。麦克白接着发出了一些关于人生空虚、毫无意义的感言。接着，又一个仆人跑来告诉他，说自己看到伯南森林正在朝着他们的城堡逼近。当士兵们到达麦克白的城堡后，他们丢开树枝准备战斗。第一个和麦克白交战的是希沃德的儿子。小希沃德自告奋勇去挑战麦克白，傲慢的麦克白宣称无人能够伤害他。尽管小希沃德很勇敢，但他很快就被麦克白杀死了。不过，英军很快攻下了麦克白的城堡，因为他的城堡几乎无人防守。麦克达夫努力寻找麦克白，为自己死去的家人报仇。两人碰面后，麦克白还扬言说麦克达夫奈何不了他，因为麦克达夫毕竟是女人所生。让他意想不到的是，麦克达夫告诉他，他还没有足月的时候就被人从他母亲的肚子里拿出来了。听闻此言，麦克白开始害怕了，他无心恋战，但麦克达夫对他说，如果他投降的话，会被苏格兰人耻笑。于是，麦克白不得不继续战斗。最后，麦克达夫杀死了麦克白，并取下了他的头颅。马尔科姆被拥戴为苏格兰王。他将那些领主们提升为伯爵，并向他们保证这个国家很快就会恢复和平和稳定。

5　Famous quotes

【Quote 1】

The three witches

Fair is foul and foul is fair;
hover through the fog and filthy air. [6]
(Act 1, Scene 1)

Unit 4　Macbeth

[**The three witches（played by Maisie MacFarquhar, Elsie Taylor and Noelle Rimmington）in a 1971 film directed by Roman Polanski.**]

◇ Paraphrase

What's fair is foul, and what's foul is fair.
We'll fly off through the fog and filthy air. [7]

◇ 原文译文

美即丑恶，丑即美，翱翔毒雾妖云里。[8]

【Quote 2】

Banquo
That, trusted home,
might yet enkindle you unto the crown,
besides the thane of Cawdor.
But 'tis strange.

[**Banquo（played by Martin Shaw）speaking to Macbeth（played by Jon Finch）in a 1971 film directed by Roman Polanski.**]

Often, to win us to our harm,
instruments of darkness tell truths,
win us with honest trifles,
to betray's in deepest consequence. [9]
(Act 1, Scene 3)

◇ Paraphrase

Banquo

If you trust them,
then it seems you might eventually become king,
not just the Thane of Cawdor.
But all of this is strange.
Often, to lead us to harm,
the agents of darkness will first tell us some bit of truth.
They win us over by telling us the truth about unimportant things,
only to betray us when the consequences will be most terrible. [10]

◇ 原文译文

您要是果然完全相信了她们的话,也许做了考德领主以后,还渴望把王冠攫到手里。可是这种事情很奇怪;魔鬼为了陷害我们,往往故意向我们说真话,在小事情上取得我们的信任,然后在重要关头我们便会落入他的圈套。[11]

【Quote 3】

Macbeth

[Aside]The prince of Cumberland!
That is a step on which I must fall down,

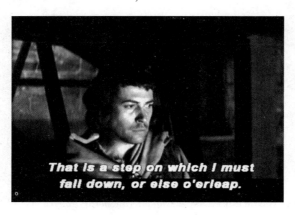

[Macbeth (played by Jon Finch) in an aside in a 1971 film directed by Roman Polanski.]

or else o'erleap, for in my way it lies.
Stars, hide your fires;
let not light see my black and deep desires.
The eye wink at the hand, yet let that be which the eye fears,
when it is done, to see. [12]
(Act 1, Scene 4)

◆ Paraphrase

Macbeth

[To himself] Malcolm is the Prince of Cumberland!
Because he is between me and the throne,
I'm either going to have to move above him,
or give up my hopes of kingship.
Stars, hide your brightness so that my evil desires are hidden from the light.
May my eye be blind to the actions of my hand.
Yet if I do the thing that my eyes fear to see,
I will be forced to see it once it's been done. [13]

◆ 原文译文

[旁白] 马尔科姆是一块横在我面前的石头,我必须跳过这块石头,否则就会被它绊倒。星星啊,收起你们的火焰!不要让光亮照见我的黑暗幽深的欲望。眼睛啊,别望这双手吧;可是我仍要下手,不管干下的事会吓得眼睛不敢看。[14]

【Quote 4】

Lady Macbeth

The raven① himself is hoarse that croaks
the fatal entrance of Duncan under my battlements.
Come, you spirits that tend on mortal thoughts, unsex me here,
and fill me from the crown to the toe top-full of direst cruelty.
Make thick my blood.
Stop up the access and passage to remorse,
that no compunctious visitings of nature shake my fell purpose,
nor keep peace between the effect and it!
Come to my woman's breasts,
and take my milk for gall, you murd'ring ministers,

---

① The raven is a symbol of bad omens.

wherever in your sightless substances you wait on nature's mischief.
Come, thick night, and pall thee in the dunnest smoke of hell,
that my keen knife see not the wound it makes,
nor heaven peep through the blanket of the dark to cry "Hold, hold!"[15]
(Act 1, Scene 5)

[**Lady Macbeth**(**played by Francesca Annis**)in a 1971 film directed by Roman Polanski.]

◆ Paraphrase

Lady Macbeth
The messenger croaks the announcement of Duncan's fatal arrival to my castle,
just like a raven would croak out a warning.
Come on, you spirits that aid thoughts of murder:
remove my womanhood and
fill me up from head to toe with terrible cruelty!
Thicken my blood.
Block my veins from all feelings of regret,
so that no natural feelings of guilt or doubt can sway me from my dark desires,
or prevent me from accomplishing them!
Demons of murder,
come to me from wherever you hide yourselves
as you wait to aid and abet corrupt and evil feelings,
and turn my mother's milk into bitter acid.
Come, thick night—wrapped in the darkest smoke of hell
—so that my sharp knife can't see the wound it makes,
and heaven can't peek through the darkness and cry: "Stop! Stop!"[16]

◆ 原文译文

报告邓肯走进我这堡门来送死的乌鸦,它的叫声是嘶哑的。来,注视着人类恶念的魔鬼们!解除我的女性的柔弱,用最凶恶的残忍从头到脚贯注在我的全身;凝结我的血液,不要让怜悯钻进我的心头,不要让天性中的恻隐摇动我的狠毒的决意!来,你们这些杀人的助手,你们无形的躯体布满在空间,到处找寻为非作歹的机会,进入我的妇人的胸中,把我的乳水当作胆汁吧!来,阴沉的黑夜,用最昏暗的地狱中的浓烟罩住你自己,让我的锐利的刀瞧不见它自己切开的伤口,让青天不能从黑暗的重衾里探出头来,高喊"住手,住手!"[17]

【Quote 5】

Lady Macbeth
O, never shall sun that morrow see!
Your face, my thane,
is as a book where men may read strange matters.
To beguile the time, look like the time.
Bear welcome in your eye,
your hand, your tongue.
Look like th' innocent flower,
but be the serpent under't.
He that's coming must be provided for;
and you shall put this night's great business into my dispatch,
which shall to all our nights and days to come
give solely sovereign sway and masterdom.[18]
(Act 1, Scene 5)

◆ Paraphrase

Lady Macbeth
That will never happen.
My thane, your face betrays your troubled thoughts,
so that others can read it like a book.
To deceive all others, you have to look exactly as they do.
When you greet the king, do so completely:
with your eyes, hands, and words.
Look like an innocent flower,
but be the snake that hides beneath it.
The king must be taken care of.
Allow me to manage everything tonight,
because the events of this night will bring us
sole mastery and power for all our nights and days to come.[19]

◆ 原文译文

啊!太阳永远不会见到那样一个明天。您的脸,我的爵爷,正像一本书,人们可以从那上面读到奇怪的事情。您要欺骗世人,必须装出和世人同样的神气;让您的眼睛里、您的手上、您的舌尖,随处流露着欢迎;让人家瞧您像一朵纯洁的花朵,可是在花瓣底下却有一条毒蛇潜伏。我们必须准备款待这位即将到来的贵宾;您可以把今晚的大事交给我去办;凭此一举,我们今后就可以日日夜夜永远掌握君临万民的无上权威。[20]

【Quote 6】

Macbeth

If it were done when 'tis done,
then 'twere well it were done quickly.
If the assassination could trammel up the consequence,
and catch with his surcease success;
that but this blow might be the be-all and the end-all here,
but here, upon this bank and shoal of time,
we'd jump the life to come.
But in these cases we still have judgment here,
that we but teach bloody instructions, which,
being taught, return to plague th' inventor:
this even-handed justice commends the ingredients of
our poisoned chalice to our own lips.
He's here in double trust.
First, as I am his kinsman and his subject,
strong both against the deed;
then, as his host, who should against his murderer shut the door,
not bear the knife myself.
Besides, this Duncan hath borne his faculties so meek,
hath been so clear in his great office,
that his virtues will plead like angels, trumpet-tongued,
against the deep damnation of his taking-off;
and pity, like a naked newborn babe,
striding the blast, or heaven's cherubim,
horsed upon the sightless couriers of the air,
shall blow the horrid deed in every eye,
that tears shall drown the wind.
I have no spur to prick the sides of my intent,
but only vaulting ambition,
which o'erleaps itself and falls on th' other.[21]

(Act 1, Scene 7)

◆ Paraphrase

Macbeth

If this will really all be over once it's done,
then it would be best to get it over with quickly.
If the assassination of the king could be like a net
—catching up all the consequences of the act within it
—then the act would be the be-all and end-all of the whole affair.
Then, at this point, I would do it and risk the afterlife.
But for such crimes there are still consequences in this world.
Violent acts only teach others to commit violence
—and the violence of our students will come back to plague us teachers.
Justice, being even-handed,
forces the cup we poisoned and gave to others back to our own lips.
The king trusts me twice over.
First, I am his kinsman and his subject.
Second, I am his host, and should be closing the door to any murderer
rather than trying to murder him myself.
Besides, Duncan has been such a humble leader
—so honest and free from corruption
—that his virtues will make angels sing for him
and cry out like trumpets against his murder.
Pity, like an innocent newborn baby,
will ride the wind like a winged angel,
or on invisible horses through the air,
to spread news of the horrible deed across the land,
so that a flood of tears will fall from the sky.
I have no reason to spur myself to act on my desires other than ambition,
which makes people leap into action and into tragedy. [22]

◆ 原文译文

要是干了以后就完了,那么还是快一点干;要是凭着暗杀的手段,可以攫取美满的结果,又可以排除了一切后患;要是这一刀砍下去,就可以完成一切、终结一切、解决一切——在这人世上,仅仅在这人世上,在时间这大海的浅滩上;那么来生我也就顾不到了。可是在这种事情上,我们往往逃不过现世的裁判;我们树立下血的榜样,教会别人杀人,结果反而自己被人所杀;把毒药投入酒杯里的人,结果也会自己饮鸩而死,这就是一些不爽的报应。他到这儿来本有两重的信任:第一,我是他的亲戚,又是他的臣子,按照名分绝对不能干这样的事；第二，我是他的主人，应当保障他身体的安全，怎么可以自己持刀行刺？并且，这个邓肯秉性仁慈，处理国政，从来没有过失，要是把他杀死了，他的生前的美德，将要像天使一般发出喇叭一样清澈的声音，向世人昭告我的弑君重罪；"怜悯"像一个赤身裸体在狂风中飘游的婴儿，又像一个御气而行的天婴，将要把这可憎的行为暴露在每一个人的眼前，使眼泪淹没叹息。没有一种力量可以鞭策我实现自己的意图，可是我的跃跃欲试的野心，却不顾一切地驱着我去冒险。[23]

【Quote 7】

Macbeth

Is this a dagger which I see before me,
the handle toward my hand?
Come, let me clutch thee;
I have thee not, and yet I see thee still.
Art thou not, fatal vision,
sensible to feeling as to sight?
Or art thou but a dagger of the mind, a false creation,
proceeding from the heat-oppressed brain?
I see thee yet, in form as palpable as this which now I draw.
Thou marshall'st me the way that I was going,
and such an instrument I was to use.
Mine eyes are made the fools o' th' other senses,
or else worth all the rest.
I see thee still, and on thy blade and dudgeon gouts of blood,
which was not so before.
There's no such thing.
It is the bloody business which informs thus to mine eyes.
Now o'er the one half-world nature seems dead,
and wicked dreams abuse the curtained sleep.
Witchcraft celebrates pale Hecate's① offerings,
and withered murder, alarumed by his sentinel, the wolf,
whose howl's his watch, thus with his stealthy pace,
with Tarquin's② ravishing strides,
towards his design moves like a ghost.
Thou sure and firm-set earth,

---

① In ancient Greek mythology, Hecate was goddess of the dark associated with witchcraft.

② Tarquin was an ancient Roman prince creeping into Lucretia's chamber to rape her. Lucretia was a nobleman's wife whose story is detailed in Shakespeare's poem *The Rape of Lucrece*.

hear not my steps, which way they walk,
for fear thy very stones prate of my whereabout,
and take the present horror from the time,
which now suits with it.
Whiles I threat, he lives.
Words to the heat of deeds too cold breath gives.[24]
(Act 2, Scene 1)

[**Macbeth** (played by Jon Finch) in his soliloquy in a 1971 film directed by Roman Polanski.]

◇ Paraphrase

Macbeth

Is this a dagger I see in front of me,
with its handle aimed toward my hand?
Come here, dagger, and let me grasp you.
[He grabs at the dagger but his hand passes right through]
I don't have you, and yet I can still see you.
Deadly apparition, is it possible to see you but not touch you?
Or are you just a dagger created by the mind,
an illusion of my feverish brain?
I still see you, and you look as real as this other dagger that I'm unsheathing now.
[He draws a dagger] You're leading me the way I was going already,
and I was going to use a weapon just like you.
Either my eyesight is the only sense of mine that isn't working,
or it's the only one that's working correctly.

I still see you

—and some spots of blood on your blade and handle that weren't there before.

This dagger doesn't exist.

It's the murder I'm planning that's affecting my eyes.

Now half the world is asleep and being attacked by nightmares.

Witches offer sacrifices to their goddess Hecate.

Meanwhile old man murder

—having been awakened by the howls of his wolf

—walks like a ghost, like that ancient Roman rapist Tarquin, to do the deed.

You firm, hard earth:

don't listen to my steps or their direction.

I fear the stones will echo and reveal where I am,

breaking the awful silence that suits what I'm about to do so well.

While I talk here about the plan, Duncan lives.

Speaking cools the heat of my willingness to act. [25]

◇ 原文译文

在我面前摇晃着、它的柄对着我的手的，不是一把刀子吗？来，让我抓住你。我抓不到你，可是仍旧能看见你。不祥的幻象，你只是一件可视不可触的东西吗？或者你不过是一把想象中的刀子，从狂热的大脑里发出来的虚妄的意匠？我仍旧看见你，你的形状正像我现在拔出的这一把刀子一样明显。你指示着我所要去的方向，告诉我应当用什么利器。我的眼睛倘不是上了当，受其他知觉的嘲弄，就是兼领了一切感官的机能。我仍旧看见你；你的刃上和柄上还流着一滴一滴刚才所没有的血。没有这样的事；杀人的恶念使我看见这种异象。现在在半个世界上，一切生命仿佛已经死去，罪恶的梦境扰乱着平和的睡眠，作法的女巫在向惨白的赫卡忒献祭；形容枯瘦的杀人犯，听到了替他巡哨、报更的豺狼的嗥声，仿佛淫乱的塔昆蹑着脚步像一个鬼似的向他的目的地走去。坚固结实的大地啊，不要听见我的脚步声音是向什么地方去的，我怕路上的砖石会泄漏了我的行踪，把黑夜中一派阴森可怕的气氛破坏了。我正在这儿威胁他的生命，他却在那儿活得好好的；在紧张的行动中间，言语不过是一口冷气。[26]

【Quote 8】

Macbeth

Methought I heard a voice cry, Sleep no more!
Macbeth does murder sleep—the innocent sleep;
sleep, that knits up the ravell'd sleave of care,
the death of each day's life, sore labor's bath,
balm of hurt minds, great nature's second course,

chief nourisher in life's feast. [27]

(Act 2, Scene 2)

(Macbeth (played by Jon Finch) speaking to Lady Macbeth (played by Francesca Annis) in his soliloquy in a 1971 film directed by Roman Polanski.)

◇ Paraphrase

Macbeth

I thought I heard a voice cry,
"Sleep no more! Macbeth murders sleep."
Innocent sleep.
Sleep that smoothes away all our fears and worries;
that puts an end to each day;
That eases the aches of the day's work;
and soothes hurt minds.
Sleep, the main and most nourishing course in the feast of life. [28]

◇ 原文译文

我仿佛听见一个声音喊着:"不要再睡了!麦克白已经杀害了睡眠。"那清白的睡眠,把忧虑的乱丝编织起来的睡眠,那日常的死亡,疲劳者的沐浴,受伤的心灵的油膏,大自然的最丰盛的菜肴,生命的盛筵上主要的营养。[29]

【Quote 9】

Lady Macbeth

Nought's had,
all's spent where our desire is got without content. [30]

(Act 3, Scene 2)

◇ Paraphrase

Lady Macbeth

When you get what you want but have no peace of mind, then you've gotten nothing, and spent everything. [31]

◇ 原文译文

费尽了一切,结果还是一无所得,我们的目的虽然达到,却一点不感觉满足。[32]

【Quote 10】

Macbeth

Tomorrow, and tomorrow,
and tomorrow creeps in this petty pace from day to day
to the last syllable of recorded time;
and all our yesterdays have lighted fools the way to dusty death.
Out, out, brief candle!
Life's but a walking shadow,
a poor player that struts and frets his hour upon the stage,
and then is heard no more.
It is a tale told by an idiot,
full of sound and fury, signifying nothing. [33]
(Act 5, Scene 5)

[Macbeth (played by Jon Finch) in his soliloquy in a 1971 film directed by Roman Polanski.]

◇ Paraphrase

Macbeth

Tomorrow, and tomorrow, and tomorrow
—creeping at this slow pace, day after day,
until the very end of time.
And the days that have gone by are just another step
for fools on the way to their deaths.
Go out, go out, brief candle.
Life is an illusion,
a pitiful actor who struts and worries for his hour on the stage
and then disappears forever.
Life is a story told by an idiot,
full of noise and emotion, without any meaning.[34]

◇ 原文译文

明天,明天,再一个明天,一天接着一天地蹑步前进,直到最后一秒钟的时间;我们所有的昨天,不过替傻子们照亮了到死亡的土壤中去的路。熄灭了吧,熄灭了吧,短促的烛光!人生不过是一个行走的影子,一个在舞台上指手画脚的拙劣的伶人,登场片刻,就在无声无息中悄然退下;它是一个愚人所讲的故事,充满着喧哗和骚动,却找不到一点意义。[35]

6　Questions for discussion

(1) Who is the protagonist① in the play and who/what is the antagonists(s)②?

(2) What role do the witches' prophesies play in this tragedy?

(3) What do darkness and light symbolize in this play?

(4) Why does Lady Macbeth keep washing her hands? What does blood symbolize in this play?

(5) Macbeth was ruined by ambition. What other great leaders in both Chinese and English history or fiction fell to ruin, or death, because of their ambition?

(6) What do you think of Lady Macbeth?

(7) Comment on this: Look like th' innocent flower, but be the serpent under't.

---

① In Shakespeare's and ancient Greek dramas, the protagonist is usually a royal or a nobleman who is brought about his downfall because of a tragic flaw such as pride, ambition, or greed.

② An antagonist is a person, a force, an emotion, an idea, or another thing opposing the protagonist. Sometimes there is more than one antagonist in a play.

7　References

［1］［2］［3］［4］［5］　Macbeth Study Guide［EB/OL］. https://www.litcharts.com/lit/macbeth.

［6］［9］［12］［15］［18］［21］［24］［27］［30］［33］　Shakespeare W. Macbeth［M］. New York：Simon & Schuster，2004.

［7］［10］［13］［16］［19］［22］［25］［28］［31］［34］　Macbeth：Shakespeare Translation［EB/OL］. https://www.litcharts.com/shakescleare/shakespeare-translations/macbeth.

［8］［11］［14］［17］［20］［23］［26］［29］［32］［35］　威廉·莎士比亚. 莎士比亚悲剧五种［M］. 朱生豪,译. 北京：人民文学出版社，2020.

Unit 5

Othello

1 Characters

Othello(奥赛罗): Black Moor and army general in Venice.

Iago(伊阿古): Othello's ancient or flag bearer.

Desdemona(戴丝狄蒙娜): Wife of Othello and daughter of a Venetian senator.

Michael Cassio(迈克尔·卡西奥): Othello's lieutenant, or second-in-command.

Duke of Venice(威尼斯公爵): Ruler who stands on Othello's side regarding his marriage to Desdemona.

Brabantio(勃拉班修): Venetian senator and father of Desdemona.

Gratiano(葛莱西阿诺): Brabantio's brother.

Lodovico(罗多维科): Brabantio's kinsman.

Roderigo(罗德里戈): Venetian gentleman who is in love with Desdemona.

Montano(蒙塔诺): Governor of Cyprus.

Clown(小丑): Servant to Othello.

Emilia(伊米莉亚): Wife of Iago.

Bianca(比安卡): A prostitute and Cassio's lover.

Minor Characters: First Senator, Second Senator, sailor, messenger, herald, officers, gentlemen, musicians, attendants.

2 Background

Since the tenth century, the Islamic Arabs and Berbers/Moors occupied Spain. Catholics fought to reseize it from the eleventh to the fifteenth century. The fight incurred deep prejudice and suspicion of the Moors even after they were overthrown. Philip III of Spain, the king of Portugal, Naples, Sicily, and Sardinia, and the Duke of Milan, from 1598 to 1621, expelled 300,000 "Moriscos" from the Iberian (Spanish) peninsula from 1609 to 1614 (*Othello* was written between 1602 and 1604 and published in 1622). The problem of the Moors was complex in England during Shakespeare's time. England was strongly anti-Catholic and had fears of the Spanish invasion. Meanwhile, England and the Moorish Northern Africa were trade partners, which was protested by Spain and Portugal. On the one hand, England benefitted from the slave trade between Africa and Europe since the mid-sixteenth century; on the other hand, England showed strong suspicion of Islam in that Elizabeth (queen of England from 1558 to 1603) had the African Moors and the Spanish "Moriscos" expelled from the English boundary from 1599 to1601. [1]

Shakespeare might have based his *Othello* on an Italian short story, *The Moorish Captain* (in Italian *Un Capitano Moro*), which appeared in *Gli Ecatommiti* or *Gli Hecatommithi* (translated into English as *One Hundred Tales*) published in Venice in 1565 or 1566 and written by Giovanni Battista Giraldi/Cinthio (1504-1573). As there was no translation of Giraldi's stories in Shakespeare's time, Shakespeare either read the original Italian version or had someone translate it for him. [2]

3　Settings

The plot takes place in Venice and Cyprus, between 1489 and 1571.

The first act of *Othello* takes place in Venice and the other acts take place in Cyprus (an island in the eastern Mediterranean).

4　Synopsis

The Moorish Othello is a general of the Venetian army. He is hated by Roderigo, a Venetian gentleman, because Othello wins Desdemona's love over him, and by Iago, Othello's flag-bearer, because Othello has promoted Michael Cassio as his lieutenant instead of him, though three noblemen in Venice have recommended Iago. Cassio doesn't know about battle. Iago complains to Roderigo, so he is worthier of that position than Cassio. He adds that Cassio is cursed with a beautiful wife who is out of his control. Roderigo complains about Iago whom he pays to help him woo Desdemona, but Desdemona has eloped with Othello. Iago comforts Roderigo that he will do his best to make Roderigo end up with Desdemona. He tells Roderigo that he serves Othello not out of love but for his own purpose. Iago goads Roderigo to wake up Brabantio, a Venetian senator and Desdemona's father, and slander Othello to the old man. This will rile up Desdemona's family and ruin Othello's happiness. As expected, Brabantio bursts up when Iago tells him that he is robbed of his daughter by Othello. Roderigo adds that Desdemona has given all her beauty, obedience, wit and wealth, to the "lascivious" Moor. Brabantio gathers his servants to look for Desdemona in his house, but in vain.

Iago finds Othello in an inn where he is lodging and tells him that he would have stabbed Roderigo hadn't he restrained himself when Roderigo said things to defame Othello. He warns Othello to avoid confronting Brabantio who is looking for him and will separate him from Desdemona. Othello appears unfazed, saying that he has a clean conscience and has served the state dutifully. Brabantio finds Othello and accuses him of seducing his daughter with magic. He will make the Duke of Venice punish the Moor. The Duke happens to summon Othello for a meeting to discuss a military affair. He needs Othello to lead the forces to repel the Turkish invaders attacking Cyprus at the moment. When Brabantio airs his grievances against Othello, the Duke gives him a chance to plead for himself. Othello explains that he didn't use magic to seduce Desdemona but won her love by his life stories of adventures and bravery, and that he loves her and is married to her. Desdemona is sent for to prove this and she confirms what Othello has said is true. Brabantio lets Desdemona choose whose obedience she is now owing to and she replies that just as her mother who shifted her obedience from her own father to Brabantio, she is now obedient to Othello, her husband. Brabantio cannot but accept the fact grudgingly. He warns Othello that now that Desdemona has disobeyed him, she might disobey Othello as well.

That very night, Othello has to depart for Cyprus with the army and Desdemona will follow him afterwards, attended by Iago's wife Emilia. Iago says there are rumors that Othello has slept with Emilia and he will take them true to justify his determination to bring Othello's downfall. Iago persuades Roderigo to go to Cyprus so that he will win over Desdemona after Othello's ruin. When they all arrive, the governor of Cyprus, Montano tells them that the Turkish fleet has been dispersed by a raging storm. Thus, they win the battle without fighting.

Iago makes use of Cassio's courtesy of taking Desdemona's hand for a brief private talk when they meet. He convinces Roderigo of love between Desdemona and Cassio. He makes Roderigo agree to challenge Cassio to a brawl which will result in the replacement of Cassio. Thus, an obstacle between Roderigo and Desdemona will be removed. Iago states in a soliloquy that he also loves Desdemona, and he wants to sleep with her to avenge the rumors regarding Othello and Emilia.

That night, Othello arranges a revelry to celebrate their victory. He commands Cassio to take charge of the situation and see to it that the soldiers will drink moderately. Iago tries to convince Cassio to take a drink, but Cassio declines, saying that he is intolerant for alcohol. Iago has made sure that the revelers are all guys touchy about honour and they will sure get drunk. Once he gets Cassio drunk too, they will create a scene. After he learns that Cassio is indeed drunk, Iago tells Roderigo to provoke Cassio to a fight. Soon Cassio is chasing Roderigo on the stage. Montano sees this and intervenes, and he is wounded by Cassio. Iago tells Roderigo to raise an alarm. Othello arrives and deprives Cassio of his position after he hears Iago's description, though Iago makes it sound he is speaking for Cassio's goodness. Cassio feels devastated by his demotion. Iago suggests that he seek the kind and generous Desdemona's help. If Desdemona pleads with Othello for Cassio, it will take effect because Othello loves Desdemona very much, and Cassio will regain his position. Meanwhile, Iago will make Othello believe that Desdemona pleads for Cassio not out of goodness but out of lust for Cassio. Iago addresses the audience that he will arrange a private meeting between Cassio and Desdemona and make sure Othello will see it.

Desdemona talks with Cassio and assures him that she will entreat Othello to restore him to his former position. Seeing Othello coming, Cassio feels ashamed of himself and exits. Othello asks Iago if it is Cassio who has just departed. Iago replies that it is unlikely to be Cassio. If it is him, why should he step away surreptitiously? When they approach Desdemona, she asks Othello to reinstate Cassio. After Desdemona exits, Iago impresses the idea in Othello's mind that Desdemona and Cassio are in an illegal relationship. But he adds that it might be his suspicion and asks Othello not to be troubled by jealousy. At the same time, he reminds Othello that Desdemona has deceived her father. Left alone, Othello thinks of his black blood and the fact that he is much older than Desdemona, so he cannot expect her to love him. He laments the fate of great men to be cuckolded. Desdemona doesn't know why Othello looks upset later. She tries to soothe him. Othello says he has a headache. Desdemona offers him her handkerchief to tie around his head to feel better, but Othello dismisses this idea, saying the handkerchief is too small. It drops onto the floor. They leave for dinner as Othello's guests are waiting.

Emilia enters. She picks up the handkerchief and shows it to Iago, saying that this is the handkerchief he has asked her to steal from Desdemona. Iago is excited and grabs it from Emilia's hands. He plants it in Cassio's room. Cassio discovers the handkerchief and likes the design on it with strawberries embroidered. He asks Bianca, a prostitute and his mistress, to make a copy of the handkerchief.

When Iago is with Othello, he tells Othello that he has slept with Cassio on the same bed recently and he heard Cassio call out Desdemona's name and puts his leg on Iago's thigh. Cassio also cursed fate for making Desdemona wife to the Moor. Othello is furious and swears he will tear Desdemona to pieces. But Iago says this is only Cassio's dream which cannot prove Desdemona's infidelity. He then asks Othello if he has given a handkerchief with strawberries embroidered on it. Othello says yes and Iago tells him that he saw it in Cassio's hands. Othello vows for revenge on the adulteress and her accomplice. He thanks Iago for his honesty and loyalty and appoints him his lieutenant.

Othello asks Desdemona about the handkerchief he gave to her. Desdemona falters. He tells her that the handkerchief was given by an Egyptian sorceress to his mother who then passed it down to Othello. This handkerchief has magic power. A woman who keeps it will be desirable to her husband and he will be in love for her helplessly, but once she loses the handkerchief or gives it away, he will hate her and love another woman. Desdemona explains that she doesn't lose it but it is just not at hand. She has asked Emilia earlier what has happened to her handkerchief and Emilia says she doesn't know.

Alone with Othello, Iago says that there are millions of women who vow that they belong to their husbands but sleep with other men. Worse than this, you kiss your wife in bed thinking she is chaste, but she is not. Iago then lets slip that Cassio has told Iago and Desdemona has slept with him. Othello is enraged. Iago adds that Cassio has talked about Desdemona in lewd language. When he sees Cassio coming, he asks Othello to hide himself and listen to their conversation. He then approaches Cassio and talks about Bianca in a voice that others cannot hear them. Every time when they talk about her, Cassio bursts into laughter. Othello cannot hear them, but is angered by Cassio's loud laughter, surmising that he laughs because of talks about Desdemona. When they are talking, Bianca enters. She makes a scene of the handkerchief and throws it at Cassio, surmising it belongs to another mistress of Cassio. Othello recognizes the handkerchief and seethes with jealousy. He swears to kill Desdemona and asks Iago to bring him poison that night. Iago suggest that he strangle her in her very bed which she has contaminated with her affair. He promises to kill Cassio for Othello.

Lodovico, Brabantio's kinsman, enters with Desdemona with the Duke's message for Othello to return to Venice and Cassio will replace him to govern Cyprus. Lodovico inquires about Cassio and Desdemona tells him that she is trying to heal a falling out between Othello and Cassio recently. This enrages Othello and he hits Desdemona, which shocks Lodovico. He asks Iago if Othello has gone mad, but Iago keeps silent.

Roderigo is angry with Iago who takes all his money and jewels as gifts for Desdemona, but no progress has been made for him to win Desdemona's hand. Iago lies to Roderigo that Othello will be sent to Mauritania with Desdemona and Cassio will govern Cyprus. To make Desdemona within his reach, Roderigo must kill Cassio so that Othello and Desdemona will stay. Roderigo agrees. Iago delivers a soliloquy that whether Roderigo kills Cassio or the other way will do him good. If Roderigo is dead, he will not ask his money and jewels back from Iago; if Cassio is killed, Iago's slander of him will not be revealed to him and Cassio's virtues will not highlight Iago's meanness.

Iago and Roderigo ambush Cassio in the darkness when he leaves Bianca's house. Roderigo thrusts his sword at Cassio, but he is stabbed by Cassio. Iago then stabs Cassio in the legs from behind. When Othello hears Cassio crying out of pain, Othello thinks Iago has killed him. He considers Iago is brave, honest and justifiable to do so. Gratiano, another kinsman of Brabantio, and Lodovico arrive. They ask Cassio and Roderigo what is happening. Iago reenters with a light. Cassio says that he has been attacked by two villains. With the light, Cassio recognizes Roderigo as one of the villains. Iago takes the chance to kill "the villain" Roderigo.

As planned, Othello enters Desdemona's bedroom with a candle. He is fascinated with her beauty but determined to kill her. Suddenly Desdemona wakes up. Othello tells her to pray for her death. She asks him why he wants to kill her. He says because he has given the handkerchief to Cassio who has admitted to having slept with her. Desdemona begs Othello not to kill her but banish her first. Othello is implacable and smothers Desdemona with a pillow.

Emilia is horrified to see Desdemona dead. She confronts Othello who insists that Desdemona cheated on him with Cassio and he is justifiable to kill her. Emilia bursts up and wails that Desdemona has never betrayed him. As regards the handkerchief, it is she who picked it up and gave it to Iago. She then realizes that Iago is all the while behind the plot. She starts to blame him. Knowing that he is ensnared by Iago, Othello attacks him but is disarmed. Iago kills Emilia and flees. Later when he is captured and brought in, Othello stabs him and is disarmed again. He then takes out a hidden dagger and kills himself. Iago is executed.

【剧情介绍】

　　奥赛罗是摩尔人,在威尼斯军队当将军。威尼斯的贵族罗德里戈憎恨他,因为奥赛罗夺走了他爱的人——戴丝狄蒙娜。奥赛罗的旗手伊阿古也痛恨奥赛罗,因为奥赛罗提拔了一个叫迈克尔·卡西奥的人做他的副将,尽管有三个威尼斯贵族都推荐伊阿古。伊阿古认为,卡西奥对打仗一窍不通,所以他不配做副将,而他自己则更有资格胜任。伊阿古还说卡西奥有一个让他头疼的妻子,因为她很漂亮,他无法驾驭她。罗德里戈抱怨伊阿古拿了他的钱,答应帮他向戴丝狄蒙娜求婚的,结果她却和那个摩尔人私奔了。伊阿古安慰罗德里戈,说自己会想方设法让戴丝狄蒙娜最终回到他身边。伊阿古还说他为奥赛罗效劳并非出自爱,而是出于私心。伊阿古怂恿罗德里戈提醒威尼斯议员勃拉班修,也就是戴丝狄蒙娜的父亲,并在他面前诋毁奥赛罗,同时激怒她的家人,破坏奥赛罗的幸福。果然,从伊阿古那里得知奥赛罗抢走了自己的女儿,勃拉班修火冒三丈。罗德里戈更是在一旁煽风点火,说戴丝狄蒙娜将她的美貌、顺从、智慧和财富都交给了奥赛罗那个淫棍。勃拉班修带着他的仆人满屋子寻找女儿,结果连她的影子也没找到。

　　伊阿古在奥赛罗下榻的旅馆找到了他。伊阿古对奥赛罗说,他听到罗德里戈在背后破坏奥赛罗的名誉时,他简直就想一剑了结罗德里戈的性命,不过他还是努力克制住了自己。他还提醒奥赛罗不要和勃拉班修对抗,因为他正在四处寻找奥赛罗和戴丝狄蒙娜,并将他们两人分开。奥赛罗一副坦然的样子,对伊阿古说他问心无愧,对国家尽职尽责。勃拉班修找到了奥赛罗,指责他使戴丝狄蒙娜中了邪。勃拉班修还说会请求威尼斯公爵来惩治他这个摩尔人。这时,公爵正好召见奥赛罗商讨战事。眼下,土耳其侵略者正想攻打塞浦路斯,公爵想派遣奥赛罗带兵前往塞浦路斯击退他们。当勃拉班修在公爵面前控诉奥赛罗的时候,公爵给了奥赛罗一个机会,让他为自己辩护。奥赛罗说,他没有用妖言引诱戴丝狄蒙娜爱上他,反而是她因为喜爱听他的传奇故事和历险事迹而对他着了迷,他爱她并且正式娶了她。于是,他们叫来戴丝狄蒙娜本人来澄清这件事。戴丝狄蒙娜说奥赛罗所说都是真的。勃拉班修让她在他和奥赛罗之间做出选择,问她到底听谁的,她回答说,正如她的母亲当初选择了顺从丈夫而不是继续顺从父亲一样,如今她也选择由顺从自己的父亲转而顺从自己的丈夫。勃拉班修只好接受这个现实。不过,他警告奥赛罗既然他女儿现在可以忤逆她的父亲,将来也会忤逆她的丈夫。

　　当天晚上,奥赛罗不得不动身率兵前往塞浦路斯。戴丝狄蒙娜随后跟上,一路上,伊阿古的妻子伊米莉亚负责照顾戴丝狄蒙娜。伊阿古说,他听到过一些关于奥赛罗和伊米莉亚奸情的流言,他相信这些流言,并把这作为他扳倒奥赛罗的正当理由。伊阿古鼓动罗德里戈跟随他们一起去塞浦路斯,等到奥赛罗垮台了,罗德里戈就可以得到戴丝狄蒙娜。等他们都到了塞浦路斯,总督蒙塔诺告诉他们,土耳其舰队被狂风暴雨冲散了,所以他们不需要动兵就赢了这场战争。

卡西奥见到戴丝狄蒙娜的时候很礼貌地和她握手,并和她单独说了几句话,伊阿古则借题发挥,让罗德里戈相信他们之间有猫腻。他鼓动罗德里戈挑战卡西奥,并让卡西奥因此丢掉他的官职。这样一来,罗德里戈和戴丝狄蒙娜之间的障碍就少了一个。伊阿古在旁白中说,他也喜爱戴丝狄蒙娜,还想和戴丝狄蒙娜发生性关系,以此报复奥赛罗和伊米莉亚之间的谣言。

那天晚上,奥赛罗安排了一场庆祝胜利的狂欢会。他命令卡西奥负责整个场面,不让士兵们酗酒。伊阿古试图劝说卡西奥喝一杯,但遭到他的拒绝,说自己不胜酒力。伊阿古确信士兵们打了胜仗很开心,肯定会喝醉。如果卡西奥也醉了,大家肯定会闹事。后来,得知卡西奥真的喝醉了的时候,伊阿古让罗德里戈挑衅卡西奥并和他决斗。很快,卡西奥就追着罗德里戈到处跑。蒙塔诺见此情形,试图阻止卡西奥,结果被他刺伤了。伊阿古让罗德里戈拉响警报。这时,奥赛罗赶来了,听完伊阿古的叙述,他立刻撤了卡西奥的职,虽然听起来伊阿古似乎是在帮卡西奥说话。被撤职的卡西奥感到很崩溃。伊阿古提议他去找好心又慷慨的戴丝狄蒙娜帮忙,让她在奥赛罗面前求求情,因为奥赛罗非常爱戴丝狄蒙娜,所以肯定会听她的,这样的话,卡西奥就可以官复原职。与此同时,伊阿古让奥赛罗相信戴丝狄蒙娜替卡西奥求情并非出自善心,而是出于她对卡西奥的私欲。伊阿古对观众说,他将安排卡西奥和戴丝狄蒙娜单独见面,并让奥赛罗看到这一幕。

戴丝狄蒙娜安慰卡西奥,说她一定会恳求奥赛罗让他官复原职。看到奥赛罗走过来,卡西奥感到羞愧不已,就出去了。奥赛罗问伊阿古刚才出去的那个人是不是卡西奥,伊阿古故意说不会是卡西奥,因为他没有理由鬼鬼祟祟地溜出去。当他们俩走到戴丝狄蒙娜跟前时,她恳求奥赛罗恢复卡西奥的官职。等她离开后,伊阿古故意为奥赛罗营造了一种错觉,使奥赛罗认为戴丝狄蒙娜和卡西奥之间有不正当关系。他又故意说,也许这些只是他个人的猜疑,让奥赛罗不要因此而感到嫉妒和困扰。他又提起了戴丝狄蒙娜欺瞒过她父亲的事。奥赛罗一个人冷静下来的时候想,他自己是黑人,年纪比戴丝狄蒙娜大很多,怎么能奢望她会爱自己呢?他哀叹,伟大的人物都难逃被妻子背叛的厄运。戴丝狄蒙娜不明白奥赛罗为何不开心。她试图安抚他。奥赛罗说他头疼,于是,戴丝狄蒙娜提出用她的手巾帮他把头扎起来,这样会舒服一些,可是奥赛罗说她的手巾太小了,没有用。正说着,手巾掉到了地上。他们匆匆离开去参加晚宴,因为客人已经在等候他们。

伊米莉亚进来捡起了手巾,然后拿到伊阿古面前,说这就是他一直想要她从戴丝狄蒙娜那里偷走的手巾。伊阿古喜出望外,赶紧一把从伊米莉亚手上抓过手巾,并放到卡西奥的房间。卡西奥看到手巾后,很喜欢手巾上绣着的草莓图案,他让他的情人,也就是妓女比安卡帮他绣一块和这个图案一模一样的手巾。

当伊阿古又和奥赛罗见面时,伊阿古告诉他,最近他和卡西奥同睡一张床的时候,听到卡西奥在睡梦中呼唤戴丝狄蒙娜的名字,并且把他的腿搭在伊阿古的大腿上。卡西奥还诅咒命运居然把戴丝狄蒙娜这样的女子安排给摩尔人做妻子。听罢此言,奥赛罗气愤地发誓要将戴丝狄蒙娜碎尸万段。可是,伊阿古说这只是卡西奥的梦话,不能证明戴丝狄蒙娜背叛了奥赛罗。接着,他问奥赛罗是不是给过戴丝狄蒙娜一块绣着草莓图案的手巾,奥赛罗说是的,然后伊阿古就说他在卡西奥的手上见过这块手巾。奥赛罗发誓要报复这对奸夫淫妇。他感谢伊阿古对自己的忠诚,并提拔他为副官。

奥赛罗问起戴丝狄蒙娜他送给她的那块手巾怎么样了。戴丝狄蒙娜说不出话来。奥赛罗接着告诉她，这块手巾是埃及的一个女巫给他妈妈的，他妈妈又传给了他。这块手巾有魔力。如果某个女人拥有它，那么她的丈夫就离不开她，会无条件地爱她，可是一旦手巾丢失，或者女人将手巾送给了别人，那么她的丈夫就会憎恨她，并且爱上别的女人。戴丝狄蒙娜解释说她并没有弄丢手巾，只是这会儿没在手上而已。在这之前，她问过伊米莉亚是否看到了她的手巾，伊米莉亚说没看到。

当奥赛罗和伊阿古在一起的时候，伊阿古说，世上有很多女人在自己的丈夫面前发誓说她们忠于自己的丈夫，可实际上却和别的男人保持不正当关系。比这更糟的是，当你在床上吻着你的妻子，以为她是一个忠贞的女人，然而并非如此。伊阿古装作不小心说出来卡西奥曾经告诉他，说他和戴丝狄蒙娜发生过性关系。奥赛罗暴怒。伊阿古接着说，卡西奥还用淫秽的语言形容过戴丝狄蒙娜。当他看到卡西奥正走进来的时候，他让奥赛罗赶紧躲到一边，偷听他们的谈话。然后，他迎着卡西奥走过去，用一种只有他俩能够听得见的声音和他谈起比安卡，每次只要一谈起她，卡西奥就止不住大笑。奥赛罗听不到他们谈话的内容，但是卡西奥大笑的样子让他很恼火，因为他以为他们在谈论戴丝狄蒙娜。他们正谈着话，比安卡走了进来。她为卡西奥给她的手巾大吵大闹，还把手巾扔到卡西奥身上，说这一定是他的另一个情妇的。奥赛罗认出了这块手巾，他怒火中烧。他发誓要杀了戴丝狄蒙娜，还让伊阿古晚上给他拿毒药来。伊阿古建议他不要使用毒药，而是把她掐死，就在那张她和别的男人睡过觉的床上。伊阿古答应替他杀了卡西奥。

勃拉班修的亲戚罗多维科和戴丝狄蒙娜一起进来了，罗多维科带来了公爵给奥赛罗的信，公爵在信中让奥赛罗赶回威尼斯，卡西奥将代替他管理塞浦路斯。罗多维科问起卡西奥怎么样了，戴丝狄蒙娜回答说他和奥赛罗之间最近发生了一点不愉快，她正在努力地修补他们之间的关系。听她这样说，奥赛罗很生气，动手打了戴丝狄蒙娜。这一举动震惊了罗多维科。他问奥赛罗是不是疯了，奥赛罗不吭声。

罗德里戈对伊阿古发脾气，说他托伊阿古送给戴丝狄蒙娜那么多钱和珠宝作为礼物，可他还是没有得到她，他要伊阿古去把他送的东西都要回来，他不打算继续追她了。伊阿古骗他说，奥赛罗马上就要被派往毛里塔尼亚，他会带上戴丝狄蒙娜一起去，塞浦路斯将由卡西奥管理。他们二人想要留住戴丝狄蒙娜，就需要把卡西奥杀了，这样奥赛罗和戴丝狄蒙娜就走不了了。罗德里戈同意了去杀掉卡西奥。伊阿古又发布了一通独白，说不管罗德里戈和卡西奥两个人谁杀了谁，对他来讲都是双赢。如果罗德里戈被杀了，那么就没人找他讨回那些钱和珠宝了。如果卡西奥被杀了，那么伊阿古对他的诽谤就没人知道了，卡西奥的美德就不会反衬伊阿古的邪恶。

卡西奥离开比安卡家时，在黑暗中遭到了伊阿古和罗德里戈的伏击。罗德里戈挥剑朝着卡西奥刺过来，没想到反被卡西奥刺中了。伊阿古趁机从卡西奥背后刺中了卡西奥的腿。听到卡西奥疼得直叫，奥赛罗以为伊阿古杀了卡西奥，便认为他勇敢、诚实，还认为卡西奥该杀。勃拉班修的另一个兄弟葛莱西阿诺和罗多维科也来了，他们问卡西奥和罗德里戈之间发生了什么。卡西奥说他遭到了坏人的暗算。这时，伊阿古提着灯过来了，卡西奥在灯光下认出了罗德里戈是其中的一个伏击者。伊阿古跟着卡西奥喊罗德里戈"坏蛋"，并趁机把罗德里戈杀了。

按照事先计划好的,奥赛罗拿着蜡烛来到戴丝狄蒙娜的卧室。她的美丽让他着迷,可他还是决定杀了她。戴丝狄蒙娜突然惊醒过来,奥赛罗让她向死神祷告,她一脸茫然地问他为何要置她于死地。他回答说,因为她把他送给她的手巾送给了卡西奥。卡西奥已经承认他们两人有不正当关系。戴丝狄蒙娜恳求奥赛罗先不要杀她,先把她流放,等查清楚真相再杀她也不迟,但是奥赛罗内心的怒火无法平息,他用枕头死死地捂住了戴丝狄蒙娜的头,戴丝狄蒙娜窒息而死。

伊米莉亚看到戴丝狄蒙娜被杀死了,她惊恐万分。她质问奥赛罗为什么要杀戴丝狄蒙娜,他坚持认为戴丝狄蒙娜背着他和卡西奥偷情,所以她该死。伊米莉亚暴跳起来,哭着说戴丝狄蒙娜从来就没有背叛过他。至于那块手巾,是她捡起来给伊阿古的。至此,伊米莉亚认识到伊阿古才是罪魁祸首。她开始责骂伊阿古。奥赛罗这才知道他上了伊阿古的当,便一剑刺过去,不过在场的人收缴了奥赛罗的武器。伊阿古杀了伊米莉亚,然后逃走了。后来,他被抓了回来,奥赛罗又朝他把剑挥过去,接着,奥赛罗取出随身携带的一把匕首,结束了自己的生命。伊阿古被判处死刑。

5　Famous quotes

【Quote 1】

Brabantio
O thou foul thief, where hast thou stowed my daughter?
Damned as thou art, thou hast enchanted her!
For I'll refer me to all things of sense,
if she in chains of magic were not bound,
whether a maid so tender, fair, and happy,
so opposite to marriage that she
shunned the wealthy curlèd darlings of our nation,
would ever have, t' incur a general mock,
run from her guardage to the sooty bosom of such a thing as thou
—to fear, not to delight.
Judge me the world if 'tis not gross in sense
that thou hast practiced on her with foul charms,
abused her delicate youth with drugs or minerals that weakens motion.
I'll have't disputed on.
'Tis probable and palpable to thinking.
I therefore apprehend and do attach thee for an abuser of the world,
a practicer of arts inhibited and out of warrant

—lay hold upon him.

If he do resist, subdue him at his peril![3]

(Act 1, Scene 2)

[Brabantio (played by Geoffrey Chater) accusing Othello (played by Anthony Hopkins) in a 1981 film directed by Jonathan Miller.]

✧ Paraphrase

Brabantio

Oh, you foul thief! Where have you hidden my daughter?

Since you're damned yourself, you probably cast a spell on her!

I'll stake my case on plain evidence and common sense

as to whether such a tender, beautiful, and happy virgin girl

—one who was so opposed to marriage that she shunned even the wealthy,

good-looking young men of our city

—would have ever risked her reputation to run away

from her protected home into the dirty embrace of such a thing as you,

a thing to be feared and not loved,

unless she had been caught by magic.

Let the world be my judge:

isn't it completely obvious that you have practiced some evil magic on her,

and abused her delicate youth with drugs or toxins that make her weak?

I'll bring you to court.

This is most likely what happened.

Therefore, I hereby arrest you as a criminal

and a practitioner of illegal black magic.[4]

Unit 5　Othello

◇ 原文译文

啊,你这恶贼!你把我的女儿藏到什么地方去了?你不想想你自己是个什么东西,胆敢用妖法蛊惑她;我们只要凭着情理判断,像她这样一个年轻貌美、娇生惯养的姑娘,多少我们国里有钱有势的俊秀子弟她都看不上眼,倘若不是中了魔,怎么会不怕人家的笑话,背着尊亲投奔到你这个丑恶的黑鬼的怀里?——那还不早把她吓坏了,岂有什么乐趣可言!世人可以替我评一评,是不是显而易见你用邪恶的符咒欺诱她的娇弱的心灵,用药饵丹方迷惑她的知觉;我要在法庭上叫大家评一评理,这种事情是不是很有可能。所以我现在逮捕你;有害风化,行使邪术,便是你的罪名。抓住他;要是他敢反抗,你们就用武力制服他。[5]

【Quote 2】

Othello
Most potent, grave, and reverend signiors,
my very noble and approved good masters,
that I have ta'en away this old man's daughter,
it is most true.
True, I have married her.
The very head and front of my offending hath this extent, no more.
Rude am I in my speech,
and little blessed with the soft phrase of peace,
for since these arms of mine had seven years' pith
till now some nine moons wasted,
they have used their dearest action in the tented field,
and little of this great world can I speak,
more than pertains to feats of broils and battle,
and therefore little shall I grace my cause in speaking for myself.
Yet, by your gracious patience,
I will a round unvarnished tale deliver of my whole course of love.
What drugs, what charms, what conjuration and what mighty magic
—for such proceeding I am charged withal
—I won his daughter.[6]
(Act 1, Scene 3)

(Othello pleading for himself in a 1981 film directed by Jonathan Miller.)

◈ Paraphrase

Othello

Most powerful, serious, and honorable sirs
—my very noble masters who have proved to be good to me
—I tell you it is absolutely true that I have taken away this old man's daughter.
It is true that I have married her.
But this is the extent of my offense—no more.
I am not good with words,
and haven't been blessed with the skill of peaceful speech.
My skill is in war:
from the time I was seven-years-old to just nine months ago,
I have used the strength of my arms on the battlefield.
I cannot speak about much in this great big world
besides wartime deeds and battle.
Therefore, I probably won't help my case much by speaking for myself.
Nonetheless, if you will be patient,
I will tell you the whole straightforward story of my love with Desdemona,
And won't embellish it at all.
I will tell you what sort of spells,
what kind of powerful magic, what drugs,
and what charms I have used to win this man's daughter
—since that is the accusation. [7]

◇ 原文译文

威严无比、德高望重的各位大人,我的尊贵贤良的主人们,我把这位老人家的女儿带走了,这是完全真实的;我已经和她结了婚,这也是真的;我的最大的罪状仅止于此,别的就不是我所知道的了。我的言语是粗鲁的,一点不懂得那些温文尔雅的辞令;因为自从我这双手臂长了七年的膂力以后,直到最近这九个月以前,它们一直都在战场上发挥它们的本领;对于这一个广阔的世界,我除了冲锋陷阵以外,几乎一无所知,所以我也不能用什么动人的字句替我自己辩护。可是你们要是愿意耐心听我说下去,我可以向你们讲述一段质朴无华的、关于我的恋爱的全部经过的故事;告诉你们我用什么药物、什么符咒、什么驱神役鬼的手段、什么神奇玄妙的魔法,骗到了他的女儿,因为这是他所控诉我的罪名。[8]

【Quote 3】

Othello

It gives me wonder great as my content to see you here before me.
Oh, my soul's joy!
If after every tempest come such calms,
may the winds blow till they have wakened death,
and let the laboring bark climb hills of seas Olympus-high,
and duck again as low as hell's from heaven!
If it were now to die, 'twere now to be most happy,
for I fear my soul hath her content so absolute
that not another comfort like to this succeeds in unknown fate.[9]
(Act 2, Scene 1)

◇ Paraphrase

Othello

I'm surprised, but happy to see that you made it here before me.
Oh, my soul is overjoyed!
If this is my reward for every sea-storm,
then let the winds rage and blow all they can,
and let my ships have to climb up mountainous waves
and drop down from their crests as if falling from heaven to hell!
If I were to die now, I'd die at my happiest moment.
I don't think my soul will ever be as happy as this again.[10]

◇ 原文译文

看见你比我先到这里,真使我又惊又喜。啊,我心爱的人! 要是每一次暴风雨之后,都有这样和煦的阳光,那么尽管让狂风肆意地吹,把死亡都吹醒了吧!让那辛苦挣扎的船舶爬上一座座如山的高浪,就像从高高的云上堕下幽深的地狱一般,一泻千丈地跌下来吧!要是我现在死去,那才是最幸福的;因为我怕我的灵魂已经尝到了无上的欢乐,此生此世,再也不会有同样令人欣喜的事情了。[11]

【Quote 4】

Iago
Good name in man and woman, dear my lord,
is the immediate jewel of their souls.
Who steals my purse steals trash; 'tis something, nothing;
'Twas mine, 'tis his, and has been slave to thousands.
But he that filches from me my good name robs me of that
which not enriches him and makes me poor indeed.[12]
(Act 3, Scene 3)

[Iago (played by Bob Hoskins) speaking to Othello about good name in a 1981 film directed by Jonathan Miller.]

◇ Paraphrase

Iago
A good reputation is the most precious jewel
of a man's or a woman's soul, my dear lord.
If someone steals money from me, it's not a big deal.
It was mine, now it's his, and it's been held by thousands of others.
But if someone steals my good reputation from me,

then he really does make me truly poor,
and steals something that doesn't even make him any richer. [13]

◇ 原文译文

我的好主帅,无论男人或者女人,名誉是他们灵魂里面最切身的珍宝。谁偷窃我的钱囊,不过偷窃到一些废物,一些虚无的东西,它只是从我的手里转到他的手里,而它也曾做过千万人的奴隶;可是谁偷去了我的名誉,那么他虽然并不因此而富足,我却因为失去它而成为赤贫了。[14]

【Quote 5】

Iago
Oh, beware, my lord, of jealousy!
'Tis the green-eyed monster,
which doth mock the meat it feeds on.
That cuckold lives in bliss.
Who, certain of his fate, loves not his wronger,
but, oh, what damnèd minutes tells he o'er who dotes, yet doubts
—suspects, yet soundly loves! [15]
(Act 3, Scene 3)

(Iago speaking to Othello about jealousy in a 1981 film directed by Jonathan Miller.)

◇ Paraphrase

Iago
Oh, my lord, beware of jealousy!
It is a green-eyed monster that mocks whoever it eats away at.

A man who knows for sure that his wife is cheating on him lives in bliss,
since he knows not to love his wife.
But, oh, what torture it is to love but doubt your wife,
suspect her of something but still love her. [16]

◇ 原文译文

啊，主帅，您要留心嫉妒啊；那是一个绿眼的妖魔，谁做了它的牺牲，就要受它的玩弄。本来并不爱他的妻子的那种丈夫，虽然明知被他的妻子欺骗，算来还是幸福的；可是啊！一方面那样痴心疼爱，另一方面又是那样满腹狐疑，这才是活活的受罪！[17]

【Quote 6】

Othello

This fellow's of exceeding honesty and knows all quantities,
with a learnèd spirit, of human dealings.
If I do prove her haggard,
though that her jesses were my dear heartstrings,
I'd whistle her off and let her down the wind to prey at fortune.
Haply, for I am black and have not
those soft parts of conversation that chamberers have,
or for I am declined into the vale of years
—yet that's not much
—she's gone, I am abused,
and my relief must be to loathe her.
Oh, curse of marriage that we can call these delicate creatures ours
and not their appetites!
I had rather be a toad and live upon the vapor of a dungeon
than keep a corner in the thing I love for others' uses.
Yet 'tis the plague to great ones,
prerogatived are they less than the base.
'Tis destiny unshunnable, like death.
Even then this forkèd plague is fated to us when we do quicken.
Look where she comes. [18]

(Act 3, Scene 3)

◇ Paraphrase

Othello

This man is very honest and knows human interactions very well.

If I find proof that Desdemona is unfaithful,
I'll let her go like I'm getting rid of a pet,
even if the leash is my own heartstrings.
Maybe since I am black and don't have the
smooth conversational skills of gallant men,
or maybe since I'm getting old
—but no, none of that's important.
She's gone, I am betrayed,
and my only recourse must be to hate her.
Oh, this is the curse of marriage,
that we can have control over our delicate wives,
but not their desires.
I'd rather be a toad who survives off the mold in a dungeon
than to share the thing I love with others.
But that's what you get for being a powerful man,
as this happens more often to noblemen than to commoners.
It's an inescapable part of fate, like death.
From the moment we're born we are fated to wear the horns①.
Look, here she comes. [19]

◇ 原文译文

这是一个非常诚实的家伙，对于人情世故是再熟悉不过的了。要是我能够证明她是一头没有驯服的野鹰，虽然我用自己的心弦把她系住，我也要放她随风远去，追寻她自己的命运。也许因为我生得黑丑，缺少绅士们温柔风雅的谈吐；也许因为我年纪老了点儿——虽然还不算太老——所以她才会背叛我；我已经自取其辱，只好割断对她这一段痴情。啊，结婚的烦恼！我们可以在名义上把这些可爱的人儿称为我们所有，却不能支配她们的爱憎喜恶！我宁愿做一只蛤蟆，呼吸牢室中的浊气，也不愿占住了自己心爱之物的一角，让别人把它享用。可是那是富贵者也不能幸免的灾祸，他们并不比贫贱者享有更多的特权；那是像死一样不可逃避的命运，我们一生下来就已经在冥冥中注定了要戴那顶倒霉的绿头巾。瞧！她来了。倘然她是不贞的，啊！那么上天在开自己的玩笑了。我不信。[20]

【Quote 7】

Desdemona

Upon my knee, what doth your speech import?
I understand a fury in your words,

---

① A cuckolded man was often depicted as having horns on his head.

but not the words. [21]

(Act 4, Scene 2)

[Desdemona (played by Penelope Wilton) trying to appease Othello in a 1981 film directed by Jonathan Miller.]

◇ Paraphrase

Desdemona

I beg you here on my knees
—tell me, what do you mean by your speech?
I can see that you are angry,
but I don't understand what you mean. [22]

◇ 原文译文

我跪在您的面前,请您告诉我您这些话是什么意思?我知道您在生气,可是我不懂您的话。[23]

【Quote 8】

Othello

O thou weed,
who art so lovely fair and smell'st so sweet that the sense aches at thee,
would thou hadst ne'er been born! [24]

(Act 4, Scene 2)

◇ Paraphrase

Othello

Oh, you weed,

you are so lovely and smell so sweet that it hurts to look at you.
I wish you had never been born![25]

◇ 原文译文

你这野草闲花啊！你的颜色是这样娇美，你的香气是这样芬芳，人家看见你、嗅到你就会心疼；但愿世上从来不曾有过你![26]

【Quote 9】

Othello

Soft you, a word or two before you go.
I have done the state some service, and they know't.
No more of that. I pray you, in your letters,
when you shall these unlucky deeds relate,
speak of me as I am.
Nothing extenuate, nor set down aught in malice.
Then must you speak of one that loved not wisely, but too well.
Of one not easily jealous, but being wrought,
perplexed in the extreme.
Of one whose hand, like the base Indian,
threw a pearl away richer than all his tribe.
Of one whose subdued eyes,
Albeit unused to the melting mood,
drop tears as fast as the Arabian trees their medicinal gum.
Set you down this, and say besides that in Aleppo once,
where a malignant and a turbaned Turk beat a Venetian and traduced the state,
I took by the throat the circumcisèd dog, and smote him, thus.[27]
(Act 5, Scene 2)

◇ Paraphrase

Othello

Wait, let me say a word or two before you go.
I have served the government of Venice well,
and they know it.
But nothing more about that.
I beg you, in your letters,
when you relate the story of these unfortunate deeds,
speak of me as I am.

Don't downplay my crime, but don't exaggerate it maliciously.
Speak of me as a man who loved not wisely, but too much;
a man who was not easily made jealous,
but was manipulated and tricked into extreme jealously;
a man who behaved like a vile Indian that
throws away a pearl worth more than his whole tribe.
Speak of me as a man who is not used to crying,
but whose eyes now drop tears
like the Arabian trees that drip with medicinal sap.
Write this, and also say that one time in Aleppo① a malicious Turk
wearing a turban beat a Venetian,
flouting the Venetian state,
and so I grabbed the circumcised Turkish dog by his throat
and struck him down like this. [28]

◇ 原文译文

且慢,在你们未走以前,再听我说一两句话。我对于国家曾经立过相当大的功劳,这是执政诸公所知道的;那些话现在也不用说了。当你们把这种不幸的事实报告他们的时候,请你们在公文上老老实实照我本来的样子叙述,不要徇私情维护我,也不要恶意构陷;你们应当说我是一个在恋爱上不聪明而过于深情的人;一个不容易嫉妒的人,可是一旦被人煽动以后,就会糊涂到极点;一个像印度人一样糊涂的人,会把一颗比他整个部落所有的财产更贵重的珍珠随手抛弃;一个不惯于流妇人之泪的人,可是当他被感情征服的时候,也会像涌流着胶液的阿拉伯胶树一般两眼泛滥。请你们把这些话记下,再补充一句:在阿勒坡,曾经有一个裹着头巾的充满敌意的土耳其人殴打一个威尼斯人,诽谤我们的国家,那时候我就一把抓住这受割礼的狗子的咽喉,就这样把他杀了。[29]

6　Questions for discussion

(1) What causes Othello's tragedy?

(2) What lessons can you learn from him regarding marriage?

(3) What do you think of Desdemona? Do you support her in her choice of a partner like Othello?

(4) What role does Iago play in this tragedy?

(5) Comment on racism in this play.

---

① Aleppo is a city in northwestern Syria.

7　References

[1][2]　Othello Study Guide[EB/OL]. https://www.litcharts.com/lit/othello.

[3][6][9][12][15][18][21][24][27]　Shakespeare W. Othello[M]. New York: Simon & Schuster, 1993.

[4][7][10][13][16][19][22][25][28]　Othello: Shakespeare Translation[EB/OL]. https://www.litcharts.com/shakescleare/shakespeare-translations/othello.

[5][8][11][14][17][20][23][26][29]　威廉·莎士比亚. 莎士比亚悲剧五种[M]. 朱生豪,译. 北京:人民文学出版社,2020.

Part Two
Shakespeare's Great Comedies

Unit 6

The Merchant of Venice

1 Characters

Antonio(安东尼奥): A merchant of Venice and a friend of Bassanio.

Shylock(夏洛克): Jewish moneylender.

Portia(鲍西亚): Rich heiress and a brilliant woman who is disguised as a lawyer named Balthazar in defense of Antonio.

Bassanio(巴萨尼奥): Friend and kinsman of Antonio.

Duke of Venice(威尼斯公爵): Ruler who takes the role of the judge in the trial of Antonio.

Prince of Morocco(摩洛哥王子), **Prince of Arragon**(阿拉贡王子): Suitors of Portia.

Nerissa(尼莉莎): Portia's maid who is disguised as a clerk in the court.

Gratiano(格莱西安诺): Friend of Bassanio who loves Nerissa.

Solanio(索拉尼欧), **Salerio**(索勒里欧): Friends of Antonio and Bassanio.

Jessica(杰西卡): Shylock's daughter.

Lorenzo(罗伦佐): Jessica's suitor and later her husband.

Tubal(图巴尔): Lorenzo's Jewish friends.

Launcelot Gobbo(朗斯洛特·戈博): Shylock's clownish servant.

Old Gobbo(老戈博): Launcelot's father.

Leonardo(里奥纳多): Bassanio's servant.

Balthasar(巴尔萨泽), **Stephano**(斯蒂芬诺): Portia's servants.

Margery(玛杰丽): Wife of Old Gobbo.

Doctor Bellario(贝拉里奥博士): Famous lawyer and Portia's cousin in Padua who is only mentioned in the play.

2 Background

Jews had restricted rights in most of the Europe. King Edward I banished Jews completely from England in 1290 and they were not allowed to return until 1655, when Oliver Cromwell gave them permission to return. The banishment took effect legally during Shakespeare's time, but according to scholars, a few hundred Jews still lived around London in the name of Christians. The Renaissance Christians didn't like Jews because Jews practiced usury—charging interest on borrowed money. According to classical and Christian tradition, it was immoral to practice usury. The English philosopher and essayist Sir Francis Bacon, Shakespeare's contemporary, wrote in his essay *On Usury* that it was "against nature for money to beget money."[1]

The chief source of this play was a tale in an Italian collection entitled *Il Pecorone* or *The Simpleton*, written in 1378 by Giovanni Fiorentino, and published in 1565. It seems that scenes of the three caskets may have been based on one of the tales in *Gesta Romanorum* (*Deeds of the Romans*) published in Latin in the late 1200s or early 1300s. Shakespeare may also have referred to his contemporary playwright, Christopher Marlowe's tragedy *The Jew of Malta* (circa 1590).[2]

3 Settings

The plot takes place in Venice, which is in northeastern Italy on the coast of the Adriatic Sea and Portia's country estate of Belmont near Venice. In late medieval and early Renaissance times, Venice was a great commercial center in Europe.[3]

4 Synopsis

Antonio, a merchant, and his friends, Solanio and Salerio, meet on a street in Venice. Later he is joined by his friend and relative Bassanio with Lorenzo and Gratiano, Bassanio's friends. Antonio tells them that he somehow feels sad. His sadness is not caused by his ships at sea, nor is he in love. Solanio says there are different kinds of people. Some people are so happy that they even smile at a funeral and some people are so sour that they cannot crack a smile even at the funniest joke. Antonio says the world is a stage and everyone has a role to play, and his role is a sad one. Gratiano says that he prefers to play the fool who is happy and to laugh without caring about wrinkles, and that he would rather drink wine to damage his liver than waste away his life groaning to make others embarrassed. Then Bassanio tells Antonio that he needs his help. Antonio says his money and his body are both at Bassanio's disposal. Bassanio says he needs 3,000 ducats to clear his current debts and to woo the rich and beautiful noblewoman Portia. Antonio tells Bassanio that he has no ready money at hand because he has invested all his money in his merchandise. He suggests that Bassanio go to a moneylender to borrow money on his credit, that is, he can use Antonio's property and reputation as collateral.

In Belmont near Venice, Portia is talking with Nerissa, her maidservant that she is tired of the world. Nerissa says she is unhappy because she is too rich. To live in excess is as unhappy as to live in starvation. A moderate life is a guarantee of happiness. Portia complains that she cannot take control over her marriage partner. She cannot act against her father's will who stipulated that whoever wants to marry Portia must choose the correct casket which contains her portrait out of three, one made of gold, one of silver and one of lead. And so far, she has been fed up with her many suitors. She shows her disapproval of them and dismisses them all. Nerissa tells Portia that since they have won no favour from her, they have decided to depart without bothering her anymore. This is fortunate for Portia. Otherwise, if one of them chooses the correct casket, she will have to marry him. When Nerissa mentions the Prince of Morocco, Portia responds that she would rather die than marry a man of dark complexion.

Bassanio goes to Shylock, a Jewish usurer to borrow the money. After some waffling, Shylock agrees to lend him 3,000 ducats for three months on Antonio's credit. But when Antonio comes in person, Shylock changes his mind. He says he will need no interest, but they must sign a bond that if Antonio fails to repay the money in three months, he will lose one pound of flesh and that Shylock is entitled to cut the flesh from any part of his body as he pleases. Confident that his ship will return at least one month before the deadline and he will get at least 9,000 ducats from his merchandise, Antonio consent to comply. Shylock thinks of this plan because Antonio has accused him many times in public places of usury, a practice against Christian morality to lend money for interest. Antonio often lends money without interest, which reduces interest rates for professional moneylenders. To boot, Antonio spits on Shylock. So this is a good chance for him to avenge the abuse inflicted by Antonio.

The Prince of Morocco has arrived at Portia's house to try his luck. He beseeches Portia not to judge him according to his complexion. He is a brave man and worthy person. Portia addresses him "Renowned Prince" and assures him that she judges a man not according to his appearance. But she cannot decide her own husband. He must choose the correct casket wherein there is her picture to marry her. She warns him that if he fails in his choice, he must not speak to another lady about marriage, and that he must leave immediately. He promises to comply. After pondering over the inscriptions on the caskets, the Prince of Morocco chooses the gold one, the inscription of which says "Who chooseth me shall gain what many men desire". After he opens it, however, he finds not Portia's picture but a skull. He departs with a grieved heart. Portia wishes that suitors of the same complexion as the Prince of Morocco would choose the same as he has done.

Launcelot, Shylock's servant, decides to leave Shylock and serve Bassanio because he thinks a Jew is a devil and serving him will corrupt his soul. He is accepted by Bassanio. He goes to bid farewell to Jessica, who feels ashamed to be Shylock's daughter. She expresses that she is only his daughter by blood but doesn't inherit his manners. She asks Launcelot to deliver a secret letter to Lorenzo, a Christian who loves her and wants to marry her. She writes in the letter that if what he says is true, she will elope with him and convert to Christianity to marry him. Gratiano, Lorenzo, Salerio and Solanio discuss a plan for Lorenzo and Jessica's elopement. They will arrange a fake masquerade and Lorenzo will bring her clothes to be dressed up as his torchbearer to elope with him. Launcelot is sent by Bassanio back to Shylock's house to invite him for dinner. Before he leaves home, Shylock bids Jessica to lock the door carefully because he had a dream that something bad will happen that night. During Shylock's absence, Jessica steals a lot of Shylock's money, gold and jewels, and runs away with Lorenzo as planned. Solanio and Salerio imitate Shylock's outburst of rage and anguish on discovery of her elopement: "My daughter! O, my ducats! O, my daughter! Fled with a Christian!" Then Salerio tells Solanio that he has heard rumors that there is a shipwreck at sea. They hope it will not be any of Antonio's ships. Antonio is such an affectionate, kind and generous gentleman that no other man can be compared with him.

The Prince of Arragon arrives in Belmont to seek Portia's hand in marriage. After he promises that if he fails, he will not tell others what he chooses, nor pursue another woman as a suitor, and will leave immediately, Portia lets him proceed. He dismisses the gold casket because he doesn't want to be one of the majority who base their choice on the appearance of things, and rejects the lead one because it looks lowly. After some puzzling and reasoning, he chooses the silver casket with the inscription "Who chooseth me shall get as much as he deserves". He thinks what property, honour, dignity one gets should be based on his merit. But when he opens it, however, he discovers a portrait of a blinking idiot, not Portrait's picture. He doesn't linger but leaves right away as he has promised, bearing his misfortune patiently. A messenger enters to announce the arrival of a young Venetian with good manners carrying a load of valuable gifts ahead of his lord. Portia is pleased with the messenger's description and Nerissa hopes the new visitor will be Bassanio.

Shylock blames Solanio and Salerio for helping Jessica to elope. They respond that she is old enough to choose her husband and do things on her own. Solanio asks Shylock if he has heard news about more shipwrecks of Antonio's. Shylock says yes. Solanio doesn't believe that Shylock really wants a pound of flesh from Antonio because it does no good for him, but Shylock answers affirmatively. At least it can feed his revenge. Shylock argues that he is the same as any Christian. When he is insulted, he thinks of revenge as well. After Solanio and Salerio exit on a message from Antonio who wants to see them, Tubal, Shylock's Jewish friend enters to tell him that he has searched in Genoa for Jessica but couldn't find her. Once again, Shylock laments his heavy financial loss. But he is consoled to learn that another ship of Antonio's is lost at sea and he will have a pound of flesh cut from Antonio's heart.

In Belmont, Bassanio and Portia have spent some happy time together and they fall in love. Portia is nervous when Bassanio wants to solve the riddle of the caskets. She tries to persuade him to delaying making the choice. If he chooses the wrong one, he will have to leave her. Bassanio insists on doing it now because he is tortured by waiting. Then they go to the caskets. Portia thinks if Bassanio truly loves her, he will make the right choice. Standing before the caskets, Bassanio says appearances are deceiving and even the wisest are sometimes tricked. Therefore, he rejects gold as gaudy and silver that is passed between men as currency. He is moved by the humble lead which implies more threat than promise and chooses it. Portia is overjoyed at his decision. Opening the casket, he finds the picture of the beautiful Portia attached with a scroll which reads "You that choose not by the view, chance as fair and choose as true. Since this fortune falls to you, be content and seek no new". Bassanio feels it is too good to be true. Portia says she is an inexperienced, unschooled and naïve girl and wishes that she would be more beautiful and wealthier for him. She declares that herself and all she has is now Bassanio's. She gives him a ring to confirm her love. At this time, Gratiano tells Bassanio that he and Nerissa have fallen in love with each other and he asks for Bassanio's permission to marry Nerissa. Bassanio consents and declares that they will have the wedding at the same time.

Salerio enters, bringing Antonio's letter to Bassanio in which he tells Bassanio that he is now in trouble with his ships missing and the pound of flesh he owes Shylock, and to pay Shylock the pound of flesh means the loss of his life. He tells Bassanio that all the debts Bassanio owes to Antonio are now cleared. He expects nothing from him except that he wants to see Bassanio before he dies. After Portia learns that they are bosom friends, she offers to pay twenty times the amount Antonio owes Shylock. Bassanio gets ready to depart for Venice. Portia hatches a plan to help Antonio out of the trouble. She asks Lorenzo and Jessica to manage her household because she will go to a monastery to pray and contemplate during Bassanio's absence, which they agree. She then writes a letter for her cousin Doctor Bellario in Padua and sends her servant Balthasar there to hand over the letter to her cousin. She tells Balthasar to bring back some documents and clothing. She then urges Nerissa to get dressed up in a man's clothes as she will do and head for Venice to see their husbands.

The Duke of Venice presides over the trial of Antonio. He tells Shylock that the law stands on his side and he is justified to have the pound of flesh, but Shylock can show mercy on Antonio so that he can get mercy from others. Shylock refuses, saying that he has done nothing wrong and doesn't need mercy. When asked why he demands Antonio's flesh, Shylock replies that he has harboured hatred for Antonio and doesn't want to explain further. Bassanio argues with Shylock and offers him twice the amount Antonio owes him, but he declines. Antonio asks Bassanio not to waste time arguing with Shylock. He has begged for Shylock's mercy and was rejected. Bassanio tells Antonio that he will follow him after he dies. Antonio asks him to give up the idea and to live to write his epitaph. The Duke tells the court that they will have a prominent lawyer, Doctor Bellario to help him judge the case. Following his words, Nerissa enters, disguised as a lawyer's clerk. She presents a letter from Doctor Bellario to the Duke, in which Doctor Bellario recommends a learned lawyer named Balthazar in lieu of him to attend the court. Shylock is whetting his knife.

Portia/Balthazar at first assures Shylock that he has Venetian law on his side and asks him to show mercy on Antonio, saying that mercy is like gentle rain from the sky which blesses both the one who gives mercy and the one who receives. Once again, Shylock refuses to spare Antonio's life. Portia asks if Antonio has prepared the money to repay Shylock and Bassanio responds that he has offered ten time the amount owed to Shylock but he declines. He then asks if the law can be altered to suit the case. Portia replies an agreed-on decree cannot be bent otherwise it will create chaos. Shylock exclaims "Daniel". Portia then asks Shylock for the bond. After reading the bond, Portia states that Shylock is entitled to cut the flesh nearest Antonio's heart and instructs Antonio to bear his chest. She begs for Shylock's mercy in vain once again and asks Shylock if he has sent for a surgeon to stop the bleeding when the flesh is cut, Shylock says this is not stated in the bond. He only prepares the scales. She tells Antonio to speak his last words, who forbids Bassanio from mourning and asks him to send his best wishes to his wife Portia. Bassanio and Gratiano wish to exchange their lives and their wives' for Antonio's life. Hearing this, Shylock says that he would rather his daughter marry a Jewish bandit than a Christian who takes his wife's life so willingly.

When Shylock is about to cut Antonio's flesh, Portia stops him, saying that according to the contract, Shylock will only take the pound of flesh, but no blood. If one drop of Christian blood is shed, according to Venetian law, all Shylock's lands and property will be confiscated to the state. Shocked by Portia's statement, Shylock flinches and decides to accept Bassanio's offer of three times the amount of the debt. Bassanio responds quickly but Portia stops him, saying that Shylock will get nothing but justice. She then states that he will cut off one pound of flesh, no more, no less. Otherwise, he will be sentenced to death and his property will be confiscated. Shylock backtracks further and asks for only his initial amount, but Portia adds that there is another Venetian law which stipulates if an alien person is proved to take the life of a Venetian citizen, half of the alien's property will be given to the citizen and the other half to the state. The Duke rules that he will show mercy on Shylock by sparing Shylock's life. Portia asks Antonio to make a decision. Antonio says that the state should disclaim the half and his half will belong to Lorenzo and Jessica, and that when Shylock dies, Jessica will inherit his wealth. Apart from these, Shylock should be converted to Christianity. Hearing this, Shylock backs off the court, saying that he is unwell to sign the deed but will sign later when it is sent to him.

In gratitude, Bassanio offers Portia 3,000 ducats. Portia declines and says she wants nothing but Bassanio's ring. Bassanio explains that the ring is a gift from his wife and he has promised never to part with it. He offers to buy another more expensive one for her. Portia rejects. Antonio persuades Bassanio to value the lawyer's help more than his wife's requirement. Bassanio relinquishes his ring. In the same way, Nerissa obtains Gratiano's ring. They rush back to Belmont, before their husbands' return. When their husbands come back in the early morning, Portia and Nerissa demands to see their rings. They admit that they were given to the lawyer, and the clerk and beg for their forgiveness. They pretend to be furious, and their fury is not out of the value of the rings but the fact that they break the oaths. They promise never to betray their wives again. Antonio offers his soul as collateral for their pledge. They forgive their husbands and give them each a new one, saying that they get the rings from the lawyer and his clerk by sleeping with them the previous night. Bassanio and Gratiano bursts up.

Unit 6　The Merchant of Venice

To placate them, Portia and Nerissa reveal the truth and clarify everything. At this time, news arrives that Antonio's ships return safely.

【剧情介绍】

　　安东尼奥是威尼斯的一个商人,他在街上偶遇了他的朋友索拉尼欧和索勒里欧。后来,安东尼奥的亲戚兼朋友巴萨尼奥,以及巴萨尼奥的朋友罗伦佐和格莱西安诺也来了。安东尼奥说不知何故他感到有些悲伤,既不是因为他在海上的商船,也不是因为恋爱了。索拉尼欧说世上的人千千万,有些人天生就是乐天派,即使在葬礼上他们也能笑得出来,有些人却生来就闷闷不乐,即使最搞笑的段子也不能让他们挤出一丝笑容。安东尼奥说在生活这个大舞台上,每个人都扮演着不同的角色,而他扮演的是一个悲伤的角色。格莱西安诺说,他宁愿扮演一个快乐的傻瓜,整天笑呵呵的,还不用担心会长皱纹,他宁愿喝酒伤肝,也不愿意整天无病呻吟浪费生命,惹得别人也不好受。接着,巴萨尼奥对安东尼奥说他需要帮助。安东尼奥说,他的钱和他的肉体都任由巴萨尼奥使用。巴萨尼奥说,他需要3000银币先偿还现在的债务,剩下的用来向美丽的富家女鲍西亚求婚。安东尼奥说他手头没有这么多现金,都投资到生意上了。他建议巴萨尼奥用安东尼奥的信誉和财产做担保,去找一个放贷人借钱。

　　离威尼斯不远,有一个叫贝尔蒙特的地方,那里就是鲍西亚的家。这天,她对女仆尼莉莎说她感到有些厌世了。尼莉莎说她不开心是因为她太富有了。太富有和一贫如洗都让人不快乐。既不缺钱也不用挨饿才是幸福的保障。鲍西亚说,她连自己的婚姻大事都做不了主。谁要是想娶她,就得从金、银、铅三个匣子中选择一个,如果选的那个匣子里装着鲍西亚的相片,那么这个人就可以和鲍西亚结婚。到目前为止,所有的求婚者都让她心生厌倦。鲍西亚对这些求婚者都不满意,这些人都不在她的考虑之列。尼莉莎说,他们得不到鲍西亚的眷顾,打算永远离开贝尔蒙特。对于鲍西亚来说这是好事,否则,万一其中一个人选中了那个装有鲍西亚相片的匣子,那她就不得不嫁给他了。当尼莉莎提到那个摩洛哥王子的时候,鲍西亚说她宁死也不愿嫁给一个黑皮肤的人。

　　巴萨尼奥找到一个名叫夏洛克的人借钱,这个犹太人专门放高利贷。思虑过后,夏洛克答应借给他3000银币,借期为3个月,由安东尼奥担保。但是见到安东尼奥本人后,夏洛克变了卦。他说这笔钱他不需要利息,但是他们之间要签订一个协议,假如安东尼奥不能如约在3个月内还钱,那么就要任由夏洛克从他身上任意一个部位割走一磅肉。安东尼奥信心满满,他认为他的船只至少会在借据到期之前一个星期回来,到时候他的收入少说也有9000银币,所以他就和夏洛克签署了这个契约。夏洛克之所以想到这一招,是因为安东尼奥多次在公共场合谴责夏洛克放高利贷这种有悖基督徒道德的做法。安东尼奥常常借钱给别人,还不收利息,他这样做相当于抢走了放贷人的生意。安东尼奥还往夏洛克身上吐口水。所以,这是夏洛克报复安东尼奥对他的侮辱的好机会。

　　摩洛哥王子来到鲍西亚家试试运气。他恳请鲍西亚不要根据他的肤色来判断他这个人。他说他是一个勇敢的男人,配得上鲍西亚。鲍西亚称他为"赫赫有名的王子",并向他保证她不以貌取人,可是,婚姻大事由不得她做主。她未来的夫君得自己选出那个装有她相片的匣子才行。她提醒他,如果他选错了匣子,他可不能再向别的女子求婚了,还必须立即离开。摩洛哥王子答应了这些条件。仔细考量了那些刻在匣子上面的题词之后,摩洛哥王子选择了那个金匣子,这上面的题词是"选择我的人将会得到多数男人想要的东西"。然而,当他打开匣子一看,却发现里面装的是一个头颅,而非鲍西亚的相片。他只好伤心地离去了。鲍西亚希望和摩洛哥王子相同肤色的男人会做出和他相同的选择。

夏洛克的仆人朗斯洛特打算离开夏洛克,去为巴萨尼奥效力,因为他认为犹太人就是恶魔,如果他一直伺候夏洛克的话,他自己的灵魂就会被玷污。巴萨尼奥接受了朗斯洛特。临走之前,朗斯洛特去和夏洛克的女儿杰西卡告别,这个姑娘也因为有夏洛克那样的父亲而感到羞愧。但她说她只是继承了她父亲的血脉,行为举止却一点也不像她父亲。她请朗斯洛特给罗伦佐带去一封密信。罗伦佐是一个基督徒,他深爱着杰西卡并且想娶她。她在信中说,如果罗伦佐真的爱她并且想娶她的话,那么她打算和他私奔,然后改信基督教,还要嫁给他。格莱西安诺、罗伦佐、索勒里欧、索拉尼欧商量出了一个计策,帮助杰西卡和罗伦佐私奔。他们会安排一场假的化装舞会,然后让罗伦佐为杰西卡换上衣服,假扮成他的火把手一起逃离。巴萨尼奥吩咐朗斯洛特去夏洛克家邀请他参加晚宴。出门之前,夏洛克叮嘱杰西卡把门窗锁好,因为他梦到今天晚上将有不好的事情发生。夏洛克走后,杰西卡偷走了父亲的现金和珠宝,然后按照计划和罗伦佐私奔了。索拉尼欧和索勒里欧学着夏洛克发现杰西卡逃离家后的样子,说:"啊,我的银币!啊,我的女儿!竟然和一个基督徒跑了!"接着,索勒里欧告诉索拉尼欧,有传闻说海上有船只失事了。他们希望不是安东尼奥的船只,安东尼奥可是举世无双的慈爱、善良、慷慨之人啊!

阿拉贡王子来到贝尔蒙特向鲍西亚求婚。他答应会做到以下几点:如果这次求婚失败,他不会对任何人讲到他选的是什么,也会不再追求别的女人,还会立即离开。于是,鲍西亚就让他在三个匣子当中选一个。他没有选择金匣子,因为他不想和多数人一样被表象左右,他也没有选择铅匣子,因为它看起来太劣质了。思来想去之后,他选择了银匣子,只见上面写着:"选择我的人会得到他应当得到的东西。"他认为一个人值当得到什么就得到什么,比如财富、荣誉、尊严等。可是,等他打开匣子一看,里面装的却是一个眨着眼睛的傻瓜,而非鲍西亚的相片。不过,他默默接受了命运的安排,按照承诺立即离开了。这时,有信使来报,有一个彬彬有礼的威尼斯年轻人带着很多值钱的礼品来访,他的主人也来了。鲍西亚听完信使的描述很高兴,尼莉莎希望这次来的人是巴萨尼奥。

夏洛克责备索拉尼欧和索勒里欧不应该协助杰西卡离家出走。他们辩解说,杰西卡已经是成年人了,她有权选择自己的结婚对象,做自己想做的事。索拉尼欧问夏洛克是否听到更多安东尼奥船只失事的消息,夏洛克说他听说了。索拉尼欧问他是不是真的想要安东尼奥的一磅肉,毕竟要了他的肉也没用。夏洛克回答说,他确确实实想要安东尼奥的一磅肉,这至少可以满足他的报复心理。夏洛克说他和基督徒一样,遭受侮辱的时候也会报复。这时,安东尼奥带信来说要见索拉尼欧和索勒里欧,于是他们俩就离开了。夏洛克的犹太朋友图巴尔进来告诉夏洛克,他帮忙在热那亚找过杰西卡了,但是没找到。夏洛克再次为自己损失的大笔钱财感到痛心。不过,一想到安东尼奥的船只失事,他很快就可以从他的心窝上割掉一磅肉,夏洛克就感到宽慰了。

巴萨尼奥和鲍西亚在贝尔蒙特度过了一段愉快的时光,他们相爱了。当巴萨尼奥打算破解那些匣子的谜题之时,鲍西亚显得很紧张。因为她担心万一他选错了的话,他们就不得不分开了。巴萨尼奥说,他一刻也不想多等了,等待是一件十分痛苦的事。于是,他们就来到匣子前面。鲍西亚想,如果巴萨尼奥真的爱自己的话,应该会做出正确的选择。巴萨尼奥面对那几个匣子说,表象具有欺骗性,就算是最明智的人也有上当的时候。因此,对于金匣子,他不予考虑,因为金子华而不实,而银子作为流通货币在人们之间传来传去,倒是那个显得卑微而又暗含危险而不是诱惑的铅匣子打动了他的心,鲍西亚看到他的选择,不由得喜出望外。巴萨尼奥打开了铅匣子,终于看到了鲍西亚的相片,相片上面还附有字轴,上面写着"你不被表象蒙蔽,你的选择漂亮又真实;红运当头,切勿贪求,知足常乐"。见自己选对了,巴萨尼奥简直不敢相信这个结果。鲍西亚说,她就是一个未见过世面的天真无知的少女,她希望自己更漂亮一些,更富有一些,以配得上巴萨尼奥。她宣布她本人以及她所拥有的一切都属于巴萨尼奥。为了证实她对他的爱,鲍西亚送给巴萨尼奥一只戒指。这时候,格莱西安诺对巴萨尼奥说他爱上了尼莉莎,她也爱他,所以请求巴萨尼奥同意他们的婚事。巴萨尼奥当即应允,并宣布他们将同时举行婚礼。

　　索勒里欧来了,他给巴萨尼奥带来了安东尼奥的信。信上说安东尼奥的船只失踪了,他现在陷入了困境。按照协议,他欠夏洛克一磅肉。让他从身上割一磅肉等于要了安东尼奥的命。安东尼奥还说,巴萨尼奥所有欠他的债都清了。他现在对巴萨尼奥别无所求,只希望临死之前和他见上一面。当鲍西亚得知他们是密友之后,她想以二十倍的银币赔付夏洛克。巴萨尼奥做好了动身前往威尼斯的准备。鲍西亚想出了一个挽救安东尼奥的办法。她拜托罗伦佐和杰西卡帮她照看家里,因为她在巴萨尼奥不在家的这段日子,她要去修道院待着。接着,她给自己在帕多瓦的表兄贝拉里奥博士写了一封信,并让她的仆人巴尔萨泽送去,贝拉里奥博士会把一些文件和服装让他带回来。同时,鲍西亚催促尼莉莎赶紧更衣,他们俩女扮男装,一起去威尼斯和她们的丈夫会合。

　　威尼斯公爵主持审理安东尼奥的案子。他告诉夏洛克,法律会维护他的利益,他有权得到那磅肉,不过夏洛克可以施舍仁慈,这样的话他也可以得到别人的仁慈。夏洛克表示拒绝,说他没有做错事,不需要别人的仁慈。当他被问及为什么想要安东尼奥的一磅肉时,夏洛克只说他对安东尼奥心怀憎恨,别的他也不想多说了。巴萨尼奥和夏洛克理论,并出价两倍偿还欠他的债,但是夏洛克拒绝接受。安东尼奥让巴萨尼奥不要浪费口舌和夏洛克争论,因为他自己也向他恳求过希望他发发慈悲,但同样遭到了拒绝。巴萨尼奥说,如果安东尼奥死了,他也会随他而去。安东尼奥劝他不要有这样的念头,巴萨尼奥得活着,为安东尼奥写墓志铭。公爵对法庭宣布即将有一个才华横溢的律师,也就是贝拉里奥博士来到这里帮助他审判这个案子。他的话音刚落,尼莉莎打扮成律师书记员的模样进来了。她递给公爵一封信,是贝拉里奥博士写给他的,他在信上说到他为公爵推荐了一位非常博学的律师来帮助公爵审理此案,这位律师叫巴尔萨泽。与此同时,夏洛克在一旁磨刀。

　　起先,鲍西亚/巴尔萨泽让夏洛克确信威尼斯法律会维护他的权益,并请他对安东尼奥施舍仁慈之心,她说仁慈就如同天空洒落的轻柔的雨滴,滋润着仁慈的布施着和接受者,可是,夏洛克再次拒绝了这样的请求,不愿意放过安东尼奥。鲍西亚问安东尼奥是否准备偿还欠夏洛克的钱,巴萨尼奥替他回答说,他已经准备好了十倍的钱偿还给夏洛克,可是夏洛克不接受,巴萨尼奥还问是否可以请求法律酌情变通一下,以便饶过安东尼奥的性命。鲍西亚说,固定的法律条款是不能随意改动的,不然就乱套了。夏洛克大声称赞鲍西亚为"丹尼尔"。于是,鲍西亚让夏洛克给她看看他们之间签订的契约。读罢契约,夏洛克便对夏洛克说他有权按照契约上的约定在安东尼奥心窝上割下一磅肉,并让安东尼奥袒露他的胸膛。鲍西亚再次恳求夏洛克施舍仁慈,但被拒绝,她便问他是否请到了外科医生替安东尼奥止血,夏洛克回复说契约上没有这一条,他只是准备好了称。鲍西亚接着让安东尼奥交代遗言,安东尼奥嘱咐巴萨尼奥不要悲伤,替他表达自己对巴萨尼奥的妻子最真心的祝福。巴萨尼奥和格莱西安诺都说他们宁愿用自己加上他们妻子的性命来换取安东尼奥的性命。听到他们这样说,夏洛克说,他宁愿自己的女儿嫁给一个犹太匪徒,也不愿她嫁给一个基督徒,因为基督徒如此轻视妻子的性命。

夏洛克正要开始割肉的时候,鲍西亚喊了一声"停下",她告诉夏洛克,契约上只说了割下一磅肉,但没用说滴下一滴血。根据威尼斯法律,谁胆敢让基督徒滴一滴血,那么他的所有财产将被充公。鲍西亚这么一说,夏洛克就退缩了,转而同意接受巴萨尼奥提出的三倍的赔偿款,巴萨尼奥欣然同意。但鲍西亚不同意,她说夏洛克什么也不需要,只需要法律的公正。然后,她又对夏洛克说,他只能割下一磅肉,不能多,也不能少,否则他将会被处死,他的财产也会被没收。夏洛克继续退步,他说只需要拿回他的本金就可以了。鲍西亚接着说,根据威尼斯另一条法律,如果一个外族人试图夺取威尼斯公民的生命,那么这个外族人的财产的一半将判给受害者,另一半充公。公爵说,他会施舍仁慈,饶夏洛克一命,鲍西亚让安东尼奥自己决定。安东尼奥说,充公的那一半财产就算了,还是给夏洛克,应判给安东尼奥的另一半财产可以留给杰西卡和罗伦佐,并且夏洛克死后他的财产也将由杰西卡和罗伦佐继承。除此之外,夏洛克还必须皈依基督教。听到这样的宣判,夏洛克匆匆离开了法庭,说他自己身体不舒服,法庭可以随后将需要他签字的文件送到他家,他签字就是。

出于感激,巴萨尼奥送给鲍西亚3000银币,鲍西亚拒收了。她说如果实在要感谢她的话,只需要他把手上的戒指给自己就可以了。巴萨尼奥有些为难地解释说,这只戒指是他妻子送给他的,他承诺永不和戒指分离。他提议为鲍西亚买一只更贵的戒指。鲍西亚说,要么给她这只戒指,要么她什么也不要。安东尼奥劝说巴萨尼奥把戒指给这位律师,因为律师的帮助比他妻子的命令重要。巴萨尼奥只得放弃了他的戒指,尼莉莎也用这种方法要到了格莱西安诺的戒指。然后,她们在她们的丈夫回家之前匆匆赶回贝尔蒙特。第二天清晨,她们的丈夫一回到家,她们两个就问他们戒指在哪里。他们回答说给了律师和律师的书记员了,并请求得到她们的谅解。她们两个假装很生气的样子,她们说不是因为戒指的价值而生气,而是丈夫违背誓言的行为让她们生气。于是,两个丈夫承诺绝不再辜负她们,安东尼奥在一边用良心为两个丈夫的承诺担保。于是,鲍西亚和尼莉莎原谅了她们的丈夫,并且给他们一人一只新戒指,告诉丈夫们这是她们昨天晚上通过和律师以及律师的书记员睡觉得来的,于是,巴萨尼奥和格莱西安诺暴怒。为了平复他们的愤怒,鲍西亚和尼莉莎只好把事情的来龙去脉告诉他们。这时候,消息传来,安东尼奥的商船全部平安归来。

5 Famous quotes

【Quote 1】

Nerissa

You would be, sweet madam,
if your miseries were in the same abundance as your good fortunes are.
And yet for aught I see,
they are as sick that surfeit with too much as they that starve with nothing.
It is no mean happiness, therefore,
to be seated in the mean.
Superfluity comes sooner by white hairs, but competency lives longer. [4]
(Act 1, Scene 2)

[Nerissa (played by Susan Jameson) speaking to Portia (played by Gemma Jones) in a 1980 film directed by Jack Gold.]

◇ Paraphrase

If your troubles were as great as your good fortune,
then you would be tired of the world.
But as I see it,
it seems that those who live in excess are
as unhappy as those who starve with nothing.

One should be happy, then,
to find oneself somewhere in the middle.
Having too much brings on gray hairs,
while having enough to get by gives you a longer life. [5]

◇ 原文译文

好小姐，您的不幸要是跟您的好运气一样多，那么难怪您会厌倦这个世界的；可是照我的愚见看来，吃得太饱的人，跟挨饿没东西吃的人一样是会害病的，所以中庸之道才是最大的幸福：富贵催人生白发，布衣蔬食易长年。[6]

【Quote 2】

Shylock
Signor Antonio, many a time and oft in the Rialto
you have rated me about my moneys and my usances.
Still have I borne it with a patient shrug,
for sufferance is the badge of all our tribe.
You call me misbeliever, cutthroat dog,
and spat upon my Jewish gaberdine
—and all for use of that which is mine own.
Well then, it now appears you need my help.
Go to, then! You come to me and you say,
"Shylock, we would have moneys." You say so!
—You, that did void your rheum upon my beard
and foot me as you spurn a stranger cur over your threshold!
Moneys is your suit.
What should I say to you? Should I not say,
"Hath a dog money?
Is it possible a cur can lend three thousand ducats?"
Or shall I bend low and in a bondman's key with bated breath
and whispering humbleness say this:
"Fair sir, you spat on me on Wednesday last;
you spurn'd me such a day, another time you call'd me dog
—and for these courtesies I'll lend you thus much monies?" [7]
(Act 1, Scene 3)

[**Shylock** (played by Warren Mitchell) accusing Antonio (played by John Franklyn-Robbins) in a 1980 film directed by Jack Gold.]

◇ Paraphrase

Sir Antonio, many times you have criticized me about
My money and habit of charging interest in the Rialto.
I have endured it all with patience and a shrug,
because we Jews are known for our ability to endure.
You say I believe in the wrong religion,
call me a cut-throat dog, and spit on my Jewish clothing,
all because I use my own money to make profit.
And now it appears that you need my help.
Okay, then! You come to me and you say,
"Shylock, I need money." You tell me this!
You who spat on my beard and kicked me
as you'd kick a stray dog away from your threshold!
You ask for money. What should I say to you?
Shouldn't I say, "Does a dog have money?
Is it possible for a dog to lend you three thousand ducats?"
Or should I get bend to my knees and with bated breath humbly whisper,
"Fair sir, you spat on me last Wednesday;
you spurned me then; another time you called me a dog
—and for all this courtesy you've shown me,
I will gladly lend you this much money?"[8]

◇ 原文译文

安东尼奥先生,好多次您在交易所里骂我,说我盘剥取利,我总是忍气吞声,耸耸肩膀,没有跟您争辩,因为忍受迫害本来就是我们民族的特色。您骂我是异教徒,杀人的狗,把唾沫吐在我的犹太长袍上,只因为我用我自己的钱博取几个利息。好,看来现在是您来向我求助了;您跑来见我,您说,"夏洛克,我们要几个钱",您这样对我说。您把唾沫吐在我的胡子上,用您的脚踢我,好像我是您门口的一条野狗一样;现在您却来问我要钱,我应该怎样对您说呢?我要不要这样说,"一条狗会有钱吗?一条恶狗能够借人三千块钱吗?"或者我应不应该弯下身子,像一个奴才似的低声下气,恭恭敬敬地说:"好先生,您在上星期三用唾沫吐在我身上;有一天您用脚踢我;还有一天您骂我是狗;为了报答您的恩典,所以我应该借给您这么些钱吗?"[9]

【Quote 3】

Prince of Morocco

Mislike me not for my complexion,
the shadowed livery of the burnished sun,
to whom I am a neighbor and near bred.
Bring me the fairest creature northward born,
where Phoebus' fire scarce thaws the icicles,
and let us make incision for your love
to prove whose blood is reddest, his or mine.
I tell thee, lady, this aspect of mine hath feared the valiant.
By my love I swear the best-regarded virgins of our clime have loved it too.
I would not change this hue
except to steal your thoughts, my gentle queen.[10]
(Act 2, Scene 1)

[The prince of Morocco (played by Marc Zuber) speaking to Portia in a 1980 film directed by Jack Gold.]

✦ Paraphrase

Don't dislike me because of my skin color,
the shadow-colored skin that results from the burning sun in Africa.
Bring me the most beautiful person born in the north,
where the light of the sun barely thaws the ice,
and let's cut both him and me so you can see whose blood is reddest,
his or mine.
I'm telling you, my lady,
this aspect of my appearance has frightened brave men.
By my love, I swear the best-regarded virgins of my land love me.
I wouldn't trade my dark skin color for anything,
my gentle queen, except to have you think kindly of me. [11]

✦ 原文译文

不要因为我的肤色而憎厌我；我是骄阳的近邻，我这一身黝黑的制服，便是它的威焰的赐予。给我在终年不见阳光、冰山、雪柱的极北找一个最白皙姣好的人来，让我们刺血查验对您的爱情，看看究竟是他的血红还是我的血红。我告诉你，小姐，我这副容貌曾经吓破了勇士的肝胆；凭着我的爱情起誓，我们国土里最有声誉的少女也曾为它害过相思。我不愿变更我的肤色，除非为了博得您的欢心，我的温柔的女王。[12]

【Quote 4】

Gratiano
That ever holds.
Who riseth from a feast with that keen appetite that he sits down?
Where is the horse that doth untread again his tedious measures
with the unbated fire that he did pace them first?
All things that are,
are with more spirit chasèd than enjoyed.
How like a younger or a prodigal the scarfèd bark puts from her native bay,
hugged and embracèd by the strumpet wind!
How like the prodigal doth she return,
with overweathered ribs and ragged sails lean, rent,
and beggared by the strumpet wind! [13]
(Act 2, Scene 6)

［Gratiano (in the middle, played by Kenneth Cranham) speaking to Salerio (played by John Rhys-Davies) in a 1980 film directed by Jack Gold.］

◇ Paraphrase

Who leaves a meal as hungry as when he sat down?
What horse retraces its steps with as much eagerness as when it went forward?
The chase is always the most exciting part.
When a ship leaves its native bay its sails are hugged
and embraced by the loving wind!
But when the ship returns it has weathered sides and ragged sails,
damaged and torn apart by the vicious wind![14]

◇ 原文译文

谁在席终人散以后,他的食欲还像初入座时候那么强烈? 哪一匹马在冗长的归途上,会像它起程时那么长驱疾驰? 世间的任何事物,追求时候的兴致总要比享用时候的兴致浓烈。一艘新下水的船只扬帆出港的当儿,多么像一个娇美的少年,给那轻狂的风儿爱抚搂抱! 可是等到它回来的时候,船身已遭风日的侵蚀,船帆也变成了百结的破衲,它又多么像一个落魄的浪子,给那轻狂的风儿肆意欺凌![15]

【Quote 5】

Jessica

Here, catch this casket. It is worth the pains.
I am glad 'tis night, you do not look on me,
for I am much ashamed of my exchange.
But love is blind and lovers cannot see the pretty follies that themselves commit,

for if they could,
Cupid himself would blush to see me thus transformèd to a boy. [16]
(Act 2, Scene 6)

[Jessica (played by Leslee Udwin) in a soliloquy in a 1980 film directed by Jack Gold.]

◇ Paraphrase

Here, catch this box. It's worth the effort.
I am glad it's dark out so you can't see me.
I'm very ashamed of how I look in my disguise.
But love is blind and lovers cannot see the little faults in their relationships.
If they could,
Cupid himself would blush at how ridiculous I look disguised as a boy. [17]

◇ 原文译文

来,把这匣子接住了,你拿了去会大有好处。幸亏在夜里,你瞧不见我,我改扮成这个怪样子,怪不好意思哩。可是爱情是盲目的,恋人们瞧不见他们自己所干的傻事;要是他们瞧得见的话,那么丘比特瞧见我变成了一个男孩子,也会红起脸来哩。[18]

【Quote 6】

Shylock

To bait fish withal. If it will feed nothing else,
it will feed my revenge.
He hath disgraced me and hindered me half a million,
laughed at my losses, mocked at my gains, scorned my nation,

thwarted my bargains, cooled my friends, heated mine enemies
—and what's his reason?
I am a Jew.
Hath not a Jew eyes?
Hath not a Jew hands, organs, dimensions, senses, affections, passions?
Fed with the same food, hurt with the same weapons,
subject to the same diseases, healed by the same means,
warmed and cooled by the same winter and summer as a Christian is?
If you prick us, do we not bleed?
If you tickle us, do we not laugh?
If you poison us, do we not die?
And if you wrong us, shall we not revenge?
If we are like you in the rest, we will resemble you in that.
If a Jew wrong a Christian, what is his humility? Revenge.
If a Christian wrong a Jew, what should his sufferance be by Christian example?
Why, revenge.
The villainy you teach me I will execute
—and it shall go hard but I will better the instruction.[19]
(Act 3, Scene 1)

(Shylock answering Salerio in a 1980 film directed by Jack Gold.)

◇ Paraphrase

I could use it as bait for fish.
If it will feed nothing else,
it will at least feed my revenge.

Half a million times he has disgraced me and hindered me.
He has laughed at my losses, mocked my profits,
scorned my people, messed with my business deals,
turned my friends against me, and encouraged my enemies.
And what's his reason for all this?
I am a Jew. Does a Jew not have eyes?
Does a Jew not have hands, organs, senses, affections, passions?
Are we not fed with the same food, hurt by the same weapons,
affected by the same diseases, healed by the same medicines,
warmed and cooled by the same winter and summer as Christians?
If you stab us, do we not bleed?
If you tickle us, do we not laugh?
If you poison us, do we not die?
And if you wrong us, should we not take revenge?
If we are like you in all the other ways,
we will resemble you in terms of revenge, too.
If a Jew wrongs a Christian, what does he do?
He takes revenge.
If a Christian wrongs a Jew, what should the Jew do,
following the Christian example?
Why, he should take revenge.
I will follow your own villainous example,
and I'll probably outdo my teachers.[20]

◇ 原文译文

拿来钓鱼也好;即使他的肉不中吃,至少也可以出出我这一口恶气。他曾经羞辱过我,夺去我几十万块钱的生意,讥笑着我的亏损,挖苦着我的盈余,侮蔑我的民族! 破坏我的买卖,离间我的朋友,煽动我的仇敌! 他的理由是什么? 只因为我是一个犹太人。难道犹太人没有眼睛吗? 难道犹太人没有五官四肢,没有知觉,没有感情,没有血气吗? 他不是吃着同样的食物,同样的武器可以伤害他,同样的医药可以治疗他,冬天同样会冷,夏天同样会热,就像一个基督徒一样吗? 你们要是用刀剑刺我们,我们不是也会出血的吗? 你们要是搔我们的痒,我们不是也会笑起来的吗? 你们要是用毒药谋害我们,我们不是也会死的吗? 那么要是你们欺侮了我们,我们难道不会复仇吗? 要是在别的地方我们都跟你们一样,那么在这一点上也是彼此相同的。要是一个犹太人欺侮了一个基督徒,那基督徒怎样表现他的谦逊? 报仇。要是一个基督徒欺侮了一个犹太人,那么照着基督徒的榜样,那犹太人应该怎样表现他的宽容? 报仇。你们已经把残虐的手段教给我,我一定会照着你们的教训实行,并且还要加倍奉还哩。[21]

【Quote 7】

Portia

Away, then. I am locked in one of them.
If you do love me you will find me out
—Nerissa and the rest, stand all aloof.
Let music sound while he doth make his choice.
Then if he lose, he makes a swanlike end, fading in music.
That the comparison may stand more proper,
my eye shall be the stream and watery deathbed for him.
He may win, and what is music then?
Then music is even as the flourish
when true subjects bow to a new-crownèd monarch.
Such it is as are those dulcet sounds in break of day that
creep into the dreaming bridegroom's ear and summon him to marriage.
Now he goes with no less presence but with much more love than young Alcides,
when he did redeem the virgin tribute paid by howling Troy to the sea monster.
I stand for sacrifice.
The rest aloof are the Dardanian wives,
with bleared visages come forth to view the issue of th' exploit.
—Go, Hercules! Live thou, I live.
With much, much more dismay I view the fight
than thou that makest the fray.[22]

(Act 3, Scene 2)

◆ Paraphrase

Let's go, then.
My picture is locked in one of the caskets.
If you truly love me, you will find it.
Nerissa and everyone else, stand back.
Let some music play while he makes his choice.
Then if he loses, he will at least have a swanlike end,
dying with a song.
To make him really like a swan,
I'll cry a river for him to swim and drown in.
And if he wins, what will be the point of the music?
In that case, the music will be like the flourish

that plays when subjects bow to a newly crowned king.
The sweet sounds that wake up a dreaming groom at dawn on his wedding day,
and announce that his wedding is here.
And now he goes to the caskets looking as noble as Hercules,
but more loving,
when Hercules rescued the Trojan princess① from the sea monster.
I am like that princess, awaiting death,
and these people standing by are like
the Trojan wives looking on with teary eyes.
Go, my Hercules!
If you live, then I live.
I am much more troubled here watching you than you are,
doing the deed.[23]

◇ 原文译文

那么去吧！在那三个匣子中间,有一个里面锁着我的小相;您要是真的爱我,您会把我找出来的。尼莉莎,你跟其余的人都站开些,在他选择的时候,把音乐奏起来,要是他失败了,好让他像天鹅一样在音乐声中死去;把这比喻说得更恰当一些,我的眼睛就是他葬身的清流。也许他会胜利的;那么那音乐又像什么呢？那时候音乐就像忠心的臣子俯身迎接新加冕的君王的时候所吹奏的号角,又像是黎明时分送进正在做着好梦的新郎的耳中,催他起来举行婚礼的甜柔的琴韵。现在他去了,他的沉毅的姿态,就像年轻的赫剌克勒斯奋身前去,在特洛伊人的呼叫声中,把他们祭献给海怪的处女拯救出来一样,可是他心里却藏着更多的爱情;我站在这儿做牺牲,她们站在旁边,就像泪眼模糊的特洛伊妇女们,出来看这场争斗的结果。去吧,赫剌克勒斯! 我的生命悬在你手里,但愿你安然生还;我这观战的人心中比你这上场作战的人还要惊恐万倍![24]

【Quote 8】

Bassanio
So may the outward shows be least themselves.
The world is still deceived with ornament.
In law, what plea so tainted and corrupt,
but being seasoned with a gracious voice,
obscures the show of evil?
In religion, what damnèd error,

---

① According to classical mythology, the Trojan princess Hesione was offered as a sacrifice to a sea monster sent by Poseidon (the Roman Neptune), god of the sea, earthquakes, and horses, but she was rescued by Hercules.

but some sober brow will bless it and approve it with a text,
hiding the grossness with fair ornament?
There is no vice so simple
but assumes some mark of virtue on his outward parts.
How many cowards whose hearts are all
as false as stairs of sand wear yet
upon their chins the beards of Hercules and frowning Mars.
Who, inward searched, have livers white as milk,
and these assume but valor's excrement to render them redoubted.
Look on beauty, and you shall see 'tis purchased by the weight.
Which therein works a miracle in nature,
making them lightest that wear most of it.
So are those crispèd snaky golden locks
which maketh such wanton gambols with the wind,
upon supposèd fairness,
often known to be the dowry of a second head,
the skull that bred them in the sepulcher.
Thus ornament is but the guilèd shore to a most dangerous sea,
the beauteous scarf veiling an Indian beauty
—in a word, the seeming truth which cunning times
put on to entrap the wisest.
Therefore then, thou gaudy gold,
hard food for Midas, I will none of thee.
Nor none of thee, thou pale and common drudge 'tween man and man.
But thou, thou meagre lead,

(Bassanio making his choice in a 1980 film directed by Jack Gold.)

which rather threaten'st than dost promise aught,
thy paleness moves me more than eloquence,
and here choose I.
Joy be the consequence![25]
(Act 3, Scene 2)

◆ Paraphrase

The appearances of these may be deceiving.
The whole world is tricked by fancy appearances.
In the court of law,
a corrupt and false plea can hide its own evil with a pleasant voice.
In religion, a damned mistake can be covered over
with the nice show of a blessing and some scripture to justify it.
Every vice has some outward appearance of virtue.
Many cowards with disloyal hearts have beards like brave Hercules and Mars,
the god of war, even though they have no guts and are easily frightened.
And think of beauty,
which can be bought by the pound in the form of cosmetics,
which work miracles on nature,
making the women that wear the most of it the most beautiful.
The curly golden locks that are tousled in the wind so nicely
and seem beautiful often turn out to be a wig,
made from a dead person's hair.
Appearances are like an inviting shore that leads to a dangerous ocean,
a beautiful scarf hiding an actually undesirable Indian "beauty".
In short, appearances can be tricky and often deceive even the wisest.
Therefore, you gold, the solid metal that Midas① couldn't eat,
I will have nothing to do with you.
And I'll have nothing to do with silver either,
that pale metal that men pass between themselves as currency.
But you, humble lead, you who threaten more than you promise,
your paleness moves me more than I can say, and I choose you.
I hope I will be happy with my decision![26]

---

① According to classical mythology, whatever the king Midas touched became gold. At first he was happy with this gift, but soon he found that even the food and drinks he had touched turned to gold, and he couldn't eat or drink. Therefore, Bassanio refers to gold as Midas' food.

◇ 原文译文

外观往往和事物的本身完全不符,世人却容易为表面的装饰所欺骗。在法律上,哪一件卑鄙邪恶的陈诉不可以用娓娓动听的言辞掩饰它的罪状?在宗教上,哪一桩罪大恶极的过失不可以引经据典,文过饰非,证明它的确上合天心?任何臭名昭著的罪恶,都可以在外表上装出一副道貌岸然的样子。多少没有胆量的懦夫,他们的心其实软弱得就像下不去脚的流沙,他们的肝如果剖出来看一看,大概比乳汁还要白,可是他们的脸上却长着天神一样威武的虬髯,人家只看着他们的外表,也就居然把他们当作英雄一样看待!再看那些世间所谓美貌吧,那是完全靠着脂粉装点出来的,越是轻浮的女人,所涂的脂粉也越重;至于那些随风飘扬像蛇一样的金色卷发,看上去果然漂亮,不知道是不是从坟墓中死人的骷髅上借来的。所以装饰不过是一道把船只诱进凶涛险浪的怒海中去的海岸,又像是遮掩着一个黑丑蛮女的一道美丽的面幕;总而言之,它是狡诈的世人用来欺诱智士的似是而非的真理。所以,你炫目的黄金,米达斯王的坚硬的食物,我不要你;你惨白的银子,在人们手里来来去去的下贱的奴才,我也不要你;可是你,寒碜的铅,你的形状只能使人退步,一点没有吸引人的力量,然而你的质朴却比巧妙的言辞更能打动我的心,我就选了你吧!但愿结果美满![27]

【Quote 9】

Portia

The quality of mercy is not strained.

It droppeth as the gentle rain from heaven upon the place beneath.

It is twice blessed.

It blesseth him that gives and him that takes.

'Tis mightiest in the mightiest.

It becomes the thronèd monarch better than his crown.

His scepter shows the force of temporal power,

the attribute to awe and majesty wherein doth sit the dread and fear of kings,

but mercy is above this sceptered sway.

It is enthronèd in the hearts of kings.

It is an attribute to God himself.

And earthly power doth then show likest God's when mercy seasons justice.

Therefore, Jew,

though justice be thy plea, consider this

—that in the course of justice none of us should see salvation.

We do pray for mercy,

and that same prayer doth teach us all to render the deeds of mercy.[28]

(Act 4, Scene 1)

Unit 6 The Merchant of Venice

(Portia disguised as a lawyer named Balthazar speaking to Shylock regarding mercy in a 1980 film directed by Jack Gold.)

◆ Paraphrase

Mercy is not something that one is forced to practice.
It falls easily like gentle rain from the sky.
It is a doubly blessed thing.
It blesses both the person showing mercy and the person receiving mercy.
Mercy is most admirable in the mightiest men.
It looks better on a king than his crown.
A king's scepter is a symbol of his earthly power,
a source of awe and majesty,
which makes people respect and fear him.
But mercy is above the power of the scepter.
It dwells in the hearts of kings.
It is an attribute of God himself.
And earthly power resembles God's power when justice is mixed with mercy.
Therefore, Jew, although you are seeking justice, consider this:
if God sought justice against all of us with no mercy,
we would all go to hell.
We pray to God for mercy,
and that same prayer should teach us all to show mercy to others. [29]

◆ 原文译文

慈悲不是出于勉强,它像甘霖一样从天上降下尘世;它不但给幸福于受施的人,也同样给幸福于施予的人;它有超乎一切的无上威力,比皇冠更足以显示一个帝王的高贵;御杖不过象征着俗世的威权,使人民对于君上的尊严凛然生畏;慈悲的力量却高出于权力之上,它深藏在帝王的内心,是一种属于上帝的德性,执法的人倘能把慈悲调剂着公道,人间的权力就和上帝的神力没有差别。所以,犹太人,虽然你所要求的是公道,可是请你想一想,要是真的按照公道,执行起赏罚来,谁也没有死后得救的希望;我们既然祈祷着上帝的慈悲,就应该按照祈祷的指点,自己做一些慈悲的事。[30]

【Quote 10】

Lorenzo
For do but note a wild and wanton herd,
or race of youthful and unhandled colts,
fetching mad bounds, bellowing and neighing loud,
which is the hot condition of their blood
—if they but hear perchance a trumpet sound,
or any air of music touch their ears,
you shall perceive them make a mutual stand,
their savage eyes turn'd to a modest gaze
by the sweet power of music.
Therefore the poet did feign that Orpheus drew trees, stones, and floods
since naught so stockish, hard, and full of rage,
but music for the time doth change his nature.
The man that hath no music in himself,
nor is not moved with concord of sweet sounds,
is fit for treasons, stratagems, and spoils.
The motions of his spirit are dull as night,

[Lorenzo (played by Richard Morant) speaking to Jessica regarding music in a 1980 film directed by Jack Gold.]

and his affections dark as Erebus①.
Let no such man be trusted.
Mark the music. [31]
(Act 5, Scene 1)

◇ Paraphrase

Take the example of a wild, wandering herd,
or a bunch of untrained young horses, running around,
bellowing and neighing loudly, as they naturally do.
If they happen to hear a trumpet play or any music,
you would see them all stand still and their savage eyes would be
turned into a modest gaze by the sweet power of music.
That's why the Roman poet Ovid wrote that the musician Orpheus made trees,
stones, and bodies of water follow him,
because there's nothing hard or strong enough not to be changed by music.
Any man who is not himself musical and is not moved by harmonious,
sweet sounds is prone to commit treason,
make tricky plots, and steal things.
His spirit is dull and he has an affinity for things dark as hell.
Don't trust a man like that.
Listen to the music. [32]

◇ 原文译文

你只要看一群不服管束的畜生,或是那野性未驯的小马,释放它们奔放的血气,乱跳狂奔,高声嘶叫,倘然偶尔听到一声喇叭,或是任何乐调,就会一齐立定,它们狂野的眼光,因为中了音乐的魅力,变成温和的注视。所以诗人会造出俄耳甫斯用音乐感动木石、平息风浪的故事,因为无论怎样坚硬顽固狂暴的事物,音乐都可以立刻改变它们的性质;灵魂里没有音乐,或是听了甜蜜和谐的乐声而不会感动的人,都是擅于为非作歹、使奸弄诈的;他们的灵魂像黑夜一样昏沉,他们的感情像鬼城一样幽暗,这种人是不可信任的。听这音乐![33]

6　Questions for discussion

(1) Is this play a sheer comedy? From whose perspective is it comedic and from whose perspective is it otherwise?

---

①　Erebus is the god of darkness, son of Chaos and brother of Night in Greek mythology.

(2) Is this play antisemitic? Why or why not?

(3) Why is the play entitled *The Merchant of Venice*? Who is the merchant?

(4) What do you think of Portia?

(5) Why doesn't Portia tell Bassanio which casket he should choose? What if the wrong man had chosen the right casket?

(6) What does the play reveal about the relationship between money and marriage? What do you think is the most important thing in a marriage?

(7) Both Antonio and Portia express their unhappiness on entering the scene. Why are they unhappy, according to their friends? What's your opinion about reasons for their unhappiness?

7 References

[1][2][3] The Merchant of Venice Study Guide[EB/OL]. https://www.litcharts.com/lit/the-merchant-of-venice

[4][7][10][13][16][19][22][25][28][31] Shakespeare W. The Merchant of Venice[M]. 3rd edition. New York: Cambridge University Press, 2018.

[5][8][11][14][17][20][23][26][29][32] The Merchant of Venice: Shakespeare Translation [EB/OL]. https://www.litcharts.com/shakescleare/shakespeare-translations/the-merchant-of-venice.

[6][9][12][15][18][21][24][27][30][33] 威廉·莎士比亚. 莎士比亚喜剧选[M]. 朱生豪,译. 北京:人民文学出版社,2013.

Unit 7

Twelfth Night

1 Characters

Orsino(奥希诺): Duke of Illyria.
Viola(维奥拉): Survivor of a shipwreck in the disguise of Cesario, a page to Duke Orsino.
Olivia(奥利维亚): Noble woman who is loved by Duke Orsino but who loves the young "man" Cesario.
Sebastian(塞巴斯蒂安): Twin brother of Viola who is married to Olivia by mistake.
Valentine(瓦伦丁), **Curio**(库里奥): Gentlemen serving Duke Orsino.
Sir Toby Belch(托比·贝尔奇): Olivia's uncle.
Sir Andrew Aguecheek(安德鲁·艾古契克): Knight who wants to marry Olivia.
Malvolio(马尔伏里奥): Steward of Olivia.
Feste(费斯特): Fool and servant of Olivia.
Fabian(费边): Servant of Olivia.
Maria(玛莉亚): Handmaid of Olivia who is married to Toby.
Antonio(安东尼奥): Sea captain who saves and attends Sebastian.
Another Sea Captain: Man who saves Viola and is kind and helpful to her.

2 Background

Twelfth Night has been known as a "transvestite comedy" and is based on an Italian comedy named *Iganni—, or the "Unknown Ones"*.[1]

Critics also argue that the plot of *Twelfth Night* is mainly based on *Apolonious and Silla*, one of the tales from *His Farewell to Military Profession*, published in 1581 by Barnabe Riche (circa 1540-1617), who in turn based his work on a tale in *Novelle*, by Matteo Bandello (circa 1480-1562).[2]

3 Settings

The plot takes place in Illyria, in the northwestern Balkans along the Adriatic Coast.

Illyrians were forefathers of modern-day Albanians. But in Shakespeare's play, Illyria is more of an imaginary country like Shangri-La, Oz, Avalon, or Prospero's island in *The Tempest*, another comedy by Shakespeare.[3]

4 Synopsis

In Illyria, Duke Orsino is giving an impassioned speech on love when his servant Valentine enters, who has got back from Olivia's house. Olivia is a noble woman whom Orsino loves. Valentine tells his master that Olivia is deep in mourning for her deceased brother. She declares that she will wear a veil and cloister herself for seven years and won't accept any man's love during these years.

Off the coast of Illyria a ship has wrecked, but its Captain, a few sailors and Viola have survived. Viola's twin brother, Sebastian is missing and she is grieved. The Captain consoles her that when he last saw Sebastian, he was holding on to the mast that was afloat and riding on the waves. Viola gives some gold to the Captain to thank him. To make a living, Viola decides to hide her aristocratic identity and look for a job. The Captain was born and grew up near Illyria and is familiar with it. He tells Viola that Illyria is governed by Duke Orsino who is in love with the gentlewoman Olivia, but his love is unrequited because Olivia is in grief since her brother died a year ago. She vows never to marry. Viola wants to work for Olivia, but the Captain tells her it's unlikely because Olivia refuses to see anyone. Then Viola decides to dress up as a pageboy and serve Duke Orsino.

Maria, Olivia's handmaid, complains to Sir Toby, Olivia's uncle, about his drinking and coming home late. Olivia expresses her disapproval of Sir Andrew, a knight and Toby's friend whom he brought to Illyria to woo her. Toby protests that Andrew is tall, rich and gifted who speaks several languages. Maria argues that he is a wastrel. Andrew tells Toby that he wants to leave the next day because Olivia refuses to see him and his courtship will be rejected, but Toby makes him stay longer, saying that he is still a prospect for Olivia's hand. It is true that the Duke is wooing her, but she will not marry a man who is above her age, wealth, status and intelligence, so she will reject the Duke.

Viola, who is disguised as young man Cesario, gets along well with Duke Orsino whose life is an open book to her after a few days. Orsino asks Cesario to woo Olivia in his stead because he assembles a woman and speaks in a woman's voice. His feminine characteristics might impress Olivia. Viola is reluctant to do so because she has got stuck in a quandary, that is, she has fallen in love with Orsino. Nevertheless, Cesario goes to Olivia's palace. As expected, Olivia refuses to see him, but he persists. At last, Olivia agrees to meet him. Olivia hides her face in a veil. After Cesario is brought in, he insists on talking with Olivia in private. Olivia bids her servants to leave them alone. Cesario then demands her to remove her veil, which she does. Cesario exclaims that she is so beautiful a picture painted by nature's skillful hand that she shouldn't be so cruel as not to pass down her beauty by bearing an heir. Cesario tells her that his master loves her so much that life is like death to him when his love is unrequited. Olivia responds that although she knows Orsino is good-looking in appearance, generous in heart and graceful in manner, she still cannot love him. Cesario says if he were the Duke, he would build a cabin outside Olivia's house, write love poems and sing them out late at night to arouse her sympathy. Olivia insists that she will not accept Orsino's love. She asks Cesario to tell Orsino not to send anymore messengers here except Cesario.

After Cesario departs, Olivia admits that she is knocked out by Cesario's features. She summons Malvolio, her steward, to catch up with Cesario and give back the ring he has left behind and tell him to come again tomorrow. When Cesario sees the ring, he is confused because he didn't give such a ring to Olivia, but he plays along and refuses to take it back. Malvolio throws it at his feet and leaves. Cesario picks it up and realizes that Olivia has fallen in love with him. By this time, Sebastian has landed on Illyria. He has been saved by a man named Antonio and stays with him in his house. Antonio is attached to Sebastian so much that he follows him wherever he goes although Sebastian prefers to be left alone. He feels sad, thinking that his twin sister has been drowned. After learning that Sebastian is an aristocrat from Messaline, Antonio offers to be his servant. Sebastian says he will head for Orsino's court, where Antonio has many enemies, and bids farewell to Antonio, who admires Sebastian so strongly as to take the risk of following him.

Toby and Andrew are drinking, eating and singing late at night again, joined by Feste, a clown. Maria warns them to keep quiet, but they ignore her. Malvolio enters and reprimands them. He shouts at Maria to prevent these lowly creatures from turning their mistress' palace into an alehouse. Maria cannot bear Malvolio's arrogance and decides to play a prank on him. She imitates Olivia's handwriting and writes a love letter. She will drop the letter for Malvolio to pick up and assume that Olivia is in love with him. The others will watch Malvolio's reaction. In the letter, Olivia asks her beloved (whom the arrogant Malvolio believes to be him) to reciprocate her love by wearing yellow stockings, crossing his garters at the knees and keeping smiling all the time. Andrew and Toby talk about Maria approvingly. Toby admires Maria so much for thinking out such a fanciful idea that he would like to marry her. As expected, Malvolio picks up the letter and believes that he is Olivia's beloved and will do as instructed in the letter. Toby, Andrew and Fabian, another attendant of Olivia, hide in the tree and they can hardly restrain from laughing while watching Malvolio's response.

Orsino asks Cesario if he is in love with a woman like he is with Olivia. Cesario answers affirmatively. He then asks how old she is. Cesario says about Orsino's age. Orsino suggests that he love a woman younger than him, because women's beauty withers soon like roses and men's love for a woman is not as constant as a woman's love for a man. Unable to confess her love for Orsino, Viola languishes in secret love. Viola asks Orsino what if a woman loves him as much as he does Olivia. He replies that no woman's love can be matched with his love for

Olivia. He says a woman's love is like a shallow appetite of the taste but not of the heart and cannot hold so much emotion. Orsino sends Cesario off with a jewel for Olivia. Cesario demands to meet Olivia in private again. He tells Olivia that the Duke loves her very much and she should reciprocate his love, but Olivia forbids him from mentioning Orsino's name. She beseeches Cesario to woo her on his own behalf. Cesario tells her that he will love no woman. After Cesario leaves, Olivia asks Maria for advice to woo Cesario when he comes again as agreed. She then sends for Malvolio for suggestions. Maria tells her that Malvolio seems to be crazy recently.

Andrew tells Toby that he decides to depart because he feels bitter to see that Olivia treats Cesario better than she treats him. Toby suggests that Andrew challenge Cesario to a duel to display his noble act of bravery which will draw Olivia's attention. After Andrew is gone, Fabian says Andrew is Toby's puppet. Toby tells Fabian that Andrew has spent about 2,000 ducats on him, so he wants him to stay and spend more money on him. By this time, Sebastian has arrived at Orsino's court, followed by Antonio. He says he will visit the city. Antonio responds that he will wait for him in the inn named Elephant. He gives Sebastian his purse to use his money freely.

When Olivia sees Malvolio wearing yellow cross-gartered stockings, she reprimands him for his weirdness, but he regards her reproach as a favour. Olivia summons Toby to take care of Malvolio. Toby offers to deliver Andrew's letter to him for a fight when he meets Cesario again, while he is clear that Cesario will not accept such a challenge. He just wants to get both sides scared of each other.

When Cesario comes again, Olivia gives Cesario a gift—a locket containing her picture and tells him that she will give him anything he wants. Cesario responds that he doesn't want anything except that she returns Orsino's love. After Olivia exits, Toby enters and warns Cesario that an assailant is going to fight with him. Cesario says he has never offended anybody and doesn't want a fight. He is honest to admit his cowardice. Toby, however, tells Andrew that he has provoked Cesario with his letter which he didn't give Cesario at all, and that Cesario is ready to fight. Andrew draws his sword and confronts Cesario who confesses aside that she is so terrified that she wants to reveal her identity of a woman. At this moment, Antonio arrives. He fights with Andrew in lieu of Cesario, mistaking him for Sebastian because the twin brother and sister look identical. When they are fighting, a few officers enter and arrest Antonio who asks Cesario for his purse back. Cesario is confused. He gives Antonio what money he has, which is only half of what Antonio has given Sebastian. Antonio is angry to see Cesario's reaction. He tells them that he has saved his life from the wild waves and helped him all the way and says Sebastian should feel ashamed of himself for treating him like this. To hear Sebastian's name, Viola is excited to learn that her brother is still alive.

Feste, Andrew and Toby encounter Sebastian, mistaking him for Cesario. Feste approaches him and asks him if he should tell his mistress that he is coming again. Sebastian gives him some money and asks him to leave him alone. Andrew is astonished to see Sebastian so soon again and he draws his sword and strikes Sebastian who strikes back. Toby seizes Sebastian and draws his sword. Feste says he will inform Olivia who doesn't want to see anybody hit Cesario. When Olivia arrives, she bids Toby to stop. She apologizes to Sebastian and invites him back to her house. Sebastian feels like he is in a dream. He thinks either of them must be crazy. After they arrive at her palace, Olivia brings a priest to marry them secretly. She tells Sebastian when he is ready, they will make it known to the public and hold a wedding ceremony. Seeing that Olivia is noble, wealthy and beautiful, Sebastian accepts her marriage proposal and they are married.

Malvolio is shut in a dark cell by Maria and Toby to cure his madness. When Feste enters, Malvolio asks him to deliver his letter to Olivia. When the Duke and Cesario are in Olivia's palace, the officers bring Antonio in, charging him of robbing their battleship and wounding the Duke's nephew. Antonio denies Orsino's accusation of him as a pirate and thief. Seeing Cesario and still mistaking him for Sebastian, Antonio accuses him of his ingratitude. He explains to the onlookers that he has saved Cesario from the shipwreck and served him and lent him his purse, but Cesario pretends as if they had never met before and hasn't returned him his purse. Orsino asks Antonio when Cesario arrived in Illyria, he replies today. Orsino says Antonio must be mad because Cesario has been in Illyria for three months. The Duke asks Antonio why he has come here since it is dangerous for him to do so, he replies that he comes here to serve Cesario, and this is out of pure love for him. Olivia blames Cesario for breaking his marriage promise by his sudden departure. Orsino is enraged, supposing that Cesario must have wooed Olivia secretly. All is in a mess.

At this time, the wounded Toby and Andrew rush in, followed by Sebastian, who apologizes to Olivia for leaving her abruptly and for wounding her kinsmen. All of them exclaim how identical Cesario and Sebastian are, like an apple cut in two halves. They clarify everything. Orsino asks Cesario if what he has said regarding his love for Orsino is still true. Cesario answers in the affirmative that he will not love a woman but the Duke. Olivia asks to be Orsino's sister, which he agrees. Cesario says that he will go to find the Captain for his old clothes. The Captain is imprisoned because he is sued by Malvolio. Olivia tells Cesario that Malvolio will release the Captain and summons Malvolio, who complains in his letter how Olivia has wronged him by instructing him to dress and behave like that. After viewing the letter which Malvolio supposes to be Olivia's writing, Olivia immediately identifies it is Maria's handwriting. Fabian instantly defends for himself and for Toby and Maria who have just got married. Orsino asks Cesario to be his mistress and queen after he changes back to his female identity. The two couples will hold a formal wedding ceremony.

【剧情介绍】

伊利里亚的公爵奥希诺正在慷慨激昂地发表他的爱情感言,他的仆人瓦伦丁从奥利维亚家回来了。奥利维亚出身贵族世家,是奥希诺爱慕的对象。瓦伦丁告诉公爵,奥利维亚正深切哀悼她的亡兄,宣称她将头戴面纱为其兄守孝七年,这七年里,她会把自己禁闭起来。

伊利里亚近海有船只失事，不过，船长和几名海员以及维奥拉都没事。但维奥拉的双胞胎哥哥塞巴斯蒂安失踪了，她很伤心。船长安慰她说，他最后一次看到塞巴斯蒂安的时候，塞巴斯蒂安正紧紧地抓着漂浮在海上的桅杆和海浪搏击。维奥拉给了船长一些金子以示感谢。为了生存，维奥拉决定隐瞒自己的贵族身份去找一份差事。船长出生于一个离伊利里亚不远的地方，并在那里长大，所以对伊利里亚的情况了如指掌。他告诉维奥拉，伊利里亚的统治者是奥希诺公爵，他爱上了贵族女子奥利维亚，但是他只不过是单相思罢了，因为奥利维亚的哥哥一年前刚刚去世，她发誓不嫁人。维奥拉想去伺候奥利维亚，但是船长告诉她这不大可能，因为奥利维亚不肯见人，于是维奥拉准备乔装成一个男仆，去伺候奥希诺公爵。

奥利维亚的女仆玛莉亚抱怨她叔叔托比爵士晚上喝酒闹到很晚。奥利维亚对她叔叔的朋友安德鲁爵士也很不满。这个安德鲁爵士被托比爵士带到伊利里亚来向奥利维亚求婚。托比说安德鲁高大、富有，很有天赋，会说好几种语言。玛莉亚却说他是一个败家子。安德鲁对托比说他打算明天就走，因为他的求婚失败了，奥利维亚甚至都不愿见他。但是托比让他再住一段时间，他说安德鲁还是有希望得到奥利维亚的爱的。虽然公爵在追求她，但她不愿意嫁给一个年龄、财富、地位、智力都在她之上的男人，所以她肯定会拒绝公爵的。

维奥拉扮成男仆后改名为西塞罗。她和公爵相处得很好，没过几天，公爵就和他无话不谈。奥希诺请西塞罗代表他去向奥利维亚求婚，因为他觉得西塞罗长得像一个女人，说话的声音也像，西塞罗的这些特点肯定会给奥利维亚留下很深的印象。这一下可把维奥拉难住了，因为她自己已经爱上了公爵。不过，她还是不负公爵所托，来到了奥利维亚的府邸。不出所料，奥利维亚不肯见西塞罗，但西塞罗坚持见她。最后，奥利维亚同意西塞罗和她见面。奥利维亚蒙上面纱。西塞罗进门之后，坚持单独和奥利维亚会面。奥利维亚只好吩咐她的下人都退下。西塞罗请求奥利维亚掀开她的面纱，她照做了。西塞罗赞叹她的美貌，大自然的手可真灵巧，居然造出了这样一个美人。如果她就这样终身不嫁的话，那她的美貌就后继无人，这样做的话，她就太狠心了。西塞罗说他的主人奥希诺非常爱她，如果得不到她的爱，奥希诺活着就像死了一样。奥利维亚说虽然奥希诺长得帅，胸怀宽广，举止文雅，但她实在对他爱不起来。西塞罗说假如他是公爵的话，就会在奥利维亚的府邸旁边建一个小屋，每晚给她写情诗并唱出来直到深夜，以打动她的芳心。但是，奥利维亚毫不动心，坚决不接受奥希诺的爱情。她让西塞罗转告奥希诺不要再派其他信使过来了，但西塞罗除外。

西塞罗离开后，奥利维亚坦言她被西塞罗的外貌迷住了。她命令管家马尔伏里奥去追上西塞罗，告诉他刚才他把戒指落在她这里了，并且让他明天再来她府上。西塞罗接过戒指一看，觉得很困惑，因为他压根没有给过奥利维亚戒指，西塞罗将计就计，一番推脱后还是不肯拿回戒指。马尔伏里奥把戒指往西塞罗跟前一丢，转身就走了。西塞罗捡起戒指，意识到奥利维亚爱上自己了。这时候，塞巴斯蒂安也来到了伊利里亚。他被一个叫安东尼奥的人救了，在他家调养了一段时间。安东尼奥太喜欢塞巴斯蒂安了，无论塞巴斯蒂安去哪里，他都想跟着，可是塞巴斯蒂安说他想要一个人静一静。因为他很伤心，自己的孪生妹妹淹死了。得知塞巴斯蒂安来自梅萨林的贵族世家，安东尼奥就提出给他当仆人。塞巴斯蒂安告别安东尼奥，说他要去奥希诺的王宫。尽管这里有很多敌人，可是安东尼奥太崇拜塞巴斯蒂安了，以至于他甘愿冒着生命危险也要跟随塞巴斯蒂安左右。

托比和安德鲁又在深夜吃喝吟唱,小丑费斯特也和他们一起。玛莉亚让他们安静,可是没人理她。马尔伏里奥来了,把他们训了一顿。他又冲着玛莉亚吼,说她应该管管这几个人,不要把主人的府邸变成酒馆。玛莉亚实在受不了马尔伏里奥的傲慢,决定搞一个恶作剧来戏弄他一番。于是,她模仿奥利维亚的笔迹写了一封情书,然后丢到地上,让马尔伏里奥在不经意中捡到这封信,让他以为奥利维亚爱上了他。他们这些人则会观察他的反应。在这封信里面,奥利维亚要求她爱的那个人(自视清高的马尔伏里奥一定会以为这个人就是他)穿着黄色的长袜,在膝盖上方交叉绑上吊袜带,并且保持微笑,以此来表示他接受了她的爱。托比和安德鲁谈到玛莉亚的时候口气中充满了赞许。托比说玛莉亚居然能想出这样的好主意来,他都想娶她为妻了。果然,马尔伏里奥捡到了这封信,读后便认为奥利维亚爱的这个人就是自己,就决定照着信上的指示去做。托比、安德鲁、奥利维亚的另一个侍从费边躲在树上偷看马尔伏里奥,看到他那副模样,他们几乎憋不住要笑出声来。

奥希诺问西塞罗是否爱过一个人,如同他爱奥利维亚那样。西塞罗点头。公爵便问西塞罗爱的人多大年纪,西塞罗说和公爵一样大。奥希诺建议西塞罗选择一个年轻一点的女人,因为女人的容颜如同玫瑰花一样很快就会凋零,并且男人对女人的爱不及女人对男人的爱那么持久。因为维奥拉无法直接表达对公爵的爱慕之情,她只好饱受单相思的苦。她问奥希诺,假如有一个女人爱他,就像他爱奥利维亚那样么深,他会怎么办。他回答说,没有一个人的爱比得上他对奥利维亚的爱。他还说女人的爱都是浅尝辄止,不会爱到灵魂深处,也没有他的感情那么丰富。接着,他命令西塞罗带上他送给奥利维亚的珠宝去找她。西塞罗再次要求单独见奥利维亚。西塞罗告诉奥利维亚公爵非常爱她,她应该回报这份爱。奥利维亚打断了西塞罗的话,让西塞罗不要再提奥希诺这个名字。她让西塞罗为自己向奥利维亚求爱。西塞罗说他是不会爱上女人的。西塞罗离开后,奥利维亚告诉玛莉亚西塞罗答应还来,还想着下次西塞罗来的时候,她应该怎样向他求婚才最合适。接着,她又让玛莉亚去找马尔伏里奥来商量,玛莉亚说马尔伏里奥最近有些不对劲。

安德鲁对托比说他打算回去,因为他看到奥利维亚对西塞罗太好了,这让他感到万分痛苦。托比建议他向西塞罗挑战,把自己勇武的气质表现出来,以吸引奥利维亚的注意力。安德鲁走后,费边说安德鲁就是托比的傀儡。托比告诉费边,安德鲁已经花了2000银币在他身上了,他当然舍不得他离去,他还想继续花他的钱呢。这时候,塞巴斯蒂安已经到了奥希诺的地盘了,安东尼奥跟随在他左右。塞巴斯蒂安说他想在城里逛逛。安东尼奥说他在大象酒吧等他,并且把自己的钱包递给塞巴斯蒂安,让他想怎么花他的钱就怎么花。

当奥利维亚看到马尔伏里奥穿着黄色长丝袜,膝盖上吊着袜带的样子,责备他怎么打扮成这副模样。见到她这样对自己说话,马尔伏里奥还以为奥利维亚对自己有别样的情愫。奥利维亚让托比好好照看着马尔伏里奥。托比对安德鲁说,等西塞罗再来的时候,他就把安德鲁的挑战信交给他。他心里清楚西塞罗不会接受安德鲁的挑战。他只想让双方都感到惧怕。奥利维亚给了西塞罗一个信物,是一个装着她的照片的小挂饰。她还对西塞罗说,只要西塞罗喜欢,她可以把自己的一切都送给他。西塞罗说他什么都不想要,只要奥利维亚回馈公爵对她的爱就行了。

奥利维亚出去之后,托比走进来告诉西塞罗有人要找他决斗。西塞罗说自己从来都没有得罪过任何人,不想决斗。西塞罗很坦率地承认自己是一个胆小鬼。另一边,托比对安德鲁说他的挑战信已经激怒了西塞罗,其实托比根本没有把这封信交给西塞罗。他告诉安德鲁,西塞罗已经做好决斗的准备了。安德鲁于是拔出剑,西塞罗吓坏了。西塞罗在旁白中说自己真的很害怕,恨不得直接告诉他们自己是女儿身。正在这时,安东尼奥来了。他代替西塞罗和安德鲁决斗,以为西塞罗是塞巴斯蒂安,因为这对孪生兄妹长得一模一样。安东尼奥一边打斗,一边找西塞罗要回他的钱包。西塞罗不知所云,但他把自己身上的钱都给了安东尼奥,这些钱只有安东尼奥给塞巴斯蒂安的一半。西塞罗的反应让安东尼奥很生气,自己在波涛汹涌的大海中救了他一命,一路对他关爱有加,可是现在塞巴斯蒂安却这样对待自己,他真应该感到羞愧才是。一听到塞巴斯蒂安这个名字,维奥拉喜出望外,原来她的哥哥还活着!

另一边,费斯特、安德鲁、托比遇到了塞巴斯蒂安,误以为他是西塞罗。费斯特走到塞巴斯蒂安跟前,问塞巴斯蒂安是否需要他去禀报女主人说塞巴斯蒂安来了。塞巴斯蒂安给了他一点钱,让他走开。安德鲁觉得很奇怪,怎么这么快又见到西塞罗了。他马上又一次拔剑朝着塞巴斯蒂安挥过来,塞巴斯蒂安也不示弱,拔出剑来回击。托比一把抓住塞巴斯蒂安,也拔出了他的剑。费斯特马上去禀报奥利维亚,他知道他的女主人可不愿意任何人伤害西塞罗。奥利维亚赶到后立刻命令托比住手,然后向塞巴斯蒂安道歉,邀请他"重新回到"她的府上。塞巴斯蒂安怀疑自己是不是在做梦。他想,要不就是这个女人疯了,要不就是自己不正常。奥利维亚把他带回家后,叫来牧师为他们秘密主持结婚仪式。她对塞巴斯蒂安说,如果他做好了心理准备,她就对外公布他们结婚的消息,然后补办婚礼。看到奥利维亚这么高贵、富有、美丽,塞巴斯蒂安就接受了她的求婚,并且让牧师主持了仪式。

马尔伏里奥被玛莉亚和托比关在一个小黑屋里,以治好他的"疯病"。看到费斯特进来,马尔伏里奥赶紧让他送一封信给奥利维亚。当公爵和西塞罗来到奥利维亚的府上,便看到几个军官把安东尼奥带了进来,指责他抢劫了公爵的战舰,还伤了公爵的侄子。安东尼奥不接受他们的指控,说他自己不是海盗,也没有做过偷盗之事。看到西塞罗,安东尼奥还以为"他"是塞巴斯蒂安,便指责"他"是一个忘恩负义的家伙。安东尼奥向众人解释说,他在海难中救了这个家伙的命,一直为他效劳,还把自己的钱包借给了他,可是这个家伙居然装作从来不认识他,更不用拒绝归还他的钱包。奥希诺问安东尼奥他所说的这个人是什么时候到达伊利里亚的,安东尼奥说是今天。奥希诺说他的脑子出了毛病,因为西塞罗三个月前就到了这里。公爵问安东尼奥,明知来到这里对他来说很危险,为什么还要来,安东尼奥回答说他纯粹出于对这个家伙的爱慕。奥利维亚也出来指责西塞罗突然离开她家,破坏了他们之间的婚约。奥希诺一听大怒,以为西塞罗瞒着自己向奥利维亚偷偷求婚了。场面一度陷入混乱。

这时,托比和安德鲁闯了进来,他们身上都带着伤,塞巴斯蒂安紧随其后。塞巴斯蒂安向奥利维亚道歉,说自己不该匆匆忙忙离开她,还把她的亲人伤着了。大家看着塞巴斯蒂安和西塞罗,惊叹他们俩长得一模一样,就像一个切成两半的苹果。大家终于弄清楚了事情的原委。奥希诺问西塞罗"他"对自己的爱还算不算数,西塞罗说自己不爱女人,只爱公爵。奥利维亚请求做公爵的妹妹,公爵答应了。西塞罗说他会找到船长拿回自己的衣服。船长被关押起来了,他受到了马尔伏里奥的指控。奥利维亚告诉西塞罗,马尔伏里奥会释放船长的。接着,马尔伏里奥被人带了上来。奥利维亚看了马尔伏里奥的信,对他所受的苦头表示歉意，奥利维亚一看马尔伏里奥说的那封是她写的信，就辨认出这是玛莉亚的笔迹。费边马上站出来，为自己、托比和玛莉亚求情，托比和玛莉亚刚刚结婚了。奥希诺请求西塞罗恢复女儿身后做他的王后，两对新人会重新举办正式婚礼。

5　Famous quotes

【Quote 1】

Orsino

If music be the food of love, play on.
Give me excess of it that, surfeiting,
the appetite may sicken, and so die.
That strain again, it had a dying fall.
O, it came o'er my ear like the sweet sound,
that breathes upon a bank of violets,
stealing and giving odor.
Enough, no more.
'Tis not so sweet now as it was before.
O spirit of love, how quick and fresh art thou,
that, notwithstanding thy capacity receiveth as the sea,
nought enters there,
of what validity and pitch soe'er,
but falls into abatement and low price even in a minute.
So full of shapes is fancy that it alone is high fantastical. [4]
(Act 1, Scene 1)

[Orsino (played by Clive Arrindell) talking about music in a 1980 film directed by John Gorrie.]

◆ Paraphrase

If music feeds love and makes it stronger,
then keep playing music.
Give me too much of it,
so much that it kills my longing for love and makes it go away.
Play that part again—it sounded melancholy.
Oh, it sounded to me like a sweet breeze blowing over a bank of violets,
stealing their scent and distributing it to everyone.
That's enough now, no more music.
It doesn't sound as sweet as it did before.
Oh, spirit of love, how restless you are!
You make me want to accept everything, like the sea does,
but then the next minute everything seems worthless,
no matter how valuable it is.
Love is like a hallucination
—nothing else is so imaginative and extravagant. [5]

◆ 原文译文

假如音乐是爱情的食粮,那么奏下去吧;尽量地奏下去,好让爱情因过饱而噎死。又奏起这个调子来了!它有一种渐渐消沉下去的节奏。啊!它经过我的耳畔,就像微风吹拂一丛紫罗兰,发出轻柔的声音,一面把花香偷走,一面又把花香分送。够了!别再奏下去了!它现在已经不像原来那样甜蜜了。爱情的精灵呀!你是多么敏感而活泼;虽然你有海一样的容量,可是无论怎样高贵超越的事物,一进了你的范围,便会在顷刻间失去了它的价值。爱情是这样充满了意象,在一切事物中是最富于幻想的。[6]

【Quote 2】

Feste

[Aside] Wit, an't be thy will, put me into good fooling!
Those wits, that think they have thee,
do very oft prove fools.
And I, that am sure I lack thee, may pass for a wise man.
For what says Quinapalus?
"Better a witty fool, than a foolish wit." [7]
(Act 1, Scene 5)

Unit 7 Twelfth Night

[Feste/the Fool (played by Trevor Peacock) talking about wit in a 1980 film directed by John Gorrie.]

◆ Paraphrase

[To himself] Come on, wit, give me something good to say now!
Those people who think they're witty often prove to be fools.
And I'm sure that I'm not witty,
so I might pass for a wise man.
For what did the philosopher Quinapalus① say?
"Better a witty fool, than a foolish wit."[8]

◆ 原文译文

[旁白]才情呀,请你帮我好好地装一下傻瓜!那些自以为满腹才华的人,实际上往往是些傻瓜;我知道我自己没有才华,因此也许可以算作聪明人。昆那拍勒斯怎么说的?"与其做愚蠢的智人,不如做聪明的愚人。"[9]

【Quote 3】

Orsino
Let still the woman take an elder than herself.
So wears she to him, so sways she level in her husband's heart.
For, boy, however we do praise ourselves,
our fancies are more giddy and unfirm,

---

① Quinapalus is a name coined by Feste.

more longing, wavering, sooner lost and worn, than women's are.
...

(**Orsino talking about a man's love for a woman in a 1980 film directed by John Gorrie.**)

There is no woman's sides can bide the beating of so strong a passion
as love doth give my heart.
No woman's heart so big to hold so much.
They lack retention.
Alas, their love may be called appetite,
no motion of the liver, but the palate,
that suffer surfeit, cloyment, and revolt;
but mine is all as hungry as the sea, and can digest as much.
Make no compare between that love a woman
can bear me and that I owe Olivia.[10]
(Act 2, Scene 4)

(**Orsino talking about a woman's love for a man in a 1980 film directed by John Gorrie.**)

◆ Paraphrase

A woman should be with a man older than she is,
so she can adapt herself to her husband and keep his love constant.
We men praise ourselves, boy,
but in reality we are more fickle and inconstant in love than women are
—our desires waver and disappear sooner and more frequently.
...
There is no woman strong enough to withstand
the passion of love that's in my heart.
No woman's heart is big enough to hold so much emotion.
Women can't carry too much.
Alas, love for them is just a shallow appetite
—a matter of taste, not a matter of the heart.
If they try to eat too much, they get sick,
but my love is as insatiable as the sea,
and can swallow just as much as the ocean.
Don't compare my love for Olivia to
any love a woman could have for me.[11]

◆ 原文译文

女人应当选一个比她年纪大些的男人,这样她才跟他合得来,不会失去她丈夫的欢心;因为,孩子,不论我们怎样自称自赞,我们的爱情总比女人们流动不定些,富于希求,易于反复,更容易消失而生厌。

……

女人的小小的身体一定受不住像爱情强加于我心中的那种激烈的搏跳;女人的心没有这样广大,可以藏得下这么多;她们缺少隐忍的能力。唉,她们的爱就像一个人的口味一样,不是从脏腑里,而是从舌尖上感觉到的,过饱了便会食伤呕吐;可是我的爱就像饥饿的大海,能够消化一切。不要把一个女人所能对我产生的爱情跟我对于奥利维亚的爱情相提并论吧。[12]

【Quote 4】

Viola

Too well what love women to men may owe.
In faith, they are as true of heart as we.
My father had a daughter loved a man as it might be,

perhaps, were I a woman, I should your lordship.

...

[**Viola (in the disguise of Cesario, played by Felicity Kendal)** expressing her love for Orsino in a roundabout way in a 1980 film directed by John Gorrie.]

She never told her love,

but let concealment, like a worm I' the bud,

feed on her damask cheek.

She pined in thought,

and with a green and yellow melancholy she sat like patience on a monument,

smiling at grief.

Was not this love indeed?

We men may say more, swear more,

but indeed our shows are more than will,

for still we prove much in our vows, but little in our love. [13]

(Act 2, Scene 4)

◇ Paraphrase

I know too well how strongly a woman can love a man.

Really, their hearts are as true as ours are.

My father had a daughter who loved a man just as strongly as I might love you,

if I were a woman.

...

She never spoke of her love,

but kept her passion concealed.

It tormented her from the inside,

like a worm trapped inside a closed flower bud,

and fed on her outer beauty until it faded.
She pined away quietly and sadly,
and sat like a sculpture of patience itself,
smiling despite her grief.
Now wasn't this true love?
We men might say more and promise more,
but indeed our words are stronger than our passions.
We are good at making vows of love, but worse at keeping them.[14]

◇ 原文译文

我知道得很清楚女人对于男人会怀着怎样的爱情;真的,她们是跟我们一样真心的。我的父亲有一个女儿,她爱上了一个男人,正像假如我是个女人也许会爱上殿下您一样。……

她从来不向人诉说她的爱情,让隐藏在内心中的抑郁像蓓蕾中的蛀虫一样,侵蚀着她的绯红的脸颊;她因相思而憔悴,疾病和忧愁折磨着她,像是墓碑上刻着的"忍耐"的化身,默坐着向悲哀微笑。这不是真的爱情吗?我们男人也许更多话,更会发誓,可是我们所表示的,总多于我们所决心实行的;不论我们怎样山盟海誓,我们的爱情总不过如此。[15]

【Quote 5】

Malvolio
[reads] "If this fall into thy hand, revolve.
In my stars I am above thee,
but be not afraid of greatness.

[Malvolio (played by Alec McCowen) reading the letter written by Maria but supposed to be written by Olivia in a 1980 film directed by John Gorrie.]

Some are born great, some achieve greatness,
and some have greatness thrust upon 'em.
Thy fates open their hands.
Let thy blood and spirit embrace them.
And, to inure thyself to what thou art like to be,
cast thy humble slough and appear fresh..." [16]
(Act 2, Scene 5)

◆ Paraphrase

[reads] "If this should fall into your hands, consider it well.
By birth I am ranked above you,
but don't be afraid of my greatness.
Some are born great, some achieve greatness,
and some have greatness thrust upon them.
Your fate welcomes you.
Accept it with your body and spirit.
And, to prepare yourself for the upper-class life you will have soon,
cast aside your lowly outer self and become a new, fresh person..." [17]

◆ 原文译文

[读信]"要是这封信落到你手里,请你想一想。虽然我的出身比你高贵,可是你不用惧怕富贵;有的人是生来的富贵,有的人是挣来的富贵,有的人是送上来的富贵。你的好运已经向你伸出手来,赶快用你的全副精神抱住它。你应该练习一下怎样才合乎你所将要做的那种人的身份,脱去你卑躬的旧习,放出一些活泼的神气来……"[18]

【Quote 6】

Viola

This fellow's wise enough to play the fool,
and to do that well craves a kind of wit.
He must observe their mood on whom he jests,
the quality of persons, and the time,
and, like the haggard, check at every feather
that comes before his eye. This is a practise
as full of labor as a wise man's art,
for folly that he wisely shows is fit.
But wise men, folly-fall'n, quite taint their wit. [19]
(Act 3, Scene 1)

[**Viola (in the disguise of Cesario) talking about the Fool in a 1980 film directed by John Gorrie.**]

◇ Paraphrase

This fellow is wise enough to play the fool,
and to do that well you have to be clever.
He has to pay attention to the mood and status of the person he's mocking,
the time, and must also pursue every target he sees.
This is a skill that requires just as much work as any wise man's job,
for he plays the fool very wisely.
Wise men, on the other hand,
ruin their reputation for intelligence when they try to play the fool. [20]

◇ 原文译文

这家伙扮傻瓜很有点儿聪明。装傻装得好也是要靠才情的:他必须窥伺被他所取笑的人们的心情,了解他们的身份,还得看准时机;然后像窥伺着眼前每一只鸟雀的野鹰一样,每个机会都不放过。这是一种和聪明人的艺术一样艰难的工作:傻瓜不妨说几句聪明话,聪明人说傻话难免笑骂。[21]

【Quote 7】

Antonio
But oh, how vile an idol proves this god!
Thou hast, Sebastian, done good feature shame.
In nature there's no blemish but the mind.

None can be called deformed but the unkind.
Virtue is beauty, but the beauteous evil
are empty trunks o'er flourished by the devil. [22]
(Act 3, Scene 4)

◇ Paraphrase

But oh, this god turned out to be a false idol!
Sebastian, you have shamed your good looks.
On the outside you seem perfect,
but you are really a deformed monster because of your unkind soul.
Virtue is beauty,
but someone beautiful and evil is like
an empty chest decorated by the devil. [23]

◇ 原文译文

可是唉！这个天神一样的人，原来却是个邪魔歪道！塞巴斯蒂安，你未免太羞辱了你这副好相貌了。心上的瑕疵是真的污垢；无情的人才是残废之徒。善即是美；但美丽的奸恶，是魔鬼雕就纹彩的空椟。[24]

【Quote 8】

Fabian
Good madam, hear me speak,
and let no quarrel nor no brawl to come
taint the condition of this present hour,
which I have wonder'd at.
In hope it shall not,
most freely I confess,
myself and Toby set this device against Malvolio here.
Upon some stubborn and uncourteous parts we had conceived against him.
Maria writ the letter at Sir Toby's great importance,
in recompense whereof he hath married her.
How with a sportful malice it was followed,
may rather pluck on laughter than revenge,
if that the injuries be justly weighed that have on both sides passed. [25]
(Act 5, Scene 1)

Unit 7　Twelfth Night

[Fabian (played by Robert Lindsay) asking for Olivia's (played by Sinéad Cusack) forgiveness in a 1980 film directed by John Gorrie.]

◇ Paraphrase

Good madam, let me speak,
and don't let any quarreling cast a shadow over
the surprised joy of these happy couples,
which I have been amazed by.
To avoid any fighting,
I'll confess that Toby and I were the ones who tricked Malvolio here,
because of the arrogant and rude behavior we had observed in him.
Maria only wrote the letter at Sir Toby's urgent request,
and he has rewarded her for it by marrying her.
The whole practical joke should inspire laughter instead of revenge,
especially if we consider that both sides injured each other equally.[26]

◇ 原文译文

好小姐,听我说,不要让争闹和口角来打断了当前这个使我惊喜交加的好时光。我希望您不会见怪,我坦白地承认是我跟托比老爷因为看不上眼这个马尔伏里奥的顽固无礼,才想出这个计策来。因为托比老爷央求不过,玛莉亚才写了这封信;为了酬劳她,他已经跟她结了婚了。假如把两方所受到的难堪酌情判断起来,那么这种恶作剧的戏谑可供一笑,也不必计较了吧。[27]

6　Questions for discussion

(1) What is dramatic irony and what other types of irony do you know? What dramatic irony can you find in this play and how it enhances the comic situations in this play?

(2) What is Orsino's opinion about a man's love for a woman and a woman's love for a man? What is Viola's response to Orsino's opinion? Do you agree with them?

(3) What is the symbolic meaning of hunting? Paraphrase Orsino's words related to hunting: "When mine eyes did see Olivia first, me thought she purged the air of pestilence. That instant was I turned into a hart, and my desires, like fell and cruel hounds, e'er since pursue me".

(4) What do you think of Orsino's love for Olivia? Are there any other characters similar to Orsino in this regard?

(5) What kind of woman is Viola?

(6) What do you think about the practical joke played by Maria and the others on Malvolio? Have you ever played practical jokes or been played on?

7　References

[1][2][3]　Twelfth Night Study Guide[EB/OL]. https://www.litcharts.com/lit/twelfth-night.

[4][7][10][13][16][19][22][25]　Shakespeare W. Twelfth Night[M]. New York: Simon&Schuster, 2004.

[5][8][11][14][17][20][23][26]　Twelfth Night: Shakespeare Translation[EB/OL]. https://www.litcharts.com/shakescleare/shakespeare-translations/twelfth-night.

[6][9][12][15][18][21][24][27]　威廉·莎士比亚. 莎士比亚喜剧选[M]. 朱生豪, 译. 北京: 人民文学出版社, 2013.

Unit 8

A Mid-Summer Night's Dream

1 Characters

Theseus(提修斯): Duke of Athens. ①

Hippolyta(希波吕忒): Theseus' wife-to-be. ②

Hermia(赫米娅): Daughter of an Athenian nobleman. She and Lysander are in love with each other.

Egeus(伊吉斯): Hermia's father.

Lysander(莱桑德): Athenian young man in love with Hermia.

Demetrius(狄米特里斯): Athenian young man in love with Hermia now, but in love with Hermia's friend Helena before.

Helena(海琳娜): Young woman in love with Demetrius.

Philostrate(菲洛斯特): Man in charge of Duke Theseus' wedding festivity.

Bottom(波屯): Weaver who plays Pyramus in a play performed with other Athenian tradesmen.

Peter Quince(彼得·奎恩思): Carpenter who writes the scripts, arranges rehearsals, directs the performances, and acts as Thisbe's father in the tradesmen's play *Pyramus and Thisbe*.

Snug(斯纳格): Joiner③ who plays a lion in *Pyramus and Thisbe*.

Francis Flute(弗朗西斯·弗鲁特): Bellows-mender who plays Thisbe in *Pyramus and Thisbe*.

Tom Snout(汤姆·思铙特): Tinker who plays Pyramus's father in *Pyramus and Thisbe*.

Robin Starveling(罗宾·斯塔夫林): Tailor who plays Thisbe's mother in *Pyramus and Thisbe*.

---

① In Greek mythology, Theseus was a hero of many accomplishments, including killing the Minotaur, a half-man and half-bull monster. He also vanquished the Amazons, a race of warrior women. Afterward, he married the queen of the Amazons, Hippolyta. In Shakespeare's play, Theseus' marriage to Hippolyta was celebrated lavishly, telling her "I will wed thee... with pomp, with triumph and with revelling".

② In Greek mythology, Hippolyta is Queen of the Amazons, a former enemy of Theseus' on the battlefield.

③ Cabinetmaker.

Oberon(奥伯龙): King of the fairies in the forest beyond Athens.
Titania(泰妲妮亚): Queen of the fairies.
Puck(帕克)(**also called Robin Goodfellow**): Mischievous sprite who serves Oberon.

2 Background

This play is partly based on *The Knight's Tale* in *The Canterbury Tales*, a masterpiece by Geoffrey Chaucer (1340? -1400). The setting and two of the main characters, Theseus and Hippolyta, are the same. Other sources of the play are Apuleius' (second century AD) *The Golden Ass*, Plutarch's (46 BC? -AD 120?) biography of Theseus in *Parallel Lives*, and possibly Robert Greene's (1560? -1592) play *King James the Fourth*. Within the play *A Mid-Summer Night's Dream*, there is a play *Pyramus and Thisbe*, which is based on the Roman poet Ovid's (43 BC-17 AD) *Metamorphoses* (Book 4). The character Puck appeared as Robin Goodfellow in Thomas Nashe's (1567-1601) play named *Terrors of the Night* in 1593. Shakespeare may have also based Puck on a devilish sprite called Pook in Edmund Spenser's *Epithalamium* (1595). Puck also appeared in Celtic and English folklore as a mischievous fairy. [1]

3 Settings

The story takes place in the city of Athens and the forest just outside, in some distant, ancient time when it was ruled by the mythological hero Theseus. [2] The time of the action is June 24, a Mid-Summer Day, a time of feasting and merriment because it was a date when the feast of Saint John the Baptist occurred in Elizabethan England. It was thought that fairies, hobgoblins, and witches held their festival on a Mid-Summer Night, and that to dream about Mid-Summer Night was to dream about weird creatures and fantastic happenings just like those in this play. [3]

4 Synopsis

In the ancient city of Athens, Duke Theseus is discussing the imminent wedding celebration with his fiancée, Queen Hippolyta of the Amazons, when Egeus, an Athenian nobleman enters with his daughter Hermia and two young men, Demetrius and Lysander. Egeus complains to the duke that he has given his consent to Demetrius to marry Hermia, but she disagrees because her heart has been stolen by Lysander. He accuses Lysander of bewitching Hermia with poems and love songs and of hoaxing her with trinkets, flowers and candies as if she were a child. Egeus demands his right as a father who, according to Athenian law, decides his daughter's husband. If she disobeys, she will have to die. Theseus advises Hermia to follow her father's order, otherwise, she will either become a nun or die. Lysander tells the duke that he is as noble and rich as Demetrius, and his prospects are as good as Demetrius', so he has the right to marry her too. Besides, Demetrius is an inconstant lover who has wooed the sweet Helena and won her love. The more important thing is that Hermia loves Lysander, not Demetrius. Hermia declares that she would rather die than marry Demetrius, who asks Lysander to give up his claim and persuades Hermia to give in to her father. Lysander responds that since Demetrius has Egeus' love, he should marry him not Hermia. Enraged, Egeus decides that all his possessions, including Hermia, who is part of his possessions, go to Demetrius.

Lysander tells Hermia that he has a widowed aunt who is wealthy and heirless. She wants him to be her heir. They can elope to her house, which is about twenty miles away, and get married there where Athenian law cannot follow them. Hermia agrees. They decide to act at midnight tomorrow. Helena enters at this moment. She wishes to be as beautiful as Hermia, who has eyes like stars and her voice is so sweet that it is more melodic than a lark's song. If she were as beautiful as Hermia, Demetrius would not have abandoned her. To comfort Helena, Hermia tells Helena their plan and hopes Demetrius will return to Helena after Hermia and Lysander leave. Helena decides to tell Demetrius this piece of information. If he appreciates this information, her betrayal of Hermia will be worth.

There is a troupe of commoners gathering in Peter Quince, a carpenter's house to discuss the role each will perform in a play named *Pyramus and Thisbe* at the duke's wedding celebration. Bottom, a weaver, is arranged to play Pyramus, but he wants to play Thisbe too, boasting that he can speak like a woman, and he also wants to play the lion and promises to roar gently so that the ladies wouldn't be scared away. Peter, the scriptwriter and director, decides that Bottom can only play one role as Pyramus. After handing out the roles, Peter asks them to meet in the forest that night to rehearse.

The forest is also a place inhabited by the fairies whose King is Oberon and the queen is Titania. Oberon asks Titania for an Indian changeling boy, which is rejected. This boy's mother had been a votary of Titania before she died of childbirth and they had spent a lot of happy time together on the beach, so Titania is bringing up the boy for this woman's sake. She will not give up the boy even for the entire fairy kingdom. They accuse each other of adultery and their fight has caused troubles such as floods and death of livestock and mixture of seasons for human beings. Oberon tells Titania that if she gives him the changeling boy to him, all the troubles will vanish. She refuses and exits. Oberon decides to play a prank on her. He summons Robin Goodfellow, a mischievous sprite who is also named Puck, and asks him to look for a magical flower named love-in-idleness. This flower changed its colour from white to purple when Cupid's arrow shot it, missing its original goal, a virgin queen of a Western land. When the juice of the flower is applied to one's eyelids during one's sleep, s/he will fall instantly for the living thing s/he sees on waking up. Oberon will apply this love juice on Titania in her sleep and he will mock her after she falls in love with another living thing until she gives up the changeling boy to him.

When Oberon is planning this, he hears human voices. Demetrius has entered the forest, chased by Helena. Demetrius bids Helena to stop following him since he doesn't and cannot love her, but she persists in her pursuit, saying that she is his spaniel and the more he beats her, the more she will fawn on him. Demetrius proclaims that he will kill Lysander and walks on fast. Helena is exhausted but continues. Seeing this, Oberon decides to help Helena to get Demetrius's love. He tells Puck to drop the love juice on the eyelids of an Athenian young man who can be identified by his Athenian dressing. Puck complies. By this time, Hermia and Lysander have arrived in the forest and got lost. They decide to lie down for a sleep because they feel exhausted. They sleep afar from each other to keep their chastity before their marriage. Discovering the sleeping lovers at a distance from each other, Puck concludes they must be the lovers referred to by Oberon. He then drops some potion on Lysander's eyelids and walks away. Now Helena walks by and sees Lysander. She wakes him up who immediately confesses his love for her and regrets for his previous love for Hermia. Shocked and annoyed, Helena walks away, followed by Lysander. Hermia wakes up from a nightmare in which a serpent is eating her heart while Lysander just stands by without offering any help. Seeing Lysander pursuing Helena, Hermia feels terrible.

The commoners happen to rehearse their play where the fairy Queen Titania is sleeping (fairies are invisible while human beings are). They have disagreements concerning the parts of Pyramus' suicide with a sword and the lion played by Snug, a joiner. They decide to add a prologue that tells the audience Pyramus is played by Bottom and the sword will do no harm to them. And Snug will reveal half of his face to reassure the audience he is not a real lion but a human being so that the audience of the fair sex will not be frightened away. While they are rehearsing, they forget their cues and make a lot of mistakes. Puck watches them performing. In a part which requires Bottom to exit for a moment, Puck takes this chance and turns Bottom's head into the head of a donkey. When Bottom shows up again, all the common actors are scared away. Bottom is left alone. He decides to keep calm and starts to sing which wakes up Titania who upon seeing him, falls for him instantly. She asks Bottom to stay with her and invites him to her chamber. She bids the fairies to serve Bottom and bring him fruits and gifts of jewels.

Meanwhile, Lysander is still chasing Helena in the forest, and Demetrius is following Hermia who accuses Demetrius of doing harm to Lysander. Otherwise, Lysander wouldn't have abandoned her. She forbids Demetrius to follow her any further. Seeing that she is so furious, Demetrius decides to obey her. Realizing that Puck has applied the love juice to the wrong person, Oberon orders him to find out Helena and bring her close to Demetrius. He will apply the love juice on Demetrius' eyelids during his sleep so that after he wakes up, he will fall in love with Helena. When Lysander is still running after Helena and swears to her that his love for her is genuine, Demetrius wakes up and sees Helena and falls for her too. The two men are quarrelling and then start to duel for Helena who is angrier to be mocked by both, as she believes. Helena thinks that Hermia, who has also arrived, takes a part in the men's mocking of her and accuses Hermia. Hermia reprimands Helena for stealing Lysander's love for Hermia. The men are fighting while the women are arguing against each other. Everything is in a mayhem. Puck honestly tells Oberon that he is amused to see the mistakes he has made but promises to redress his wrongs.

Titania is still doting on Bottom. Oberon takes the chance to mock her and sends Puck back to her for the changeling boy, which she gives in. Oberon then tells Puck to restore Bottom's human head. Puck also plays tricks to make the four young people fall asleep and applies antidote to restore things to normal. Duke Theseus, Hippolyta and Egeus have also arrived in the forest to hunt. They are surprised to see the four young people sleeping peacefully together. After they wake up, Lysander admits to his plan to elope with Hermia, for which Egeus asks the duke to punish him. But Demetrius says that somehow, he doesn't love Hermia now but Helena. The duke rules that the couples can get married at the same time as his own wedding. The young people talk about the weird dream that they all had the previous night. The labourers, however, are unable to find Bottom and afraid that their play will be ruined when they see Bottom enter. Hearing that there will be three marriages, the labourers think that they are going to make a fortune to perform their play.

At the wedding, Philostrate, a character in charge of entertainment in the court, presents Theseus a list of entertainment. He chooses the play *Pyramus and Thisbe* when he learns that it is performed by a group of uneducated simple labourers. He thinks that they will have fun to watch them making mistakes during their performance of the play. When it begins, Peter enters and introduces a ridiculous prologue as well as the plot and the characters and their roles. When he exits, Snout, who plays the role of a wall between Pyramus and Thisbe, explains to the audience that the two lovers will talk through a hole played by Snout's separate fingers. Then Bottom shows up to tell the audience his role as Pyramus who curses the wall for dividing Thisbe from him and his curse is a cue for Flute, a bellows-mender to appear as Thisbe. The two lovers then start a conversation through the hole of the wall about love with a lot of erroneous references to classical mythology. Pyramus and Thisbe decide to meet and elope on a moonlit night at Ninus' tomb which they pronounce wrongly as "Ninny's tomb". They exit and Starveling shows up, carrying a lantern to indicate the moonlight. Then Snug enters the stage as the lion. Before he roars, he explains to the audience that he is not a real lion. Hearing his roar, Thisbe is scared away, leaving a mantle behind. When the lion is gone, Pyramus comes and sees Thisbe's mantle and blood (the lion's) on it, he assumes that his lover has been eaten by the lion and stabs himself. Thisbe returns to the stage. Seeing the dead Pyramus, she stabs herself too. While they are performing, they are interrupted and commented by the audience amusingly and they end the play with a dance. After all of them are gone, Puck enters to give blessings to the married couples and their future children.

【剧情介绍】

在雅典古城,提修斯公爵和亚马逊女王希波吕忒在商量他们的婚礼事宜,这时,贵族伊吉斯带着女儿赫米娅、两个贵族青年狄米特里斯和莱桑德走了进来。伊吉斯对公爵抱怨道,他本来把女儿许配给了狄米特里斯,可是赫米娅的心却被莱桑德偷走了,她不肯嫁给狄米特里斯。他指责莱桑德用他的情诗蛊惑赫米娅爱上他,还把她当小孩一样用一些小玩意儿、鲜花、糖果等哄着她。伊吉斯要求行使他作为父亲的权力,按照雅典的法律,女儿的婚事必须由父亲做主。如果她违抗的话,她就是不想活了。提修斯劝说赫米娅听从父亲的安排,否则她要么当尼姑,要么被处死。莱桑德对公爵说,他和狄米特里斯一样出身高贵,一样富有,和他一样有前途,所以他也有权娶赫米娅。何况狄米特里斯这个家伙用情不专,他之前还向赫米娅的闺蜜,也就是乖巧的海琳娜求爱并得到了她的钟情。关键问题是莱桑德和赫米娅彼此相爱,赫米娅根本不爱狄米特里斯。赫米娅宣布,她宁死也不嫁给狄米特里斯。伊吉斯勃然大怒,宣布他所有的财产都将由狄米特里斯继承,而赫米娅作为她父亲的财产的一部分,也归狄米特里斯所有。

莱桑德告诉赫米娅,他有一个有钱的姑姑想让他做继承人,因为她没有子嗣。他们俩可以逃到她那里去,那里离雅典大概二十英里,他们可以在他姑姑家结婚,因为雅典法律在他姑姑那个地方没有效力。赫米娅同意了。他们于是决定第二天晚上就开始行动。这时,海琳娜走了进来。她希望自己像赫米娅那样漂亮,有着她那星星般闪闪发光的眼睛,还有她那说起话来就像云雀歌唱一样的甜美嗓音。如果她拥有赫米娅那样的美貌,那么狄米特里斯就不会抛弃她了。赫米娅安慰海琳娜,说她打算和莱桑德一起逃离这里,把狄米特里斯留给她。海琳娜打算把这个消息告诉狄米特里斯。如果他会因此而感激她的话,那她对赫米娅的背叛也值了。

木匠彼得·奎恩思家里聚集着一群平民演员,他们正在商讨即将在公爵的婚礼上表演的那部《皮拉摩斯和提丝柏》的戏剧角色分配的问题。纺织工波屯被安排扮演皮拉摩斯,但他还想同时扮演提丝柏,他吹嘘说自己可以像女人那样说话。他还想扮演狮子,并保证他的吼声会很温柔,不会吓跑女性观众。彼得是这部剧的编剧和导演,他认定波屯只能扮演皮拉摩斯这个角色。角色分配完毕,彼得吩咐他们晚上到森林里去排练。

这个森林也是仙子们居住的地方。仙人国的国王叫奥伯龙,王后叫泰妲妮亚。奥伯龙向泰妲妮亚讨要一个被仙子调包了的印度男婴,遭到王后的拒绝。这个男婴的母亲生前崇拜泰妲妮亚,后来分娩的时候不幸去世。泰妲妮亚和这个男婴的母亲一起在海边度过了很多愉快的时光,因此她想替这个女人把男婴养大。就算奥伯龙用整个仙人国来和她交换,泰妲妮亚也不答应。他们互相指责对方和别人通奸,他们的打闹给人间带来了洪水和牲畜的死亡,还有四季的颠倒。奥伯龙答应泰妲妮亚,只要她把那个调包男婴给他,他就让一切人间疾苦立刻消失。王后拒绝,并离开了。奥伯龙决定好好戏弄一番王后。于是,他叫来好心肠的罗宾,又名帕克,吩咐他去帮自己寻找一种神奇的叫作三色堇的花,这种花原本是白色,可是丘比特的箭错过了它的既定目标——西方世界的一位贞洁的女王——反而射中这种花,之后这朵花就变成了紫色。如果向睡眠中的人的眼皮上滴上几滴这种花汁,那么这个人醒来后将会爱上他/她第一眼看见的人/动物。奥伯龙打算趁王后睡觉的时候,往她的眼皮上喷洒这种花

Unit 8　A Mid-Summer Night's Dream

汁(爱的甘露)，等到她爱上第一眼看上的人/动物，他就趁机嘲笑她，然后把那个调包的男婴要过来。

　　正当奥伯龙策划如何捉弄王后的时候，突然传来人类的说话声。狄米特里斯来到了森林，海琳娜紧随其后。狄米特里斯让海琳娜不要跟着他，并且明确对她说他不爱她，也不可能爱她。可是海琳娜还是对狄米特里斯紧追不放，还说自己是他身边的一条狗，他越是打她，她越是对他摇尾巴。狄米特里斯一边扬言要杀了莱桑德，一边继续往前赶。海琳娜筋疲力尽，可还是没有停下脚步。见此情景，奥伯龙决定帮助海琳娜得到狄米特里斯的爱。于是，他命令帕克找到一个穿着雅典服装的男青年，趁他睡觉的时候往他的眼皮上喷洒爱的甘露，帕克按照他的吩咐去做了。这时，赫米娅和莱桑德早已来到了森林里，他们迷路了。筋疲力尽的两人决定躺下来休息一下。他们睡觉的地方保持着一定的距离，因为他们还没有结婚，要守住他们的童贞。看到他们两个各睡各的，中间还隔着那么远的距离，帕克断定他们就是奥伯龙所说的那对冤家，于是帕克就往莱桑德的眼皮上滴了爱的甘露，然后走开了。这时，正好海琳娜经过，她看到了莱桑德。海琳娜叫醒了他，醒来的莱桑德立刻就爱上了她，表达对她的爱，还说自己很后悔爱上赫米娅。海琳娜对莱桑德的求爱感到又惊又气，不理他，转身走开了，莱桑德追着她。赫米娅醒来了，她刚刚做了一个噩梦，梦见一条蛇在咬她的胸口，可是莱桑德居然袖手旁观，也不救她。现在看到莱桑德追求海琳娜，赫米娅心里痛苦万分。

　　平民演员正在森林里排练他们的戏剧，他们排练的地方正好是泰姐妮亚睡觉的地方（人眼是看不见仙子的）。关于皮拉摩斯自杀和焊接工斯纳格表演的狮子吼叫这几个部分，他们产生了分歧。他们决定插进一段序言，向观众解释皮拉摩斯是纺织工波屯扮演的，他的剑不伤人，并且斯纳格要露半边脸，表明他是人而不是狮子，免得女性观众被他吓跑了。他们在排练的时候总是忘词，闹出很多笑话。帕克看着他们的排练，然后趁波屯暂时退场的时间，把波屯的头变成了一个驴头。当波屯再次入场的时候，那些演员都被他吓跑了。波屯一个人留在那里。他决定保持镇定，开始唱起歌来，他的歌声吵醒了泰姐妮亚，当她睁开眼看到波屯的时候，泰姐妮亚立即迷上了他。她邀请波屯留下来，把他带到她的卧室，让仙子们伺候他，给他端来水果，还把珠宝当作礼物送给他。

　　这时，莱桑德还在森林里继续追逐海琳娜，狄米特里斯则追逐着赫米娅，赫米娅斥责狄米特里斯一定对莱桑德做了什么，不然莱桑德不会抛弃她。她命令狄米特里斯不要继续跟在她后面了。看到她真的很气愤的样子，狄米特里斯不敢造次。奥伯龙已经看出帕克乱点鸳鸯谱，就命令帕克找到海琳娜，并指引她到狄米特里斯跟前来，然后他会趁狄米特里斯睡着的时候往他的眼皮上滴爱的甘露，这样他就可以一醒来就看到海琳娜并且爱上她。莱桑德一边继续追逐海琳娜，一边信誓旦旦地说他对她的爱是真真切切的。狄米特里斯醒来后看到海琳娜，立刻爱上了她。于是两个男人争吵起来，并且开始为争夺海琳娜而决斗。海琳娜则认为这两个人都在戏弄她，于是她更加生气了。海琳娜认为，这两个家伙之所以这样愚弄她，赫米娅也脱不了干系，于是她开始指责赫米娅。赫米娅也斥责海琳娜偷走了莱桑德对她的爱，于是，在两个男人决斗的时候，两个女人也在争吵，现场一片混乱。帕克坦率地说，看到这样的情景，他觉得很好玩，不过，他答应把自己造成的错误纠正过来。

　　泰姐妮亚还在继续宠溺着波屯。奥伯龙趁机嘲笑她，并派帕克去找她要那个调包的男婴，泰姐妮亚只好屈服。奥伯龙命令帕克恢复波屯的人头。帕克略施小计，让四个年轻人入睡,然后给他们滴上解药,让一切回到正常。这时,提修斯公爵、希波吕忒、伊吉斯都来到森林打猎。看到四个年轻人相安无事地睡在一起,他们很诧异。他们醒来后,莱桑德交代了他原本准备和赫米娅私奔的计划,伊吉斯请求公爵处罚他。但是狄米特里斯声明他现在不知道怎么的已经不爱赫米娅了,现在他爱的人是海琳娜。公爵于是下令他们四个人可以和他一起举行婚礼。年轻人接着谈论他们昨晚做的奇怪的梦。那群平民组成的临时演员因为波屯不见了而害怕他们的戏演不了、坏了大事的时候,波屯突然出现了。听说将有三对新人结成连理,这群平民乐坏了,他们觉得到时候可以赚得盆满钵满。

婚礼上,主管宫廷娱乐的菲洛斯特给提修斯呈上了一份节目单。当提修斯得知表演《皮拉摩斯和提丝柏》这部剧的演员是一群单纯无知的平民的时候,他决定就选这个节目。他认为这群人在表演的时候一定会漏洞百出,十分滑稽。表演开始的时候,彼得入场,用十分滑稽的语言做了一个开场白,介绍了故事情节、剧中人物以及每个角色的扮演者。他退场后,思铙特进场,他扮演的是皮拉摩斯和提丝柏之间的那堵墙。他向观众解释说,这两个有情人将会通过他扮演这堵墙上面的一个洞说话,他用岔开的手指表示这个洞。接着,波屯入场,他向观众解释他扮演的是皮拉摩斯,接着,他就诅咒那堵墙把他和他的爱人提丝柏分割开来。他的诅咒就是一个提示,提醒下一个演员弗鲁特入场。弗鲁特扮演的是提丝柏。这两个有情人于是隔着墙说起了情话,他们提到了很多经典神话里面的故事,错误不断。皮拉摩斯和提丝柏决定在一个月光皎洁的晚上私奔,他们约定在尼纳斯(他们误读成了尼尼)的坟前碰头,然后他们就退场了。接着,斯塔夫林入场,他手里提着一个代表月亮的灯笼。然后,斯纳格登场,他扮演的是狮子。在他吼叫之前,他向观众解释说他不是真的狮子。他一声吼叫,把提丝柏吓跑了,只留下她的披风。当狮子离开后,皮拉摩斯出现了,他看到提丝柏的披风和上面沾着的狮子的血,便以为他的爱人已经成了狮子的腹中食,于是皮拉摩斯自刎。提丝柏回到舞台看到提修斯已死,也一刀结果了自己的性命。本剧以舞蹈表演收场。等到人群都散去之后,帕克入场,祝福这些新婚夫妇以及他们的子孙后代。

5 Famous quotes

【Quote 1】

Helena
Call you me "fair?" That "fair" again unsay.
Demetrius loves your fair. O happy fair!
Your eyes are lodestars,
and your tongue's sweet air more tunable than
lark to shepherd's ear when wheat is green,
when hawthorn buds appear.
Sickness is catching. Oh, were favor so,
yours would I catch, fair Hermia, ere I go.

My ear should catch your voice. My eye, your eye.
My tongue should catch your tongue's sweet melody.
Were the world mine, Demetrius being bated,
the rest I'd give to be to you translated.
O, teach me how you look, and with what art
you sway the motion of Demetrius' heart. [4]
(Act 1, Scene 1)

[Helena (played by Cherith Mellor) speaking to Hermia (played by Pippa Guard) in a 1981 film directed by Elijah Moshinsky (The man in the middle is Lysander played by Robert Lindsay).]

◆ Paraphrase

Did you call me "beautiful?" Take it back.
Your beauty is what Demetrius loves. Oh, lucky beauty!
Your eyes are like stars, and your sweet voice is more melodic
than a lark's song is to a shepherd in the springtime,
when the wheat is green and hawthorn buds appear.
Sickness is contagious. Oh, I wish beauty was also.
I would catch yours, beautiful Hermia, before I left.
My ear would be infected by your voice, my eye by your eye,
and my tongue would catch your tongue's musical voice.
If I owned the world, I'd give it all up
—with the exception of Demetrius
—to be transformed into you.
Oh, teach me how you look at Demetrius,
and the tricks you use to make him fall in love with you. [5]

◇ 原文译文

你称我"美丽"吗?请你把那两个字收回了吧!狄米特里斯爱着你的美丽;幸福的美丽啊!你的眼睛是两颗明星,你的甜蜜的声音比之小麦青青、山楂蓓蕾的时节送入牧人耳中的云雀之歌还要动听。疾病是能染人的;唉!要是美貌也能传染的话,美丽的赫米娅,我但愿染上你的美丽;我要用我的耳朵捕获你的声音,用我的眼睛捕获你的凝视,用我的舌头捕获你那柔美的旋律。要是除了狄米特里斯之外,整个世界都是属于我所有,我愿意把一切抛弃,但求化身为你。啊!教给我怎样流转眼波,用怎么一种魔力操纵着狄米特里斯的心。[6]

【Quote 2】

Helena

How happy some o'er other some can be!
Through Athens I am thought as fair as she.
But what of that? Demetrius thinks not so.
He will not know what all but he do know.
And as he errs, doting on Hermia's eyes,
so I, admiring of his qualities.
Things base and vile, holding no quantity,
love can transpose to form and dignity.
Love looks not with the eyes but with the mind,
and therefore is wing'd Cupid① painted blind.
Nor hath love's mind of any judgment taste
—wings and no eyes figure unheedy haste.
And therefore is love said to be a child,
because in choice he is so oft beguiled.
As waggish boys in game themselves forswear,
so the boy Love is perjured everywhere.
For ere Demetrius looked on Hermia's eyne,
he hailed down oaths that he was only mine.
And when this hail some heat from Hermia felt,
so he dissolved, and showers of oaths did melt.[7]
(Act 1, Scene 1)

---

① Cupid, or Eros, was the ancient Greek god of love.

Unit 8　A Mid-Summer Night's Dream

[Helena (played by Cherith Mellor) in a soliloquy in a 1981 film directed by Elijah Moshinsky.]

◆ Paraphrase

How happy some people can be compared to others!
Throughout Athens, people think I'm as beautiful as Hermia.
But what does that matter? Demetrius doesn't think so.
The only opinion he has is his own.
And as he wanders, idolizing Hermia's eyes,
likewise I admire his beauty.
Love can transform crude and horrible things of
no worth into beautiful and dignified things.
Love doesn't look with eyes, but with the mind.
That's why they paint winged Cupid blind.
And love doesn't have good judgment or taste
—wings and blindness make for undue speed in falling in love.
Thus, love is thought of as a child,
because he often makes the wrong choice.
Just like mischievous boys who go back on their word as they play games,
so too does the boy love perjure himself everywhere.
Because before Demetrius saw Helena's eyes,
he swore that he belonged to only me.
And when he felt attracted to Hermia,
He dissolved. His promises melted down like hail in the heat. [8]

◆ 原文译文

有些人比起其他的人来是多么幸福！在全雅典大家都认为我跟她一样美，但那有什么相干呢,狄米特里斯不是这么认为的;除了他一个人之外,大家都知道的事情,他不会知道。正如他那样错误地迷恋着赫米娅的秋波一样,我也是只知道爱慕他的才智;一切卑劣的弱点,在恋爱中都无足重轻,而变成美满和庄严。爱情是不用眼睛而用心灵看着的,因此生着翅膀的丘比特常被描述为盲目的;爱情的判断全然没有理性,光有翅膀,不生眼睛,一味表示出鲁莽的急躁,因此爱神据说是一个孩儿,因为在选择方面他常会弄错。正如顽皮的孩子惯爱发假誓一样,司爱情的小儿也到处赌着口不应心的咒。狄米特里斯在没有看见赫米娅之前,也曾像下冰雹一样发着誓,说他是完全属于我的,但这阵冰雹一感到身上的一丝热力,便立刻融化了! 无数的誓言都化为乌有。[9]

【Quote 3】

Demetrius

Do I entice you? Do I speak you fair?
Or rather, do I not in plainest truth tell you I do not,
nor I cannot, love you?[10]
(Act 2, Scene 1)

[**Demetrius (played by Nicky Henson)** blaming Helena for following him in a 1981 film directed by **Elijah Moshinsky.**]

◆ Paraphrase

Do I invite you to follow me? Do I speak to you kindly?
Instead, don't I tell you as clearly and plainly as possible
that I do not and cannot love you?[11]

◇ 原文译文

是我引诱你跟着我的吗?我有对你好言相向吗?我不是曾经明明白白地告诉过你,我不爱你,并且也不能爱你吗?[12]

【Quote 4】

Helena

And even for that do I love you the more.
I am your spaniel.
And, Demetrius, the more you beat me,
I will fawn on you.
Use me but as your spaniel
—spurn me, strike me, neglect me, lose me.
Only give me leave, unworthy as I am, to follow you.
What worser place can I beg in your love
—and yet a place of high respect with me
—than to be usèd as you use your dog?[13]
(Act 2, Scene 1)

◇ Paraphrase

And for that I love you even more. I'm your little dog.
And, Demetrius, the more you beat me, the more I'll love you.
Treat me like a dog
—kick me, hit me, ignore me, try to lose me.
Just allow me to follow you,
even though I'm not good enough for you.
Is there a worse position I could ask to be held
in your heart than to be treated as you would treat a dog?
And yet I would consider it a place of honor.[14]

◇ 原文译文

即使那样,也只是使我爱你爱得更加厉害。我是你的一条狗,狄米特里斯;你越是打我,我越是向你献媚。请你就像对待你的狗一样对待我吧,踢我,打我,冷落我,不理我,都好,只容许我跟随着你,虽然我是这么不好。在你的爱情里,我要求的地位还不如一条狗,这还不行吗?但那对于我已经是十分可贵了![15]

【Quote 5】

Helena

We cannot fight for love as men may do.
We should be wooed and were not made to woo.
I'll follow thee, and make a heaven of hell,
to die upon the hand I love so well.[16]
(Act 2, Scene 1)

(Helena pursuing Demetrius in a 1981 film directed by Elijah Moshinsky.)

◇ Paraphrase

We can't fight for love as men can.
We should be pursued. We weren't made to be the pursuer.
I'll follow you and turn this hell of mine into a heaven,
By ensuring that I am killed by the one I love so much.[17]

◇ 原文译文

我们是不会像男人一样为爱情而争斗的;我们应该被男人追求,而不是追求男人。我就要跟随你;我愿死在我所深爱的人的手中,好让地狱化为天堂![18]

【Quote 6】

Bottom

I have had a most rare vision.
I have had a dream
——past the wit of man to say what dream it was.

Unit 8 A Mid-Summer Night's Dream

Man is but an ass if he go about to expound this dream.
Methought I was—there is no man can tell what.
Methought I was, and methought I had
—but man is but a patched fool
if he will offer to say what methought I had.
The eye of man hath not heard,
the ear of man hath not seen,
man's hand is not able to taste,
his tongue to conceive,
nor his heart to report what my dream was.
I will get Peter Quince to write a ballad of this dream.
It shall be called "Bottom's Dream" because it hath no bottom.
And I will sing it in the latter end of a play before the duke.
Peradventure, to make it more gracious,
I shall sing it at her death. [19]
(Act 4, Scene 1)

[Bottom (played by Brian Glover) in a soliloquy in a 1981 film directed by Elijah Moshinsky.]

◇ Paraphrase

I have had the strangest dream.
I have had a dream so strange that it's beyond explanation.
A man would be a fool if he tried to explain this dream.
I thought I was—well, nobody could describe what I was.
I thought I was, and I thought I had
—but a man would have to be a true fool
to try and say what I thought I had.

My dream was so odd that no man's eyes have heard,
or his ears have seen, or his hands have tasted,
or his tongue felt, or his heart described what it was like.
I will get Peter Quince to write a ballad about this dream.
It will be called "Bottom's Dream"
because it's so complex that it has no bottom.
And I'll sing it for the duke at the end of the play.
Or, better yet, to make it more pleasing,
I'll sing it when Thisbe dies. [20]

◇ 原文译文

我做了一个奇怪得不得了的梦,我的这个梦奇怪得难以描述,要是谁想把这个梦解释一下,那他一定是一头驴子。咱好像是——没有人说得出那是什么东西,咱好像是——咱好像有——但要是谁敢说出来咱好像有什么东西,那他一定是一个蠢材。咱那个梦啊,人们的眼睛从来没有听到过,人们的耳朵从来没有看见过,人们的手也尝不出来是什么味道,人们的舌头也想不出来是什么道理,人们的心也说不出来究竟那是怎样的一个梦。咱要叫彼得·奎恩思给咱写一首歌儿歌颂一下这个梦。题目就叫作"波顿的梦",因为这个梦可没有个底儿;咱要在演完戏之后当着公爵大人的面前唱这首歌——或者更好些,还是等咱死了之后再唱吧。[21]

【Quote 7】

Lion/Snug
You, ladies, you whose gentle hearts do fear
the smallest monstrous mouse that creeps on floor,
may now perchance both quake and tremble here,

[**The Lion/Snug (played by Ray Mort) in a 1981 film directed by Elijah Moshinsky.**]

when lion rough in wildest rage doth roar then know that I,
as Snug the joiner, am a lion fell, nor else no lion's dam.
For if I should as lion come in strife
into this place, 'twere pity on my life. [22]
(Act 5, Scene 1)

◆ Paraphrase

You gentle-hearted ladies
—who fear even the smallest monstrous mouse that sneaks along the floor
—may shake and tremble when the wild lion roars in its most violent rage.
Therefore, know that I, Snug the carpenter,
am neither a cruel lion nor a lioness,
because if I were a lion that had come to this place in order to fight,
then it would cost me my life. [23]

◆ 原文译文

各位太太、小姐,你们那柔弱的心一见了地板上爬着的一只小小的老鼠就会害怕,现在看见一头凶猛的狮子发狂地怒吼,多少要发起抖来吧。但是请你们放心,咱是细木工匠斯纳格,既不是凶猛的公狮,也不是一头母狮;要是咱真的是一头狮子冲到了这儿,那咱才倒了大霉![24]

6 Questions for discussion

(1) What do you think of Helena's love for Demetrius? If you were Helena, would you love a man as she does Demetrius? At the end of the play, they are married. Do you think their marriage will last long?

(2) Which is more important to Helena, love or friendship? How would you deal with love and friendship?

(3) Comment on Duke Theseus' words to Hermia, "To you, your father should be as a god".

(4) What is Snug's opinion about women's nature? Do you agree with him?

(5) In the fairy land, Oberon does what he can to get the changeling boy for Titania. What male characters are similar to him in dealing with women in the human world?

7 References

[1][2][3]   A Midsummer Night's Dream Study Guide [EB/OL]. https://www.

litcharts. com/lit/a-midsummer-nights-dream.

［4］［7］［10］［13］［16］［19］［22］ Shakespeare W. A Midsummer Night's Dream［M］. New York：Simon & Schuster,2004.

［5］［8］［11］［14］［17］［20］［23］ A Midsummer Night's Dream：Shakespeare Translation［EB/OL］. https：//www. litcharts. com/shakescleare/shakespeare-translations/a-midsummer-nights-dream.

［6］［9］［12］［15］［18］［21］［24］ 威廉·莎士比亚. 莎士比亚喜剧选［M］. 朱生豪,译. 北京：人民文学出版社,2013.

Unit 9

As You Like It

1 Characters

Duke Senior(大公爵): Rightful duke banished by his brother.
Duke Frederick(弗雷德里克公爵): Usurper of Duke Senior's dukedom.
Amiens(亚眠), **Jaques**(杰奎斯): Followers and attendants of Duke Senior.
Orlando(奥兰多): Youngest son of the late Sir Rowland de Boys.
Oliver(奥利弗): Eldest son of the late Sir Rowland de Boys.
Jaques de Boys(杰奎斯·德·博伊斯): Middle son of the late Sir Rowland de Boys.
Rosalind(罗莎琳德): Daughter of Duke Senior.
Celia(西莉亚): Daughter of Duke Frederick, cousin and best friend of Rosalind.
Le Beau(勒·博): Courtier attending upon Duke Frederick.
Charles(查尔斯): Wrestler in Duke Frederick's court.
Adam(亚当): Servant for the household of de Boys, who is loyal to Orlando.
Dennis(丹尼斯): Servant of Oliver.
Touchstone(试金石)[①]: Clown who follows Celia and Rosalind to the Forest of Arden.
Sir Oliver Martext(奥利弗·马特克斯): A vicar.
Corin(科林): Old fellow Shepherd and friend of Silvius.
Silvius(西尔维厄斯): Young Shepherd in love with Phebe.
Audrey(奥黛丽): Country wench who marries Touchstone.
William(威廉): Country man in love with Audrey.
Hisperia(希斯皮里亚): Celia's handmaid.
Hymen(海门): The god of marriage in Greek mythology.
Phebe(菲比): Shepherdess who marries Silvius.

[①] Literally a touchstone is a black stone used to test the purity of precious metals. This character lives up to his name because his presence makes other characters reveal their personal qualities.

2　Background

　　This play was based on Thomas Lodge (1557-1625)'s *Rosalynde*: *Euphues Golden Legacie* (1590), a prose romance which in turn, was based on *The Tale of Gamelyn*, a narrative poem of nine published anonymously in the middle of the fourteenth century. The poem tells the story of Gamelyn de Boundys, a young man whose inheritance is confiscated by his brother. Gamelyn is forced to live in the forest as an outlaw but eventually restored to his rightful position. [1]

　　Shakespeare wrote this play at the end of Elizabeth's reign over England. Elizabethan society was highly patriarchal. Women had very limited rights and there was no freedom of marriage. That the characters in the play love and marry freely reveals the playwright's wish for marriage out of love. [2]

3　Settings

　　The plot takes place in the French court and in the Forest of Arden. There is an Arden Forest in Warwickshire, England, and an Ardennes Forest in continental Europe. The latter forest covers parts of Belgium, Luxembourg, and France. Thomas Lodge, who wrote a play which was one of the sources of Shakespeare's *As You Like It*, studies for a medical degree in France and practiced medicine in Belgium, near the Ardennes Forest. [3]

4　Synopsis

　　In the French court, Orlando, the youngest son of the late Sir Rowland de Boys, who was a nobleman favoured by the banished Duke Senior, complains to Adam, a servant about Oliver, Orlando's eldest brother. He tells Adam that his father left only 1,000 crowns for him and asked Oliver to take care of him. But he feels that even Oliver's livestock is treated better than he is. Oliver deprives him of the right to receive education while his elder brother Jacques is at school. He decides to rebel against his position of servitude. Seeing Oliver approaching, Orlando asks Adam to hide and observe how his brother treats him. Orlando tells Oliver that though Oliver is superior to him in age and importance, he is of noble birth as Oliver. Hearing this, Oliver strikes him. Orlando reacts by grabbing him and Oliver calls Orlando villain. Orlando is insulted. He protests that when Oliver calls him villain, he is humiliating their father. Orlando also protests that Oliver tries every means to prevent Orlando from becoming a gentleman and that he is changing him into a peasant. He demands that either Oliver give him freedom or give him his share of their father's inheritance as he deserves. Oliver orders Orlando to go away with Adam. He is shocked at Orlando's rebellion and decides not to give him the 1,000 crowns.

Oliver summons Dennis, another servant, to call in Charles, a professional wrestler. He inquires Charles the recent news about the court. Charles tells him that Duke Senior, whose dukedom is usurped by his brother, the new Duke Frederick, is still in banishment. Duke Senior has gone to live in the Forest of Arden with a group of followers, his faithful lords. But Duke Senior's daughter Rosalind remains in the court because Frederick's daughter Celia loves Rosalind deeply. They were brought up together from childhood and Celia cannot be separated from Rosalind. If Rosalind is banished, she will follow her in exile or die in grief, so Rosalind stays. Frederick treats Rosalind like his own child. Oliver asks Charles if he will wrestle in front of the new duke tomorrow and Charles answers in the affirmative. Charles wants Oliver to warn Orlando, who is supposed to wrestle with him, to quit the match because Orlando is young and inexperienced. Otherwise, it's quite likely that Orlando will be seriously injured or even lose his life. Oliver responds that Orlando is stubborn, ambitious, jealous, villainous and treacherous. He will kill his opponent by poison or whatever means if he is defeated, so Charles should be alert.

Rosalind is dejected thinking of her father. Celia tries to lighten her up and asks her to treat Frederick as her own father. She assures Rosalind that she will return to Rosalind with affection what her father has taken from Rosalind's father by force and that when Frederick dies Rosalind will be his heir. They continue talking about love, fortune and nature when one of Duke Frederick's courtiers, Monsieur Le Beau, enters to report the latest sport news to them. The duke's wrestler Charles has just defeated three brothers who are good-looking and charismatic. They are mortally injured and their old father is lamenting their doom. Le Beau informs the two cousins of the next wrestling match between a young man and Charles, which is scheduled to take place where they stay, so they decide to watch. Frederick enters and tells them that he doesn't want to see the young man become another victim and has tried to dissuade him from participating, but to no avail. He tells his daughter and niece to have a try to stop him. They then summon Orlando and propose that he quit the match, but Orlando responds that if he is beaten to death, he is willing to die in this world, where he has nothing and no friends to grieve over his death. The ladies cannot but encourage him. Unexpectedly, Charles is defeated by the young man and carried off, unable to speak. They all hail for Orlando. Frederick admires the brave young man and asks for his name. When he hears that he is Orlando, the youngest son of Sir Rowland de Boys, Frederick feels disappointed to learn that he is the son of his enemy, though Sir Rowland de Boys was an honourable man. Celia and Rosalind come up to Orlando to congratulate him. Rosalind takes off the chain from her neck and gives it to Orlando. They all exit except Orlando.

Le Beau reenters to tell Orlando to leave the court because the duke is displeased with him. Orlando asks him about the two ladies and learns that Rosalind is Duke Senior's daughter. Le Beau adds that Frederick makes her stay to keep company with Celia. Their love is stronger than the bond of blood. But lately Frederick has harboured malice against Rosalind because the people praise her virtues and pity her for the usurped duke's sake. Soon Frederick declares that Rosalind is banished and must leave his court as soon as possible, or else she will die. When she asks him what crime she has done, he charges her as traitor because she is her father's daughter and he doesn't trust her. Celia tells her father that she wants to be banished too, because she cannot be parted from Rosalind. Because Rosalind is tall, she will disguise herself as a brave young man named Ganymede carrying sword in her belt and spear in her hand. Celia will be disguised as Aliena. She suggests that they go to look for Duke Senior in the Forest of Arden, where he and his attendants enjoy a life of natural beauty and free from worldly things. Celia adds that they will gather heir jewels and wealth and arrange the best time and safest way to go, so that they will not be chased down. They will take Touchstone, the Fool and a comfort during their travels. They will not go to banishment but to liberty. When Frederick finds Celia missing, he sends his men to track down Orlando because he hears from Hisperia, the Princess' gentlewoman that the ladies are in high praise of Orlando and he is certain to be with them.

When Orlando comes home, Adam expresses his love for him as a living memory of his father—noble, virtuous, strong and brave. He then tells him to escape because Oliver has decided to kill him by burning the hut where he sleeps or by other means after he has learnt of his victory. Adam offers Orlando all his savings in his life as a servant in this house—five hundred gold coins. He will follow him as his true and loyal servant. Though he is almost eighty, he is still strong and healthy.

In the Forest of Arden, Touchstone, Ganymede/Rosalind and Aliena/Celia come upon an old and a young shepherd, Corin and Silvius, who are talking about love. Silvius tells Corin that he has never loved as passionately as he now does Phebe. Their conversation reminds Touchstone of his previous love for a woman named Jane Smile and strange things he has done for love. Ganymede also admits that the young shepherd's passion is like hers. Aliena requests them to get food from the two shepherds. Touchstone calls out to them arrogantly, referring to himself as their superior. Ganymede stops him, approaches Corin, and asks politely if they have food to sell them and a place for a rest. Corin replies that he has no food and tells them that he is employed by a miser whose cottage, pastures and flocks are all for sale. Rosalind and Celia like the place and decide to buy it and stay here. In another part of the forest, Duke Senior and his followers are eating their food, when Orlando intrudes and bids them to stop eating, drawing his sword to demand food from them for Adam who is too tired and hungry to walk any further. Unexpectedly, they treat him gently with hospitality and generosity and ask him to join them. Orlando apologizes for his bad manners. He assumes that people living in wilderness all behave rudely. He requests them to wait till he gets his servant Adam here.

Frederick demands Oliver to bring Orlando back to him, otherwise, he will forfeit all his lands and property. Orlando carves his poems on the bark of trees to express his love for Rosalind. Ganymede pulls one down from a tree and reads it. Touchstone improves it by making it rhymed. Aliena enters, reading another love poem written by Orlando, which praises Rosalind for a beautiful face like Helen's, Cleopatra's majesty, Lucretia's modesty and the best parts of Atalanta. She then tells Rosalind that she knows who wrote these poems. Rosalind immediately demands to know its name. At first, Celia teases her. Rosalind says though she is dressed up as a man, she doesn't have a man's patience. Celia then reveals Orlando's name and tells her that she has seen Orlando under a tree, dressed like a hunter. When Ganymede meets Orlando, "he" promises to cure Orlando of his lovesickness. "He" tells Orlando to call "him" Rosalind and treat "him" as Rosalind and expresses his love to "him". In this way, Rosalind enjoys hearing Orlando's confession of love for her. When Orlando doesn't show up, she feels upset. She tells Celia that she has met Duke Senior the day before and she asks him not to talk about parentage but Orlando.

Touchstone falls in love with the goatherd Audrey and wants to marry her. Audrey is pretty but not very intelligent. Touchstone thinks that it is rare for a woman to be both beautiful and honest. And he is not afraid of having horns to grow from his forehead, saying it is more desirable and honourable to have horns than be a bare-browed bachelor. Touchstone wants vicar Oliver Martext to marry them, but Jacques suggests that they get married in a church. Touchstone agrees with him, saying that a poorly managed marriage will give a man a good excuse to step out of the marriage afterwards. Corin enters and invites Rosalind and Celia to watch the passionate Silvius wooing Phebe. Silvius begs Phebe to pity him and not to be so hard-hearted to him. He says her eyes are so cruel that they inflict harm to him. Phebe refutes his statement and tells him not to approach her unless she feels his invisible wounds. Rosalind intervenes and points out that Phebe is plain and arrogant and that her arrogance is fed on Silvius' infatuation with her. Phebe falls for Ganymede.

Orlando plays along the love game with Ganymede as Rosalind, who accuses him of missing their meeting that morning. Rosalind makes fun of Orlando by telling him that if "he" were Rosalind, "he" wouldn't accept his love. Orlando responds that he would die in this case. They have a mock marriage with Celia playing the minister. Orlando leaves for a lunch date with Duke Senior, to Rosalind's disapproval, and he promises to come back by two o'clock. When Rosalind is waiting impatiently for Orlando's return, Silvius enters and delivers a letter from Phebe to Ganymede who reads it and tells them that it is an insulting letter full of rude words, but actually it is a love letter full of Phebe's adoration and praise for Ganymede. Ganymede makes Silvius carry "his" message to Phebe and says "he" will not accept her love unless she accepts Silvius' love.

Oliver shows up. He finds Ganymede and Aliena and gave them a bloody napkin. He tells them that he is sent by Orlando here. Oliver came to the forest searching for Orlando as demanded by Frederick and fell asleep under an old oak tree. Orlando passed by and spotted a man sleeping under the tree. Orlando noticed a snake coiled around Oliver's neck. When Orlando approached, the snake unwound itself and slithered into the bush where a hungry lioness was crouching and waiting to see if Olive was dead or alive. If alive, she would prey on him.

Seeing the lioness, Orlando woke up the man, and recognized him as his vicious brother. Orlando had intended to walk away, but his kindness overwhelmed him. Then he came back and fought the lioness away. During the fight, Orlando was wounded and his blood stained his napkin. Hearing this, Rosalind swoons. Oliver ridicules Ganymede that "he" has the appearance of a man but lacks a man's brave heart. Aliena explains that Ganymede faints at the sight of blood. When Ganymede regains her consciousness, "he" tells Oliver that "his" swoon was fake. Oliver responds that "his" blushing face reveals that it was authentic. Oliver adds that Orlando saved his life and brought him to the noble duke who gave him food and clothing and asked Orlando to take care of him. Orlando then led Oliver into his cave, but his wound was bleeding all the time and he fainted murmuring Rosalind's name. Oliver dressed his wound and nursed him back to life. Then Orlando sent Oliver here to apologize for being unable to keep his promise. Oliver reveals his identity as the malicious brother of Orlando, but adds that he has been reformed by Orlando's kindness and generosity.

Oliver confesses to Orlando that he has fallen in love with the shepherdess Aliena at the first sight. Orlando and Ganymede talk about this when they meet. Orlando says he feels happy for his brother but upset for himself, because his Rosalind is not to be seen. Ganymede promises to bring his Rosalind tomorrow so that they can get married. Phebe comes to complain to Ganymede that "he" has shared her letter with others. Ganymede agrees to marry her unless she retreats. If she does, she should marry Silvius. Duke Senior talks about Ganymede with Orlando and exclaims that how much "he" resembles his Rosalind in appearance and courtly manners. Orlando dissolves his suspicion by telling him that Ganymede has learned "his" courtly manners from an uncle who is familiar with these.

The next day, four couples are married: Celia and Oliver, Rosalind and Orlando, Silvius and Phebe, Touchstone and Audrey. When they see the properly dressed Rosalind, Duke Senior and Orlando are amazed and rejoiced. Phebe immediately withdraws her love on discovering that Ganymede is a woman and keeps her promise to marry the faithful Silvius who has interpreted love as made of sights, tears, duties and service, and declares that his love for Phebe is all of these. To add joy to their happiness, Jaques de Boys enters to bring the good news that Frederick has decided to return the dukedom to Duke Senior with all his previous lands. Frederick is now converted to love of peace and will spend the rest of his life in a monastery after he meets a religious man and falls under his influence.

【剧情介绍】

在法国宫廷里，奥兰多——已故的罗兰·德·博伊斯大人最小的儿子——向他们家的仆人亚当抱怨他的长兄奥利弗。罗兰·德·博伊斯大人生前很受大公爵的恩宠。奥兰多对亚当说，他父亲只给他留下1000克朗，让奥利弗照顾他。可是他感觉哥哥家的牲畜都比他的待遇好。奥利弗剥夺了他受教育的权利，而他的二哥杰奎斯却可以上学。奥兰多决定摆脱这种受奴役的地位。看到奥利弗走过来了，奥兰多让亚当躲在一边看看他哥哥是如何对待他这个弟弟的。奥兰多对哥哥说,虽然哥哥在年龄和地位上比他优越,但是他好歹也和哥哥一样出身贵族。奥利弗听他这样一说,当即打了他一下。奥兰多抓住哥哥进行反抗。奥利弗就喊弟弟是恶棍。奥兰多受到侮辱,抗议道,哥哥称他为恶棍是对他们父亲的侮辱。接着,奥兰多指责哥哥想尽一切办法不让他接受贵族应该接受的教育,哥哥是想让他变成一个平民。他要求哥哥要么给他自由,要么就把他们的父亲分给他的那份遗产给他。奥利弗让他跟亚当一起离开。奥兰多的反抗让奥利弗感到震惊,决定不给他那1000克朗。

奥利弗叫来了他家的另一个仆人丹尼斯,让他去请那个职业摔跤手查尔斯到家里来。他问查尔斯宫廷里最近有些什么消息。查尔斯说,大公爵被他的弟弟,也就是现任的弗雷德里克公爵夺去了爵位后如今还在流放中。大公爵如今以阿尔丁森林为家,和一群忠实的随从在一起。不过,大公爵的女儿罗莎琳德仍然留在王宫,因为弗雷德里克的女儿西莉亚和罗莎琳德形影不离。如果罗莎琳德被流放,西莉亚也会和她一起流放,否则她就会伤心而死,因此罗莎琳德只好留下。弗雷德里克将罗莎琳德视如己出。奥利弗问查尔斯第二天是否在新公爵面前表演摔跤,查尔斯说是的,他让奥利弗奉劝奥兰多放弃和他比赛,因为奥兰多太年轻了,又没经验。如果奥兰多非要摔跤的话,他可能会伤得很严重,甚至丢掉性命。奥利弗回答说,奥兰多就是一个顽固的家伙,他野心勃勃,嫉妒心强,甚至背信弃义。如果他输了,他会毒死他的对手,或者想尽一切办法置他的对手于死地,所以查尔斯自己要小心才是。

罗莎琳德一想到父亲,就不禁沮丧起来。西莉亚努力想让她开心起来,安慰她说,她也可以把弗雷德里克当作自己的父亲。她向罗莎琳德保证,将来她会诚心诚意地把她父亲从大公爵手里夺过来的一切都还给罗莎琳德。如果她父亲死了,罗莎琳德就会成为他的继承人。接着,她们就讨论起了爱情、命运和性格这些话题。这时,弗雷德里克公爵的廷臣勒·博大人进来,向两位公主报告最新的体育消息。公爵的摔跤手查尔斯刚刚打败了一家三兄弟,这三兄弟个个都长得很帅,而且魅力四射。他们的伤是致命的,他们的老父亲为他们不久于人世而伤心欲绝。勒·博大人说,下一场比赛是查尔斯和一个年轻人,比赛地点就是她们现在待的地方,所以她们决定观看这场比赛。弗雷德里克进来对她们说,希望她们能够去劝劝这个年轻人放弃比赛,不要成为下一个悲剧中的人物。他自己已经劝过他了,但是他不听。于是,她们就让人把奥兰多喊过来,劝他不要参加比赛,不料,奥兰多回答道,假如他在比赛中丧命,他无怨无悔,因为他在这世上一无所有,并且也没人会为他的死而悲伤。两位公主只好鼓励了他一番。让所有人感到意外的是,查尔斯居然被打到抬出去了,连话都说不了。他们为奥兰多欢呼喝彩。弗雷德里克非常钦佩这个勇敢的年轻人,于是问他叫什么名字。当得知他叫奥兰多,他的父亲是已故的受人尊敬的罗兰·德·博伊斯大人,也就是他的死对头的时候,弗雷德里克大失所望。西莉亚和罗莎琳德走到奥兰多面前祝贺他。罗莎琳德把她脖子上的项链取下来送给了他。然后,他们都离开了,只有奥兰多一个人还留在那里。

勒·博大人又跑进来,让奥兰多赶紧离开王宫,因为他让公爵很不悦。奥兰多向他打听两位女士,得知罗莎琳德是大公爵的女儿。勒·博还告诉他,弗雷德里克让罗莎琳德留在王宫是为了让她给西莉亚做伴,她们俩的感情比血缘关系还亲。可是,最近弗雷德里克对罗莎琳德心怀怨恨,因为法国人都称赞罗莎琳德的美德,还因为大公爵的遭遇而同情这个不幸的女孩。很快,弗雷德里克宣布罗莎琳德被流放,她必须马上离开王宫,否则就定她死罪。当罗莎琳德问她叔叔自己犯了什么罪的时候,弗雷德里克说她犯了叛国罪,理由是因为她是大公爵的女儿,所以他不信任她。西莉亚对她父亲说,她希望和堂姐一起被放逐,因为她不能和堂姐分开。因为罗莎琳德个子比较高,她打扮成了一个勇敢的男青年,改名叫伽倪墨得,她将手持长矛,腰佩宝剑。西莉亚则化名为阿列娜。西莉亚提议她们去阿尔丁森林寻找大公爵。大公爵和他的随从在那里过着逍遥的日子,他们远离尘世的烦恼,享受着美丽的大自然。西莉亚还说她们将把她们所有值钱的宝贝都打包带上,还要找个最佳时间,选择最好的路线出发,这样就算西莉亚父亲的人追过来,也找不到她们。她们还会带上小丑试金石,这样她们一路上就不会无聊了。她们将要踏上的不是流放之行,而是自由之旅。弗雷德里克发现西莉亚不见了,马上派人去追踪奥兰多,因为西莉亚的女佣希斯皮里娅报告说她曾听到过两位公主对奥兰多赞誉有加,弗雷德里克猜想他们三个人肯定在一起。

奥兰多回到家后,亚当对他说从他的身上可以看到已故的罗兰·德·博伊斯大人的影子——出身高贵、品德高尚、坚强勇敢。接着,他让奥兰多赶快逃走,因为奥利弗得知他打败了查尔斯后正打算杀了他,他准备趁奥兰多睡觉的时候放火烧了他住的那个棚子,或者采取别的手段除掉他。亚当把自己当仆人以来攒下的所有积蓄——500个金币送给奥兰多,他说他会跟着奥兰多,仍然做他最忠实的奴仆,尽管他已经80岁了,但他的身体还硬朗着呢。

在阿尔丁森林,试金石、伽倪墨得/罗莎琳德和阿列娜/西莉亚遇到一老一幼两个牧羊人,分别叫科林和西尔维厄斯,他们正在谈论关于爱情的话题。西尔维厄斯说,科林这辈子绝对没有像他爱菲比那样强烈地爱过一个女人。他们的对话让试金石想起他曾经对一个名叫简·斯迈尔的女人的爱,以及他因为爱她而做过的一些荒唐的事情。伽倪墨得也说西尔维厄斯的爱让她感同身受。阿列娜要求他们俩去找这两个牧羊人要点吃的。于是,试金石趾高气扬地对那两个人牧羊人喊话,伽倪墨得让他打住,然后她走到科林跟前,很有礼貌地问他可不可以卖一点吃的东西给他们,并且给他们提供一个歇脚的地方。科林说他没有吃的,他自己也是受雇于人,而他的雇主是一个吝啬鬼。如今,主人的小屋、牧场、羊群都在出售中。罗莎琳德和西莉亚很喜欢这个地方,决定买下来,在这里安家。在森林的另一处,大公爵和他的随从正在享用他们的美食,此时奥兰多闯了进来,拔出剑来命令他们不许吃,要他们给他一些吃的,因为亚当这时又累又饿,走不动了。没想到这群人很温和,也很热情,大方地接待他,还邀请奥兰多坐下来和他们一起吃。奥兰多为他的粗鲁的行为致歉。他还以为生活在这种荒郊野外的人行为举止都很粗鲁呢。他让他们等他一会儿,他去把亚当叫过来。

弗雷德里克命令奥利弗把奥兰多交出来,否则他的一切房产和钱财都将被没收。奥兰多把情诗刻在树皮上,抒发他对罗莎琳德的爱。伽倪墨得从树上剥下一首诗来读。试金石改了一下这首诗,让它读起来更押韵。阿列娜进来了,口里读着另一首奥兰多的情诗,这首诗赞扬罗莎琳德有着海伦绝世的美貌、克利欧佩特拉的端庄、卢克丽霞的矜持以及阿塔兰特的绝妙身材。接着,西莉亚告诉罗莎琳德她知道这些情诗的作者是谁。罗莎琳德立刻追问她到底是谁写的。起先,西莉亚一直逗她,罗莎琳德说虽然她的外表是男人的装扮,但她可不像男人那样有耐心。西莉亚只好告诉她这些诗是奥兰多写的,她还看到奥兰多以一身猎人的装扮站在一棵树下。伽倪墨得遇到奥兰多的时候,自称可以治好奥兰多的相思病。"他"让奥兰多叫自己罗莎琳德,并把自己当作罗莎琳德,向"他"倾诉他对罗莎琳德的爱。这样一来,罗莎琳德就可以享受奥兰多对她的爱情表白。如果奥兰多没有出现在她面前,她就会感到难过。她告诉西莉亚,她前一天碰到过自己的父亲大公爵,但她让他不要聊为人父母的话题,而是让他聊聊奥兰多这个人。

试金石爱上了牧羊女奥黛丽,并且想娶她。奥黛丽很漂亮,但是不怎么聪明。试金石认为,在世上很难找到一个又漂亮又忠诚的女子。不过,他认为额头上长角的男人总比额头上光光的单身汉强点。试金石想要奥利弗·马特克斯牧师为他和奥黛丽主持婚礼,可杰奎斯建议他还是去教堂结婚比较好。试金石觉得这个提议也好,随随便便结婚会让男人更有借口离婚。科林来邀请罗莎琳德和西莉亚去看西尔维厄斯向菲比求爱。西尔维厄斯请求菲比可怜可怜他,不要那么狠心肠。他说菲比眼露凶光,让他感到受伤。菲比反驳他,让他不要靠近她,除非他的伤痛实实在在看得见。伽倪墨得插嘴说,菲比相貌平平,却很傲慢,她说正是西尔维厄斯对她的爱恋助长了她的嚣张气焰。菲比立刻爱上了伽倪墨得。

奥兰多继续和伽倪墨得扮演的罗莎琳德玩爱情游戏。罗莎琳德责备奥兰多那天上午怎么爽约。她逗奥兰多说,如果她真的是罗莎琳德,她就不会接受他的爱。奥兰多说,假如罗莎琳德拒绝了他的爱,他会去死的。他们让西莉亚假扮牧师为他们主持婚礼。让罗莎琳德感到不快的是,奥兰多要赴大公爵的午餐之约,不过他说两点钟之前一定回来。当她焦急地等待奥兰多回来之际,西尔维厄斯来了,他给罗莎琳德带来了菲比写给伽倪墨得的信。罗莎琳德看罢信,故意说这封信满纸都是粗鲁的语言,太伤人了。其实,这是一封菲比表达对伽倪墨得的崇拜和赞美的情书。罗莎琳德,此时在大家眼里依然是伽倪墨得,让西尔维厄斯转告菲比,说"他"不会接受菲比对"他"的爱,除非菲比接受西尔维厄斯对她的爱。

这时,奥利弗来了。他找到伽倪墨得和阿列娜,递给她们一块带血的手巾,还告诉他们是奥兰多派他来找她们的。奥利弗按照弗雷德里克的命令,到森林里来找奥兰多,中途他在一棵古老的橡树下睡着了。奥兰多正好从这个地方经过,看到了正在树下睡觉的人。奥兰多发现有条蛇正盘在这个人的脖子上,奥兰多走近后,这条蛇便松开奥利弗溜走了,钻进了一旁的灌木丛,正好灌木丛里蜷伏着一只饥饿的母狮,她在等待确认奥利弗是死是活,如果他活着,母狮就能饱餐一顿。看到母狮,奥兰多赶忙叫醒奥利弗,认出了他正是自己那个歹毒的哥哥。他本来想一走了之,但是他的善良让他回过头来帮助奥利弗赶走了母狮。在和母狮搏斗的过程中,奥兰多受了伤,鲜血染红了他的手巾。听到这里,罗莎琳德当即晕过去了。奥利弗嘲笑罗莎琳德空有男人的外表,却没有属于男人的一颗勇敢之心。阿列娜赶紧掩饰说,伽倪墨得是晕血。当伽倪墨得恢复意识后,他对奥利弗说刚才他是假装晕过去的。奥利弗却说他的脸都红了,这可不像是装出来的。奥利弗又说奥兰多救了他的命,把他带到高贵的大公爵面前,大公爵给了奥利弗食物和衣服,还让奥兰多照顾他。奥兰多把奥利弗带到他住的山洞里,这才发现奥兰多的伤口一直在流血,后来奥兰多就晕过去了,嘴里还念叨着罗莎琳德的名字。奥利弗帮他包扎好伤口,照顾他直到他苏醒过来。奥兰多于是请奥利弗帮他找到伽倪墨得,并且替他向伽倪墨得道歉,因为他不能前来赴约。奥利弗向伽倪墨得和阿列娜表明了他的身份,他就是奥兰多那个恶毒的哥哥,不过他说奥兰多的善良和大度让他改邪归正了。

奥利弗对奥兰多说他对牧羊女阿列娜一见钟情。奥兰多和伽倪墨得再次见面后谈论起了这件事。奥兰多说,他为哥哥找到爱情而高兴,但是自己却因见不到心爱的罗莎琳德而难过。伽倪墨得答应他明天一定帮他把罗莎琳德带到他面前和他结婚。菲比来找伽倪墨得抱怨,说伽倪墨得不该把她写的信给别人看。于是,伽倪墨得答应和她结婚,只要她不反悔。如果她反悔的话,她就要嫁给西尔维厄斯。大公爵和奥兰多谈到伽倪墨得,他们惊叹伽倪墨得和罗莎琳德长得太像了,连他们表现出的宫廷礼仪都如出一辙。奥兰多打消了公爵的疑虑,他说伽倪墨得是向一个熟悉宫廷礼仪的叔叔学的这些。

第二天,四对新人喜结连理:西莉亚和奥利弗,罗莎琳德和奥兰多,西尔维厄斯和菲比,试金石和奥黛丽。当看到女装打扮的罗莎琳德,大公爵和奥兰多又惊又喜。菲比发现伽倪墨得是女儿身,立刻收回了对她的爱,并且遵守承诺,嫁给了痴情的西尔维厄斯。西尔维厄斯说爱情里有叹息,有眼泪,还有责任和照顾,他对菲比的爱包含了这一切。喜上加喜的是,杰奎斯·德·博伊斯跑来告诉了他们一个好消息:弗雷德里克决定把爵位连同他夺取的土地都还给大公爵,因为他遇到一个道人,在他的熏陶下皈依了宗教,将在修道院度过他的余生。

5 Famous quotes

【Quote 1】

Duke Senior

Now, my co-mates and brothers in exile,

hath not old custom made this life more sweet than that of painted pomp?

Are not these woods more free from peril than the envious court?

Here feel we not the penalty of Adam, the seasons' difference,

as the icy fang and churlish chiding of the winter's wind,

which, when it bites and blows upon my body,

even till I shrink with cold, I smile and say,

"This is no flattery.

These are counselors that feelingly persuade me what I am."

Sweet are the uses of adversity,

which, like the toad, ugly and venomous,

wears yet a precious jewel in his head.

And this our life, exempt from public haunt,

finds tongues in trees, books in the running brooks,

sermons in stones, and good in everything. [4]

(Act 2, Scene 1)

[**Duke Senior (played by Tony Church) with his followers living in the Forest of Arden in a 1978 film directed by Basil Coleman.**]

◆ Paraphrase

Now, my companions and brothers in exile,
hasn't our long experience shown this simple life
to be sweeter than one of superficial luxury?
Aren't these woods less dangerous than
the jealousies and treachery of the court?
Out here we don't feel the penalty resulting from Adam's sin
—the changing seasons.
When the icy fangs of the scolding winter wind
bite and blow upon my body
—even though I shiver with cold
—I smile and say to myself:
"The wind isn't flattering me.
It is like a counselor who makes me feel what I truly am."
Adversity has sweet benefits, just like the ugly,
venomous toad who wears a precious jewel in his forehead. ①
And in this new life, far away from society,
we can hear the voices of the trees,
read books in the running brooks, hear sermons in the stones,
and find the good in everything. [5]

---

① Folklore held that poisonous toads grew jewels in their foreheads that could be used as medicine.

◇ 原文译文

我的流放中的同伴们,我们不是已经习惯了这种生活,觉得它比矫饰的浮华有趣得多吗?这些树林不比猜忌的朝廷更为安全吗?我们在这儿所感觉到的,只是时间的改变,那是上帝对于亚当的惩罚。冬天的寒风挥舞着冰雪的爪牙,发出暴虐的呼啸,即使当它鞭笞着我的身体,使我冷得发抖的时候,我也会微笑着说:"这不是谄媚啊;它们就像忠臣一样,循循善诱地提醒我所处的境况。"逆境也有它的好处,就像丑陋而有毒的蟾蜍,它的头上却顶着一颗珍贵的宝石。我们的这种生活,虽然远离尘嚣,却可以听树木的谈话,溪中的流水便是大好的文章,一石之微,也暗寓着教训!我们在每一件事物中都可以找到些益处来,我不愿改变这种生活。[6]

【Quote 2】

Silvius

If thou rememb'rest not the slightest folly

that ever love did make thee run into,

thou hast not loved.

Or if thou hast not sat as I do now,

wearying thy hearer in thy mistress' praise,

thou hast not loved.

Or if thou hast not broke from company abruptly,

as my passion now makes me,

thou hast not loved.[7]

(Act 2, Scene 4)

[Silvius (on the left, played by Maynard Williams) talking to Corin (on the right, played by David Lloyd Meredith) about love in a 1978 film directed by Basil Coleman.]

◆ Paraphrase

Oh, then you never loved as fully as I do.
If you cannot remember even the smallest foolish act
that love drove you to,
then you have not loved.
Or if you have not sat as I do now,
wearying your listener with the praise of your beloved,
then you have not loved.
Or if you have not broken away from all company,
as my passion now leads me to do,
then you have not loved. [8]

◆ 原文译文

假如你记不得你为了爱情而做出来的一件最琐碎的傻事,你就不算真的恋爱过。假如你不曾像我现在这样坐着絮絮叨叨讲你的姑娘的好处,使听的人不耐烦,你就不算真的恋爱过。假如你不曾突然离开你的同伴,像我的热情现在驱使着我一样,你也不算真的恋爱过。[9]

【Quote 3】

Touchstone

And I mine. I remember when I was in love I broke my Sword upon
a stone and bid him take that for coming a-night to Jane Smile.
And I remember the kissing of her batler,
and the cow's dugs that her pretty chapped hands had milked.
And I remember the wooing of a peascod instead of her,
from whom I took two cods and, giving her them again,
said with weeping tears, "Wear these for my sake."①
We that are true lovers run into strange capers.
But as all is mortal in nature,
so is all nature in love mortal in folly. [10]
(Act 2, Scene 4)

---

① According to folklores, by giving a beloved a peapod, or "cod", one could win his/her love.

[Touchstone (played by James Bolam) talking to Rosalind who is disguised as Ganymede (played by Helen Mirren) about his love experience in a 1978 film directed by Basil Coleman.]

◆ Paraphrase

I remember when I was in love,
I broke my sword upon a stone and told the sword
to "take that" for coming at night to visit Jane Smile.
And I remember kissing Jane's washing stick,
and the cow's udders that her pretty chapped hands had milked.
And I remember wooing a peapod,
and taking two peas from it and giving them to her,
and tearfully asking her to "wear these for my sake".
We who are true lovers do many strange things.
But just as everything in nature is mortal,
so all lovers show their humanity through their foolishness.[11]

◆ 原文译文

我记得我在恋爱的时候,曾经把一柄剑摔断在石头上,叫夜里来和琴·史美尔幽会的那个家伙留心着我,我记得我曾经吻过她的洗衣棒,也吻过被她那双皲裂的手挤过的母牛乳头;我记得我曾经把一个豌豆荚当作她而向她求婚,我剥出了两颗豆子,又把它们放进去,边流泪边说:"为了我,请您留着做个纪念吧。"我们这种多情的人都会做出一些古怪事儿来,但是我们既然都是凡人,一着了情魔,是免不得要发痴劲的。[12]

【Quote 4】

Amiens
Under the greenwood tree who loves to lie with me
and turn his merry note unto the sweet bird's throat,
come hither, come hither, come hither.
Here shall he see no enemy but winter and rough weather. [13]
(Act 2, Scene 5)

[**Amiens** (sitting in the middle, played by Tony Church) with his followers living in the Forest of Arden in a 1978 film directed by Basil Coleman.]

◆ Paraphrase

Who wants to lie with me, under the greenwood tree,
and tune his merry notes to the sweet bird's singing,
come here, come here, come here.
Here he will see no enemy but winter and rough weather. [14]

◆ 原文译文

绿树高张翠幕,谁来偕我偃卧,翻将欢乐心声,学唱枝头鸟鸣:盍来此? 盍来此? 盍来此? 目之所接,精神契一,唯忧雨雪之将至。[15]

【Quote 5】

Jacques
All the world's a stage,

and all the men and women merely players.
They have their exits and their entrances,
and one man in his time plays many parts,
his acts being seven ages.
At first the infant, mewling and puking in the nurse's arms.
then the whining schoolboy with his satchel and shining morning face,
creeping like snail unwillingly to school.
And then the lover, sighing like furnace,
with a woeful ballad made to his mistress' eyebrow.
Then a soldier, full of strange oaths and bearded like the pard,
jealous in honor, sudden and quick in quarrel,
seeking the bubble reputation even in the cannon's mouth.
And then the justice, in fair round belly with good capon lined,
with eyes severe and beard of formal cut,
full of wise saws and modern instances;
and so he plays his part.
The sixth age shifts into the lean and slippered pantaloon
with spectacles on nose and pouch on side,
his youthful hose, well saved,
a world too wide for his shrunk shank,
and his big manly voice, turning again toward childish treble,
Pipes and whistles in his sound.
Last scene of all,
that ends this strange eventful history,

[Jacques (the one facing the audience, played by Richard Pasco) talking about one's life in the Forest of Arden in a 1978 film directed by Basil Coleman.]

is second childishness and mere oblivion,
sans teeth, sans eyes, sans taste, sans everything. [16]
(Act 2, Scene 7)

◆ Paraphrase

The whole world is a stage,
and all the men and women merely actors.
They have their exits and their entrances,
and in his lifetime one man plays many parts,
with the ages of his life in seven acts.
In the first act he is the infant, crying and puking in the nurse's arms.
Then he plays the whining schoolboy
with his book bag and bright youthful face,
creeping like a snail unwillingly to school.
And then he is the lover, sighing like a furnace and
writing sad songs about his beloved's eyebrows.
Then he is a soldier,
full of foreign curses and bearded like a leopard,
quick to fight and jealously responding to any slight to his honor,
Seeking fleeting fame and reputation even if
it means putting himself in front of the cannon's mouth.
Then he plays the judge,
with a nice round belly lined with the bribes he's taken,
with stern eyes and a beard cut to a respectable shape,
full of wise sayings and everyday examples of his points;
and in this way he plays his part.
In the sixth act he shifts into the skinny, ridiculous old man,
wearing slippers on his feet, glasses on his nose,
and a money bag at his side.
The stockings he has saved since his youth are
now way too wide for his shriveled legs,
and his big manly voice becomes like a child's voice,
squeaking and whistling.
In the last scene of all, which ends this strange, eventful story,
the man enters his second childhood and goes mentally blank
—without teeth, without eyes, without taste, without everything. [17]

◇ 原文译文

全世界是一个舞台,所有的男男女女不过是一些演员;他们都有下场的时候,也都有上场的时候。一个人在一生中扮演着好几个角色,他的表演可以分为七个时期。最初是婴孩,在保姆的怀中啼哭呕吐。然后是背着书包、满脸红光的学童,像蜗牛一样慢腾腾地拖着脚步,不情愿地呜咽着上学堂。然后是情人,像炉灶一样叹着气,写了一首悲哀的诗歌,咏着他恋人的眉毛。然后是一个军人,满口发着古怪的誓,胡须长得像豹子一样,爱惜名誉,动不动就要打架,在炮口上寻求着泡沫一样的荣名。然后是法官!胖胖圆圆的肚子塞满了阉鸡,凛然的眼光,整洁的胡须,满嘴都是格言和老生常谈;他这样扮了他的一个角色。在第六个时期,他变成了精瘦的趿着拖鞋的龙钟老叟,鼻子上架着眼镜,腰边悬着钱袋;他那年轻时候节省下来的长袜子套在他皱瘪的小腿上,显得异常宽大,他那明朗的男子的口音又变成了孩子似的尖声,像是吹着风笛和哨子。终结这段古怪的多事的历史的最后一场,是孩提时代的再现,全然的遗忘,没有牙齿,没有眼睛,没有口味,没有一切。[18]

【Quote 6】

Rosalind

Love is merely a madness and, I tell you,
deserves as well a dark house and a whip① as madmen do,
and the reason why they are not so punished and cured is that
the lunacy is so ordinary that the whippers are in love, too.
Yet I profess curing it by counsel.[19]
(Act 3, Scene 2)

[**Rosalind** promising to cure Orlando (on the left, played by Brian Stirner) of his lovesickness in a 1978 film directed by Basil Coleman. The one on the right is Celia (played by Angharad Rees).]

---

① In Shakespeare's time, darkness and the whip were often used as a remedy for insanity.

Unit 9 As You Like It

◇ Paraphrase

Love is merely insanity, I tell you.
And lovers deserve the madhouse just like insane people do.
The only reason they don't get the punishment and cure of the madhouse
is that this form of insanity is so common that all the doctors have it too.
But I claim that it can be cured with counseling. [20]

◇ 原文译文

爱情不过是一种疯狂;我对你说,对待痴迷于爱情的人,是应该像对待一个疯子一样,把他关在黑屋子里用鞭子抽一顿。那么为什么他们不用这种处罚的方法来医治爱情呢?因为那种疯病是极其平常的,就是拿鞭子的人也在恋爱哩。可是我有医治它的法子。[21]

【Quote 7】

Phebe
Dead shepherd, now I find thy saw of might:
"Who ever loved that loved not at first sight?"[22]
(Act 3, Scene 5)

[Phebe (played by Victoria Plucknett) falling in love with Ganymede (Rosalind in disguise) in a 1978 film directed by Basil Coleman.]

◇ Paraphrase

Dead shepherd①,

---

① This refers to Christopher Marlowe, a contemporary playwright of Shakespeare's who had been killed before Shakespeare wrote this play. Marlowe's most famous play is *Doctor Faustus*.

now I understand the power of what you said earlier:
"You only truly love when you fall in love at first sight."[23]

◇ 原文译文

过去的诗人,现在我明白了你的话果然是真:"一见钟情的爱才真切。"[24]

【Quote 8】

Rosalind

For your brother and my sister

no sooner met but they looked,

no sooner looked but they loved,

no sooner loved but they sighed,

no sooner sighed but they asked one another the reason,

no sooner knew the reason but they sought the remedy;

and in these degrees have they made a pair of stairs to marriage,

which they will climb incontinent,

or else be incontinent before marriage.

They are in the very wrath of love, and they will together.

Clubs cannot part them.[25]

(Act 5, Scene 2)

(Rosalind talking to Orlando about love between Oliver and Celia in a 1978 film directed by Basil Coleman.)

◇ Paraphrase

Your brother and my sister had no sooner met

than they looked closely at each other;

had no sooner looked than they fell in love;
had no sooner loved than they sighed;
no sooner sighed than they asked each other why they sighed;
and no sooner learned the reason than they
looked for the solution to their mutual "problem".
And in this way the degrees of their courtship
made a flight of stairs leading up towards marriage.
They'll climb those stairs immediately,
or else they'll sleep together before they get married.
They are in the heat of passion, and must be together.
You couldn't beat them apart with a club. [26]

◆ 原文译文

令兄和舍妹刚见了面,便对上眼了;一瞧便相爱了;一相爱便叹气了;一叹气便彼此问为的是什么;一知道了为的是什么,便要想补救的办法;这样一步一步地走到了结婚的阶段,不久他们便要喜结连理了,否则他们等不到结婚便要放肆起来。他们简直爱得慌了,一定要在一块儿;棒打鸳鸯也散不了。[27]

6　Questions for discussion

(1) Rosalind falls in love with Orlando upon first seeing him. Likewise, Oliver falls in love with Celia when they first meet. Phebe cites Christopher Marlowe's words: "You only truly love when you fall in love at first sight." Comment on "love at first sight".

(2) Does Duke Senior enjoy his banished life? How do you know? Which do you prefer, rural or urban life?

(3) Why does Rosalind disguise as Ganymede? What related information do you know about this name?

(4) Which character is more admirable, Celia or Rosalind? Why?

(5) Paraphrase and comment on Touchstone's words: "As a walled town is more worthier than a village, so is the forehead of a married man more honorable than the bare brow of a bachelor."

(6) Do you think Frederick's conversion convincible? Why or why not?

7　References

[1][2][3]　As You Like It Study Guide[EB/OL]. https://www.litcharts.com/lit/as-you-like-it.

［4］［7］［10］［13］［16］［19］［22］［25］　Shakespeare W. As You Like It［M］. New York：Simon & Schuster, 2004.

［5］［8］［11］［14］［17］［20］［23］［26］　As You Like It：Shakescleare Translation［EB/OL］. https：//www. litcharts. com/shakescleare/shakespeare-translations/as-you-like-it.

［6］［9］［12］［15］［18］［21］［24］［27］　威廉·莎士比亚. 皆大欢喜［M］. 方平,译. 上海：上海译文出版社,2016.

Unit 10

Much Ado about Nothing

1 Characters

Hero(希罗): Leonato's daughter, Beatrice's cousin.
Claudio(克劳迪奥): A friend of Benedick and a young Florentine soldier fighting for Don Pedro.
Benedick(班尼迪克): A soldier and Lord of Padua who is tricked into falling in love with Beatrice.
Beatrice(碧翠丝): Hero's cousin and Leonato's niece.
Don① Pedro(佩德罗阁下): The Prince of Aragon②.
Don John(约翰阁下): The bastard brother of Don Pedro.
Leonato(里昂纳多): Hero's father and Governor of Messina③.
Antonio(安东尼奥): Leonato's brother.
Balthazar(巴尔萨泽): A servant of Don Pedro's.
Borachio(博拉奇欧): A minion of Don John's.
Conrade(康拉德): A minion of Don John's.
Dogberry(多格博利): A constable of Messina.
Verges(维吉斯): A headborough of Messina.
Friar Francis(弗朗西斯牧师): A vicar who conducts the two weddings.
Margaret(玛格丽特): Hero's handmaid.
Ursula(厄秀拉): Another handmaid of Hero's.

2 Background

Much Ado about Nothing probably takes place during the 16th century Italian Wars (1494-

---

① "Don" in both Spanish and Italian is tantamount to "Sir" or "Lord" in English.
② Aragon was a kingdom in Spain.
③ Messina is a busy port and trading center near the mainland of Italy. Messina is a fertile mountainous province whose capital is also named Messina.

1559), which involved France, the Holy Roman Empire, the Spanish Kingdom of Aragon, England, Scotland, the Ottomans, the Swiss and various Italian states. This is why the characters in the play are of diverse origins: Don Pedro and Don John come from Aragon, Benedick comes from Padua, and Claudio comes from Florence. For some time during the Italian Wars, Naples and Sicily (where Messina is located) were controlled by Aragon. [1]

One source for this play was one of the tales written by Italian writer Matteo Bandello (1485-1561). Another source was an Italian epic poem entitled *Orlando Furioso*, which was published in 1516 by Lodovico Ariosto (1474-1535). This poem was translated into English by Sir John Harington and published in 1591. Shakespeare may also have based this play on *Il Libro del Cortegiano* (*The Book of the Courtier*), published in Italian in 1528 by Baldassare Castiglione (1478-1529). It was translated into English by Sir Thomas Hoby (1530-1566) and published in 1561. [2]

3 Settings

The plot takes place in the province of Messina in northeastern Sicily, Italy in the 16th Century. [3]

4 Synopsis

In Messina, Governor Leonato is waiting for the arrival of Don Pedro, the Spanish Prince of Aragon, Count Claudio, a soldier from Florence, and Benedick, a noble young man from Padua. They have won a battle during the Italian Wars without losing a single man of high rank or reputation. The messenger reports that Claudio fought very bravely like a lion unexpectedly. Beatrice, Leonato's niece, inquires the messenger about Benedick, and he tells her that Benedick is brave too, and witty and virtuous as well. Beatrice responds that Benedick is a dummy with a good stomach for eating. After the guests have entered and exchanged greetings, Benedick and Beatrice start another battle—a battle of wits—as Leonato has called. When Benedick says that he is not a hard-hearted man, but he doesn't love any woman, Beatrice immediately scoffs at him that it is a blessing for women, otherwise, they will be in trouble. She adds that she doesn't love a man either. Benedick calls her Lady Scorn and responds that since she doesn't love a man, he will escape from the misfortune of having his face being scratched up. Beatrice retorts that if he were the man, even scratching wouldn't make his face look worse.

Claudio tells Benedick that he has fallen in love with Hero, Leonato's daughter. Benedick doesn't think much of Hero, who is short and too ordinary and not as pretty as Beatrice. When Claudio says that he is serious and wants to marry her if Hero consents, Benedick regrets that now it is rare to find a man who maintains a bachelor, and that they are not fearful of horns sprouting from their foreheads. When Don Pedro learns that Claudio is in love with Hero, he approves that Hero is a worthy woman. Seeing Benedick always dissenting regarding love, Don Pedro says he will live to see that Benedick will turn pale with lovesickness. Benedick responds that he might turn pale with anger, illness or hunger, but not with love. After Benedick exits, Claudio confesses to Don Pedro that he liked Hero before he left for the battle and now he is lovesick. Don Pedro comforts him that he will discuss this with Leonato and Hero to make Hero his wife.

Don John, Don Pedro's bastard brother who hates Don Pedro, learns that he will propose on behalf of Claudio and determines to ruin the marriage proposal. He conspires with his minions, Conrad and Borachio, to botch up the coming dinner or the masquerade afterwards. Leonato, Antonio (Leonato's brother), Hero, Beatrice, Ursula (Hero's handmaid), and Margaret (another handmaid of Hero) enter. They discuss the two brothers, Don Pedro and Don John, who didn't show up at dinner. Hero and Beatrice comment that Don John always looks sour and sad. Beatrice remarks that Don John is like a statue who doesn't talk, while Don Pedro is like a spoiled child babbling on. She adds that a man between them will be perfect. For such a man who has handsome legs and feet and a full purse, he will win all women in the world once he has won her goodwill. Leonato warns his niece that if she keeps such a sharp tongue, no man would like to marry her. She responds that she doesn't want to get married because she doesn't like beard. Her uncle responds that she can find a beardless man and she remarks that such a man is not manly. Then they talk about the supposed courtship of Claudio. Antonio hopes that Hero will obey her father. Beatrice interjects that if he finds a handsome husband for her, her cousin should curtsy and say "father, as it pleases you"; otherwise, she might say, "father, as it pleases me".

When the dance begins, Don Pedro hides his face under a mask and pass for Claudio to woo Hero on Claudio's behalf and wins Hero and Leonato's approval. Don Pedro's servant Balthazar woos Margaret but is rejected. Don John approaches Claudio, pretending to take him as Benedick and tells him that his brother is in love with Hero and making a marriage proposal. He hopes that "Benedick" would persuade his brother to change his mind because Hero's social position doesn't match Don Pedro's. Claudio feels insulted and betrayed by Don Pedro and regrets having confiding in him to court Hero. When Beatrice comes to tell Claudio that Don Pedro has proposed for him, he disbelieves it. But when Don Pedro declares the news that Claudio and Hero will get married, he is too excited to speak. Don Pedro also hatches out a plan for them to bring Benedick and Beatrice together and to prove that they are better love gods than Cupid. Don John plots with Borachio to ruin Claudio's imminent marriage. They will make them believe that Hero is a promiscuous woman that doesn't deserve Claudio.

Alone in the garden, Benedick complains that Claudio has forsaken his bachelorship to get married. He then wonders if he should change his mind concerning love and marriage. He makes a list of personal qualities that a woman should possess to become his wife. Seeing Don Pedro, Claudio, and Leonato entering, Benedick hides himself from them. Knowing well that Benedick is listening to them from behind the tree, they discuss the beautiful Beatrice's passionate and hopeless love for Benedick and sympathize with her in such a desperate situation because Benedick will spurn her love and scorn it as a joke. They criticize Benedick for not deserving Beatrice's love. Judging from their serious attitudes and apparent earnestness, Benedick concludes that it is true that Beatrice has fallen in love with him. He relents and decides to requite Beatrice's love.

When Beatrice is sent to invite Benedick for dinner, he replies with courtesy and friendliness and addresses her "fair Beatrice". Beatrice feels weird at his abrupt change. Thinking that he is not in the mood for another war of wits, she departs rudely. But Benedick begins to interpret her words from the implied meanings of love rather than their literal meanings of sarcasm, thus believing that she is really in love with him. He decides to pity and love her, or else he will be a hard-hearted villain.

As another part of Don Pedro's plan proceeds, Hero, Margaret, and Ursula meet and talk about how to make Beatrice overhear their discussion about Benedick's love for Beatrice. Margaret whispers to Beatrice that she has heard Hero and Ursula gossiping about her in the garden. As expected, Beatrice falls into their trap. She enters the garden and creeps up on Hero and Ursula and eavesdrops their argument about Benedick's love for Beatrice. Hero thinks Benedick had better keep his love to himself, or else Beatrice will "mock him to death". After they exit, Beatrice believes what they have said and decides to marry Benedick.

When Don Pedro, Leonato and Claudio are chatting, Benedick comes up. His face is pale with toothache. They notice that he has shaved his beard and changed his dressing and tease him that he must have fallen in love. At this time, Don John enters to tell Claudio and Don Pedro that Hero is an unfaithful woman who has another man. He invites them to watch her tryst with that man from her window that evening. Don Pedro declares that he will accuse Hero of disloyalty publicly if this is true. On the previous night before the wedding, Dogberry, the magistrate of Messina warns the watchmen to be cautious and keep watch over Leonato's house. When they are sheltering under a roof from the rain, they overhear Conrade and Borachio talking. Borachio boasts that Don John has offered him 1,000 ducats for arranging Don Pedro and Claudio into believing that Hero is promiscuous. Borachio then changes the topic to fashion and refers it to a deformed thief. The night watchmen misunderstand that they are talking about a thief named deformed and arrested them.

Hero is dressed up for the wedding when Beatrice enters. She tells her and the two handmaids that she has caught a cold. They tease her that she has fallen in love. Dogberry comes to Leonato's house to inform him of the two suspicious men they have caught, but he has a problem to get to the point by using fancy words incorrectly which are confusing. Leonato is impatient to go on listening to him. He departs to prepare for the wedding. As the wedding ceremony progresses in the church, Friar Francis asks Claudio and Hero if either of them has known any secret impediment that stops them from being conjoined, Hero answers that there is none. Leonato answers the same on behalf of Claudio. To Leonato's dismay, Claudio gives Hero back to him and declares that he cannot marry his daughter because she has cheated on him. He calls her "rotten orange" and wanton, accuses her of a deceiving virginal appearance, and claims that her blush indicates her guilt. Don Pedro and Don John confirm Claudio's accusation. Don Pedro refers Hero to a prostitute and proves that they have witnessed her tryst at her window with a villain who has confessed to have had a thousand such encounters. Claudio resumes his criticism of Hero. Leonato feels so ashamed that he asks if anyone has a dagger for him to kill himself. Hero collapses with a swoon. Don Pedro, Don John and Claudio exit.

When Hero comes to, Leonato feels ashamed for her and wishes that she were dead. Beatrice weeps for her cousin and is certain she is slandered. Friar Francis also believes that her blush indicates her innocence. But Leonato decides that it's impossible for the two princes to provide perjury and for Claudio to give false accusations. Benedick supposes that Prince Pedro and Claudio are honourable men and if one of them is a culprit, it must be the wicked-natured Don John. Friar Francis suggests that they hold a mock funeral for Hero to make Claudio remorse for his rashness and cruelty while they will investigate the whole case secretly. Benedick swears to carry out this plan secretly and honourably.

When they are all gone except Beatrice and Benedick, they swear their love for each other. Benedick pledges to do anything for Beatrice, who then asks Benedick to kill Claudio who has wronged, slandered and ruined her cousin. When Benedick refuses to do so, Beatrice tells him that she is killed by his refusal and is about to leave. Benedick stops her and assures her that he will challenge Claudio.

Dogberry, Verges, the night watch, and the Sexton interrogate the two suspects, Conrade and Borachio, whose conspiracy with Don John to frame Hero for infidelity is revealed. They set out for Leonato's house to report the result. Leonato is impatient to listen to Antonio's advice, but he begins to believe his daughter has been wronged. Supposing that Hero is dead, Antonio is about to duel with Claudio, but is stopped by Leonato. Don Pedro and Claudio are dispirited. They hope that Benedick will lighten them up. To their shock, Benedick challenges them to a fight instead of comforting them. They think he is crazy out of love for Beatrice. Benedick tells them that Don John has fled the city, indicating that he must have done something wrong. Dogberry and watchmen bring in the two culprits. Borachio is forced to admit their conspiracy to bring disrepute to Hero and ruin Claudio's marriage. Not until then do Don Pedro and Claudio regret for what they have done. Leonato agrees to forgive Claudio if he writes an epitaph on Hero's tomb to clear her reputation. After he has done this, Leonato will marry him to his niece. Claudio accepts. Benedick asks Leonato for the permission to marry Beatrice and he is granted.

Back from the visit to Hero's grave, Claudio and Don Pedro head for the church where Claudio's second marriage is to be proceeded with Benedick's. When they all arrive, two masked brides are brought forward to the bridegrooms. When Claudio unmasks Leonato's niece, he is overjoyed to see Hero instead. It is not until their wedding that Beatrice and Benedick discover they are deceived by Leonato and their friends into believing that each is in love with the other. When they deny their love, Claudio presents Benedick's letter about love for Beatrice and Hero shows Beatrice's for Benedick. Benedick suggests a dance before the wedding. The play ends with a message that Don John is captured and will be delivered back for punishment.

【剧情介绍】

墨西拿总督里昂纳多正在等待作战归来的西班牙阿拉贡王子佩德罗阁下、来自佛罗伦萨的贵族克劳迪奥，以及来自帕多瓦的年轻贵族班尼迪克。他们刚从意大利战争的一场战役中凯旋，在这场战争中没有一名高官伤亡。信使称克劳迪奥作战时如同狮子一般骁勇，这一点很出人意料。里昂纳多的侄女碧翠丝向信使打听班尼迪克的情况。信使告诉她，班尼迪克非常勇敢，品德高尚，并且才华横溢。碧翠丝却说班尼迪克就是个蠢货，还是个酒囊饭袋。客人到了，一番寒暄过后，班尼迪克和碧翠丝就开始唇枪舌剑地争辩起来，里昂纳多称这是智慧之战。班尼迪克说，他不能算是一个硬心肠的人，可就是对女人爱不起来。碧翠丝马上说，这对女人来说是好事，不然她们可就麻烦了。她还说自己也对男人爱不起来。班尼迪克称碧翠丝为"嘲讽达人"，并回击说她不爱男人最好，不然哪个男人被她爱上，他的脸可就要遭殃了，一定会留下她的抓痕。碧翠丝说，如果班尼迪克是那个男人，即便他的脸被她抓破，也不会比现在更难看。

克劳迪奥告诉班尼迪克，他爱上了里昂纳多的女儿希罗。班尼迪克觉得希罗相貌平平，还没有碧翠丝漂亮，并且个子也矮。克劳迪奥说他是动真格的，只要希罗同意，他就会娶她为妻。班尼迪克说，如今想当单身汉的人太少了，他们也不担心额头上会长犄角，真遗憾。佩德罗阁下得知克劳迪奥爱上了希罗，他马上表示认同。他说希罗值得爱。看到班尼迪克总是在爱情这个问题上唱反调，佩德罗阁下说他希望有生之年能够看到班尼迪克有一天会因为害相思病而面色苍白。班尼迪克立刻说，生气会让他面色苍白，生病或者饥饿也会让他面色苍白，但他唯独不会因得相思病而面色苍白。班尼迪克出去后，克劳迪奥向佩德罗阁下坦言他去参战之前就喜欢上了希罗，现在他已经因爱成疾了。佩德罗让他放心，他会去找里昂纳多和希罗谈一谈，让希罗嫁给他。

约翰是佩德罗的弟弟，他是一个私生子。约翰憎恨佩德罗。当他得知佩德罗会代表克劳迪奥向希罗求婚的消息时，他就下定决心要坏了他们的好事。约翰和他的手下康拉德、博拉奇欧策划如何搞砸即将开始的晚宴或者接下来的化装舞会。里昂纳多、他的兄弟安东尼奥、希罗、碧翠丝，还有希罗的女佣厄秀拉和玛格丽特都进来了。他们谈论着佩德罗和约翰两兄弟。这两个兄弟都没有参加晚宴。希罗和碧翠丝说，约翰总是板着脸，一副悲催相。碧翠丝说，约翰像一座雕塑沉默不语，而佩德罗就像个受宠溺的小孩子叽叽喳喳说个不停。她又说，如果他们之间互相调和一下就完美了。对于一个有着健美腿脚和鼓囊钱包的男人来说，他简直可以征服天底下的所有女人，只要他能得到这个女人的芳心。里昂纳多警告他的侄女说话不要那么尖刻，不然没有哪个男人愿意娶她。碧翠丝说她才不想结婚呢，因为她不喜欢男人的胡子。她叔叔让她找一个没有胡子的男人，碧翠丝又说没有胡子的男人缺乏男子气概。接着，他们就谈到克劳迪奥将要向希罗求婚的事。安东尼奥希望希罗听从她父亲的安排。碧翠丝说,如果希罗的父亲帮她找的男人是她喜欢的美男子,希罗就会顺从父亲,否则她就应该按自己的心意行事。

舞会开始了。佩德罗在面具的掩护下以克劳迪奥的名义向希罗求婚并且得到了希罗本人和她父亲的同意。佩德罗的仆人巴尔萨泽向玛格丽特求爱,却遭到拒绝。约翰走近克劳迪奥,假装把他认作班尼迪克,对他说他的哥哥爱上了希罗并且已经向她求婚了。他希望"班尼迪克"劝劝他哥哥打消这个念头,因为希罗的社会地位和他哥哥不般配。听闻此言,克劳迪奥立刻感到很沮丧,认为佩德罗辜负了他的信任,他不该相信他,不该让他代表自己去和希罗求婚。当碧翠丝过来告诉克劳迪奥,佩德罗已经代表他向希罗求婚了,克劳迪奥不相信。可是,当佩德罗宣布克劳迪奥和希罗将要喜结连理的时候,克劳迪奥激动得说不出话来。佩德罗还想到了趁机把班尼迪克和碧翠丝凑成一对的主意,如果这事成了,他们就是比丘比特更称职的月老。约翰和博拉奇欧策划如何搞砸克劳迪奥的婚事。他们将设法让大家认为希罗是一个水性杨花的女人,不值得克劳迪奥去爱。

班尼迪克独自待在花园里,感叹克劳迪奥这么快就要告别单身身份。他想自己是不是要改变自己的婚恋观了。他列举了他的恋爱对象必须具备的很多品质,如此她才配做他的妻子。这时,佩德罗、克劳迪奥和里昂纳多走了进来,班尼迪克赶忙躲了起来。他们很清楚班尼迪克就躲在树丛后面听他们说话,于是故意讲到漂亮的碧翠丝不可救药地爱上了班尼迪克,可是班尼迪克一定看不上她,甚至会嘲笑她,这个女孩真可怜。他们批评班尼迪克不值得碧翠丝去爱。从他们说话的严肃神情和认真劲儿来看,班尼迪克断定他们不像是在开玩笑。于是,他认定碧翠丝真的爱他,他立刻心软了,准备对碧翠丝的爱做出回应。

碧翠丝被派去请班尼迪克用晚餐,他很礼貌、很友好地做出回应,还称碧翠丝为"美丽的女士"。对他突如其来的变化,碧翠丝有些不习惯。她想,他可能没心情和她再来一场智慧之战,于是就没好气地拂袖而去。可是,班尼迪克却通过碧翠丝带讽刺意味的话解读出了暗含的爱慕之情,便认定碧翠丝爱上了他。于是,他决定同情她、爱她,否则他就是一个铁石心肠的坏蛋。

佩德罗计划的另一部分也在按部就班地实施。希罗、玛格丽特和厄秀拉一起商量如何让碧翠丝听到她们讲班尼迪克爱上了她的消息。玛格丽特悄悄在碧翠丝耳边说,她听到希罗和厄秀拉在花园里聊她的事情。碧翠丝果然落入了她们的圈套。她来到花园里,慢慢走近希罗和厄秀拉,偷听她们俩的谈话。只听她们俩讲到班尼迪克爱上了碧翠丝,并且对于这事她们发生了争执。希罗认为,班尼迪克不如把他对碧翠丝的爱放在心里,因为碧翠丝会笑死他的。她们离开之后,碧翠丝对这些话信以为真,准备嫁给班尼迪克。

佩德罗、里昂纳多、克劳迪奥正在聊天的时候,班尼迪克走了过来。他的脸因为牙疼而变得苍白。他们还注意到他剃了胡子,连装束也变了,于是他们就笑他坠入爱河了。这时,约翰走进来对他们说,他发现希罗是一个不检点的女人,因为她有别的男人。约翰让他们当天晚上从她房间的窗户偷看她和别的男人幽会的情景。佩德罗当即宣布,假如这是真的,那么婚礼当天他将当众指责她,让她出丑。婚礼的头天晚上,墨西拿的执法官多格博利提醒值班人员要注意警惕里昂纳多家附近的安全隐患。当他们在一个屋檐下躲雨的时候,他们听到康拉德和博拉奇欧的谈话。博拉奇欧向康拉德吹嘘道,约翰给了他1000银币,命令他想办法让佩德罗和克劳迪奥相信希罗是一个滥交的女人。博拉奇欧将话题转到时尚方面,把时尚比作一个畸形的小偷。守夜人以为他们在谈论一个名叫畸形的小偷,便将他们捉拿归案。

当希罗正在为婚礼梳洗打扮的时候,碧翠丝走了进来,对希罗和她的两个女佣说她感冒了。他们取笑她坠入了爱河。多格博利到里昂纳多家里来,向他报告他们抓获了两个嫌疑人,但是他的表达有问题,说话总是抓不住重点,别人不知道他要表达什么意思,里昂纳多没有耐心听他啰唆,说他还要张罗婚礼的事,就径自走了。婚礼在教堂进行,弗朗西斯牧师问克劳迪奥和希罗是否知晓有什么阻挡他们结为夫妻的障碍,希罗回答说没有。里昂纳多擅自替克劳迪奥回答说他也没有。然而,令里昂纳多惊愕的是,克劳迪奥把希罗的手重新交回到他手上,对他说自己不能娶她的女儿,因为希罗背叛了他。克劳迪奥说希罗是一个"烂橙子",说她是荡妇,指责她长着一副贞洁的模样,话说她涨红了的脸就是心里有鬼的证据。佩德罗和约翰也出来指证希罗。佩德罗也称希罗是一只破鞋,并说他们都看到了她和一个坏蛋的约会,那个坏蛋已经交代他们私会过上千次了。克劳迪奥还在继续谴责希罗。里昂纳多无地自容,希望有人能够给他一把匕首好结束自己的老命。希罗突然晕过去了。佩德罗、约翰以及克劳迪奥退下了。

希罗苏醒过来后,里昂纳多替她感到羞耻,他希望她已经死掉了。碧翠丝为她的堂姐哭泣,她确信是有人故意中伤希罗。弗朗西斯牧师也相信希罗是无辜的,她涨红了的脸就是证明。但里昂纳多说,佩德罗和约翰两位王子不可能做伪证诋毁自己的女儿,克劳迪奥也没有理由故意败坏希罗的名声。班尼迪克推断,佩德罗和克劳迪奥是值得尊敬的人;如果他们三个人当中有一个是坏蛋的话,那一定是生性狡诈的约翰。牧师提议他们先为希罗举办一场假葬礼,让克劳迪奥为他的冲动和残忍感到后悔,同时他们会暗中将这件事查个水落石出。班尼迪克以他的名誉发誓,他会保守秘密并协助调查此事。

当所有人都离开之后,班尼迪克和碧翠丝互诉衷肠,坦言了对彼此的爱。班尼迪克保证他会为碧翠丝做任何事。碧翠丝趁机让他把克劳迪奥杀了,这个家伙竟然冤枉、中伤她的堂姐,破坏她的名声。但班尼迪克表示不愿意去杀人的时候,碧翠丝有些伤心,她正要拂袖而去,班尼迪克拦住她,向她保证会找克劳迪奥决斗。

多格博利、守夜人维吉斯、教堂执事在盘问那两个嫌疑人——康拉德和博拉奇欧,他们交代了和约翰串通起来陷害希罗的事。多格博利等人于是前往里昂纳多家,去向他汇报情况。经过安东尼奥的提醒,里昂纳多开始相信自己的女儿是清白的。安东尼奥以为自己的侄女真的死了,于是打算找克劳迪奥决斗,里昂纳多拦住了他。佩德罗和克劳迪奥情绪低落,他们希望班尼迪克能够让他们开心起来。想不到班尼迪克不但不安慰他们,反倒提出要和他们决斗。他们心想,这个家伙因为爱碧翠丝而疯了。班尼迪克告诉他们,约翰已经逃离了这座城市,很明显他是畏罪潜逃。多格博利和守夜人把两个嫌疑人带进来了。博拉奇欧只好承认他们合伙玷污希罗的名声,并毁掉他们的婚礼的犯罪事实。佩德罗和克劳迪奥立刻后悔他们对希罗做过的事。里昂纳多答应原谅克劳迪奥,但他必须为希罗写上墓志铭,以还她一个清白。然后,他再把自己的侄女嫁给他。克劳迪奥同意了。班尼迪克请求克劳迪奥允许他和碧翠丝结婚,里昂纳多点了头。

克劳迪奥和佩德罗从希罗的墓地回来,然后直接到了教堂,他们俩的婚礼都在这里举行。当人员都到齐后,两位戴着面纱的新娘被带到两位新郎面前。当克劳迪奥掀起他的新娘的面纱时,惊奇地发现里昂纳多说的侄女竟是希罗本人。直到婚礼这天,班尼迪克和碧翠丝才得知,原来里昂纳多和他的朋友们合起伙来让他们俩相信对方爱上了自己。于是,他们马上否认他们不爱对方,结果克劳迪奥拿出班尼迪克写给碧翠丝的情书,希罗也拿出了碧翠丝写给班尼迪克的情书。班尼迪克于是建议他们在婚礼开始之前先跳舞。在本剧的结尾,消息传来,约翰被抓回来了,正在等待惩处。

5　Famous quotes

【Quote 1】

Claudio

Friendship is constant in all other things
save in the office and affairs of love.
Therefore all hearts in love use their own tongues.
Let every eye negotiate for itself and trust no agent,
for beauty is a witch against whose charms faith melteth into blood. [4]
(Act 2, Scene 1)

[Claudio (played by Robert Sean Leonard) complaining about Don Pedro's friendship in a 1993 film directed by Kenneth Branagh.]

✥ Paraphrase

Friendship is loyal in all things except for the business of love.
Therefore all lovers should speak only for themselves.
Let everyone do their own courting,
and not trust any middle-men.
Beauty is a witch whose spells melt honor into passion. [5]

◆ 原文译文

友谊在别的事情上都是可靠的,在恋爱的事情上却不能信托;所以恋人们都是用他们自己的唇舌。谁生着眼睛,让他自己去传达情愫吧,总不要请别人代劳;因为美貌是一个女巫,在她的魔力之下,忠诚是会在热情里溶解的。[6]

【Quote 2】

Claudio

Silence is the perfectest herald of joy.

I were but little happy if I could say how much.

—Lady, as you are mine, I am yours.

I give away myself for you and dote upon the exchange.[7]

(Act 2, Scene 1)

[Claudio (on the left) expressing his happiness to Hero (on the right, played by Kate Beckinsale) in a 1993 film directed by Kenneth Branagh.]

◆ Paraphrase

Silence is the best announcer of joy.
If I were only a little happy, I could say how much,
but as it is I'm speechless.
Lady, you are mine, and I am yours.
I give myself away for you, and I delight in the trade.[8]

◆ 原文译文

无以言表是此刻的我无比欣喜的写照;如果言语能够表达出我此刻的欢欣,那说明我的喜悦程度不深。尊贵的小姐,我们现在属于彼此了。现在我把自己交给你,感到非常快乐。[9]

Unit 10 Much Ado about Nothing

【Quote 3】

Benedick

I will not be sworn but love may transform me to an oyster,
but I'll take my oath on it, till he have made an oyster of me,
he shall never make me such a fool.
One woman is fair, yet I am well;
another is wise, yet I am well;
another virtuous, yet I am well;
but till all graces be in one woman,
one woman shall not come in my grace.
Rich she shall be, that's certain; wise, or I'll none;
virtuous, or I'll never cheapen her;
fair, or I'll ever look on her;
mild, or come not near me;
noble, or not I for an angel;
of good discourse, an excellent musician,
and her hair shall be of what color it please God.
Ha! The prince and Monsieur Love!
I will hide me in the arbor. [10]
(Act 2, Scene 3)

[Benedick (played by Kenneth Branagh) talking about his ideal wife in a 1993 film directed by Kenneth Branagh.]

✧ Paraphrase

I can't promise that love won't change me.
But until I have really fallen in love,
I'll never act like such a fool.
One woman is beautiful, but I don't care.

Another woman is wise, but I don't care.
Another is virtuous, but I don't care.
I won't pay attention to anyone until all three of
these qualities come together in one woman.
She must be rich, that's for sure, and wise
—or else I'll have nothing to do with her.
She must be virtuous, or I won't consider her;
beautiful, or I won't look at her;
mild-mannered, or else she shouldn't come near me;
noble, or I won't have her even if she's an angel.
She must be well-spoken, an excellent musician,
and her hair should be whatever color God wants it to be.
Ha! Here come the prince and Mister Love!
I'll hide myself in the garden alcove. [11]

◇ 原文译文

我不敢说爱情是否也会改变我,让我变成一个牡蛎;可是我可以发誓,在它没有把我变成牡蛎以前,它一定不能把我变成这样一个傻瓜。好看的女人,聪明的女人,贤惠的女人,我都碰见过,可是我还是原来的我;除非在一个女人身上能够集合一切女人的优点,否则没有一个女人会中我的意的。她一定要有钱,这是不用说的;她必须聪明,不然我就不要;她必须贤惠,不然我也不敢领教;她必须漂亮,不然我看也不要看她;她必须举止文雅,否则我不准她靠近我;她必须有高贵的人品,这样我就不会贬低她;她必须会讲话,精通音乐,并且她的头发必须是天然的颜色。哈!亲王跟咱们这位多情种子来啦!让我到凉亭里去躲他一躲。[12]

【Quote 4】

Benedick

Well, everyone can master a grief but he that has it. [13]

(Act 3, Scene 2)

◇ Paraphrase

Well, everyone knows how to cure a pain
except the person actually feeling it. [14]

◇ 原文译文

会驾驭痛苦的人是因为他们没有身陷痛苦之中。[15]

【Quote 5】

Dogberry

I think they that touch pitch will be defiled.
The most peaceable way for you, if you do take a thief,
is to let him show himself what he is and steal out of your company. [16]
(Act 3, Scene 3)

◇ Paraphrase

I think that those who touch tar will become unclean themselves.
If you do find a thief, the most peaceable thing to do is to let
him prove himself a thief by stealing away from your presence. [17]

◇ 原文译文

可是我想,谁把手伸进染缸里,总要弄脏自己的手;为了省些麻烦,要是你们碰见了一个贼,顶好的办法就是让他显露出他的小偷本色,悄悄溜走。[18]

【Quote 6】

Don John

Fie, fie, they are not to be named, my lord,
Not to be spoke of!
There is not chastity enough in language,
without offense, to utter them.
—Thus, pretty lady,
I am sorry for thy much misgovernment. [19]
(Act 4, Scene 1)

◇ Paraphrase

Shame, shame! Those sins are not to be named, my Lord
—not to be spoken of!
Language itself is not innocent enough to
describe them without offending everyone here.
So, pretty lady,
I'm sorry about your great wickedness. [20]

◇ 原文译文

呸！呸！王兄,那些话还是不要说了吧,说出来也不过污了大家的耳朵。美貌的姑娘,你这样不知自重,我真替你可惜![21]

【Quote 7】

Beatrice
Is he not approved in the height a villain,
that hath slandered, scorned, dishonored my kinswoman?
Oh, that I were a man!
What, bear her in hand until they come to take hands and then,
with public accusation, uncovered slander, unmitigated rancor
—O, God, that I were a man!
I would eat his heart in the marketplace.[22]
(Act 4, Scene 1)

◇ Paraphrase

Hasn't he proved to be the worst kind of villain by
slandering, scorning, and dishonoring my cousin?
Oh, if only I were a man!
What, he just leads her on until the moment
they were exchanging vows, and then,
with public accusation, open slander, pure hatred
—Oh, God, if only I were a man!
I would rip out his heart and eat it in the marketplace.[23]

◇ 原文译文

他不是已经充分证明了他是一个恶人,把我的妹妹这样横加诬蔑,信口毁谤,破坏她的名誉吗？啊！我但愿自己是一个男人！嘿！不动声色地搀着她的手,一直等到将要握手成礼的时候,才翻起脸来,当众宣布他那恶毒的谣言！——上帝啊,但愿我是个男人！我要在市场上吃下他的心。[24]

【Quote 8】

Leonato
Men can counsel and speak comfort to
that grief which they themselves not feel but tasting it,

their counsel turns to passion which
before would give preceptial med'cine to rage,
fetter strong madness in a silken thread,
charm ache with air, and agony with words.
No, no, 'tis all men's office to speak patience
to those that wring under the load of sorrow,
but no man's virtue nor sufficiency to be so moral
when he shall endure the like himself.
Therefore give me no counsel.
My griefs cry louder than advertisement. [25]
(Act 5, Scene 1)

[**Leonato (on the left, played by Richard Briers) talking about grief with his brother Antonio (on the right, played by Brian Blessed) in a 1993 film directed by Kenneth Branagh.**]

◇ Paraphrase

It's easy for men to comfort and advise about
sorrows that they themselves don't feel.
But once they taste them too,
their advice turns into passion.
You can't cure rage with advice,
bind up madness with silk thread,
treat aches with hot air,
or fix agony with words.
No, no, every man thinks it's his duty
to advise patience to those who bear the burden of sorrow,
but no man has the ability or power to live up

to his own advice when he's in the same situation.
So don't give me advice.
My griefs drown out whatever you have to say.[26]

◇ 原文译文

人们对于自己并不感觉到的痛苦，是会用空洞的话来劝告慰藉的，可是他们要是自己尝到了这种痛苦的滋味，他们的理性就会让感情来主宰了，他们就会觉得他们给人家服用的药饵，对自己也不会发生效力；极度的疯狂，是不能用一根丝线把它拴住的，就像空话不能止痛一样。不，不，谁都会劝一个在悲哀的重压下辗转呻吟的人安心忍耐，可是谁也没有那样的修养和勇气，能够叫自己忍受同样的痛苦。所以不要给我劝告，我的悲哀的呼号会盖住劝告的声音。[27]

6　Questions for discussion

（1）Comment on Claudio's words："Friendship is constant in all other things save in the office and affairs of love. Therefore all hearts in love use their own tongues." Do you agree with him? Do you know examples of friendship betrayed in the face of love in real life or literary works?

（2）Do you agree with Claudio in that "Silence is the perfectest herald of joy"? Are there other occasions when we lose words to express ourselves?

（3）If you were Hero, would you still marry Claudio after having been wronged and insulted?

（4）Do you agree with Leonato on this：Men can counsel and speak comfort to that grief which they themselves not feel? Why or why not?

（5）Why does Leonato disown Hero and act so tempestuously on hearing Claudio's accusation of her? Is it fair to Hero? If you were Hero's father, what would you do to your daughter on this occasion? Is Leonato's attitude towards his daughter unique or typical in Shakespeare's time? Use examples in the previous plays we have learned to demonstrate.

（6）Does Beatrice meet with Benedick's standard of his ideal wife? Does such an ideal wife exist in real life? Why or why not?

7　References

[1][2][3]　Much Ado About Nothing Study Guide[EB/OL]. https：//www. litcharts. com/lit/much-ado-about-nothing.

[4][7][10][13][16][19][22][25]　Shakespeare W. Much Ado About Nothing [M]. New York：Simon & Schuster, 2018.

[5][8][11][14][17][20][23][26] Much Ado About Nothing: Shakescleare Translation [EB/OL]. https://www.litcharts.com/shakescleare/shakespeare-translations/much-ado-about-nothing.

[6][9][12][15][18][21][24][27] 威廉·莎士比亚.莎士比亚喜剧选[M].朱生豪,译.北京:人民文学出版社,2013.